'One of the year's most beautif... ...es the path to womanhood of Alannah from disastrous affair to no-less-comfortable marriage and beyond'   *The i*, Best Books of 2020 So Far

'Sharply written . . . The quality of the writing is top-notch. Page after page of astute, deft observations . . . Campbell holds her own against her contemporaries, writers like Claire-Louise Bennett, Sally Rooney, Nicole Flattery and Lucy Sweeney Byrne . . . The novel is full of sensual, offbeat descriptions'   *Irish Times*

'Engaging . . . Plot isn't the point here; rather, the novel gets its energy from the sour kick to its intelligently disaffected narration, as Campbell pins down fleeting impressions from a life textured by memory'   *Daily Mail*

'Campbell's debut is a novel of psychological texture, rather than plot, but its opulent unhappiness and mordant observations make it superb'   *The Daily Telegraph*

'What sets it apart is also its greatest strength: a well-constructed non-linear form . . . The story of this relationship is interweaved with the present so closely that it feels almost overlaid, reading convincingly like a memory. There's also interesting commentary on class . . . *This Happy*'s retrospective narration allows Alannah to accept responsibility gradually for her past actions, ultimately making her a fuller, more satisfying character than others of this ilk . . . a quietly exhilarating story'   *The Sunday Times*

'Astute . . . As she explores her ambivalence and unrest, each refracted through the prism of her experience and each considered in her sharp, antic and candid voice, we are offered a dazzling array of thoughts . . . Campbell leads us to these insights with freshness and resonance . . . The ghosts of our past might refuse to go away. But, as this book so stirringly shows, you can write them into edifying life'   *The i*

'There are impressively toe-curling set pieces detailing awkward encounters between families . . . Campbell's language is striking'
John Self, *The Spectator*

'If you loved Sally Rooney's *Normal People*, read this novel . . . It's become *de rigeur* to label any young Irish writer the 'next Sally Rooney' over the last few years, but Niamh Campbell has a stronger claim to the title than most . . . darkly romantic . . . The moral ambiguities (and irreconcilable power struggles) inherent in the relationship are familiar territory for fans of *Conversations with Friends*, but in many ways, the prose is less reminiscent of Rooney's clipped, email-honed style than of Eimear McBride's lyrical Joycean sentences'   *Vogue*

'She has already been compared with writers such as Eimear McBride, Ali Smith and Claire Louise Bennett, and indeed Niamh Campbell's debut novel does add a distinctive new voice to Irish literature . . . Campbell has produced a thought-provoking piece. With her interior monologue, written in the first person, this creates a claustrophobic ambience . . . At times witty, fiery, wistful and even shocking, with engrossing heady prose, Campbell's style is unique'   *Irish Independent*

'A triumph of style . . . This book is made of ancient stuff. It is of the land and the landscape – replete with unashamedly ornate, arguably extraneous detail . . . She writes against the style *du jour* – sparse prose; tight, fast plots – in favour of something more rich and rebellious . . . I heard tones of Joyce as I read – not only in the direct references ('the snot-green sea', Alannah's remark: 'he was my epiphany') – but also in the muscular, myth-laden prose . . . it is the best novel I have read all year. It snuck up on me like a ghost in the night. It spoke on a different frequency'   *Sunday Business Post*

'An intense, evocative read'   *Irish Country Magazine*

'Campbell evokes vivid nostalgia with her clear-eyed prose that is a compelling combination of candid and droll'
Book Riot, Best Books of Summer 2020

Niamh Campbell holds a PhD in English literature from King's College London and works as a postdoctoral fellow for the Irish Research Council at Maynooth University. She was the winner of the 2020 Sunday Times Audible Short Story Award and her short fiction and essays have appeared in *The Dublin Review, 3:AM Magazine, The Penny Dreadful, Banshee, gorse*, and the collection *Autonomy* (New Binary Press, 2018), published in aid of the campaign to repeal the eighth amendment in Ireland. She was awarded a 'Next Generation' literary bursary by the Arts Council of Ireland in 2016, and an annual literary bursary in 2018. She is based in Dublin.

This Happy

First published in Great Britain in 2020 by Weidenfeld & Nicolson
This paperback edition published in 2021 by Weidenfeld & Nicolson
an imprint of The Orion Publishing Group Ltd
Carmelite House, 50 Victoria Embankment
London EC4Y 0DZ

An Hachette UK Company

1 3 5 7 9 10 8 6 4 2

A CIP catalogue record for this book is
available from the British Library.

ISBN (Paperback) 978 1 4746 1168 8
ISBN (eBook) 978 1 4746 1169 5

Typeset by Input Data Services Ltd, Somerset
Printed in Great Britain by Clays Ltd, Elcograf S.p.A.

www.weidenfeldandnicolson.co.uk
www.orionbooks.co.uk

This Happy

Niamh Campbell

WEIDENFELD & NICOLSON

When I awoke to find him gone I was not immediately surprised. After all we had argued the previous night and I had broken a plate with a chaffinch on it, one part of a set decorated with thrushes and various tits. I had broken it emphatically but, surprised at myself, snapped back at the sandy *crack*: I felt remorse, as if I had let slip something I didn't mean.

As I lay in the bed it occurred to me that he could not have gone for a walk in the lane, or to visit the landlady, or to buy supplies, because the sun still hadn't come up. The kitbag that he travelled with was gone from the top of the inlaid chest. And then, Oh hell, I thought: he's gone back to his wife.

It was early. The window was a coffer in the wall and the room was filled with moonlight, and in the faded wallpaper were putti, Virgins, wolfhounds, hags, calligraphy. The moon lit the wardrobe and the horse-bits on the windowsill. It was an austere room. There was only the chest, the wardrobe, the bed with its cakey eiderdown, and a stack of mildewed books. Mice lisped in panels and the boards groaned underfoot. I lay in the hollow he'd left, beginning to feel afraid.

I listened for the ring of his weight on the ladder, for the creak of his tread in the lower room, for a boot or a cough or the rustle of clothes. I heard nothing but the wind rinsing the trees as shadows tossed along the wall.

After a time I rose from the bed and pulled on his expensive peacoat, which hung on a nail. The motorbike was gone from the yard below. Across the stubble field I saw the brick factory piped like a candle shrine, its tusks and stacks macabre against the sky.

What to do? It was cold in the room. It was five o'clock – this I knew because the cat was crying outside the window now: meowing in outrage, meow! The cat was like clockwork at five a.m. When I rushed to the pane we looked at one another before he leapt out of sight, and where his yellow eyes had been an oak tree rolled in the wind. I went downstairs and let the animal in; it wrapped itself around my legs. It climbed up onto the pulverised loveseat to look at me. I knew the soles of both my feet were black.

What to do? I walked a thoughtful circuit through the house. The main room was cavernous with deep windows, and, in one of these, books had been crushed together on the sill. In this room there was also a fireplace of wood-chocks and a crisp corona-shaped grate. A corridor of Perspex ran adjacent, lapped with leaves and seedpods. A lamp like a smoky bowl, upturned, ridged and twisted at the neck by the glass-blower, was always left on. I'd never seen it being switched on or off. It gave a waxy colour to the room.

Outside, I knew, the painful business of daybreak was beginning. The sky was gashed with grey and yellow to the east. Cold beaches without colour lay in low-tide, just a few miles away, and this was relevant to me, as was the bicycle beneath tarpaulin in the yard.

Every light out but the yellow of the lamp.

Every light out but the eyes of the cat.

Every light out but the truly indifferent moon.

Part One

Part One

One day in autumn when I had been married for less than four months I saw the landlady. I saw her in Cow Lane – such a strange place to be, cobbled self-consciously – and when I caught sight of her I turned and pretended to be distracted by the surplus of a shop door, a banal glass-panelled door, swinging and releasing people with shopping bags.

The landlady was standing on the pavement. It had been raining, all was shining, it was mild: she was pausing and reading something on her phone. In the years since I had seen her last, when she oversaw my disgrace, she hadn't changed. Even without preparation – nothing that had taken place during the day to indicate this encounter would occur – I felt generosity rise within me, a desire to tell her so – to tell her, you look great, you always do, you have such *style*. She must, I thought, be fifty now at least.

I weighed my options and eventually pivoted, prevaricated, walked away. I swept off before she could see me. My footsteps clacked on the cobblestones.

Dame Street was like coming ashore, and here I halted. I began to click the fingers of my hands. This is something

I do when I want to summon a decision from within or without me. Behind, the chute leading back into Temple Bar was desultory. Buses broke from the Cathedral and brayed towards College Green.

Even now, I thought. Even now this minute I feel exhilarated to think about it, all of it, although I must confess it had been crushed into a kind of pinhead, a pinprick, a *punctum*, something severe, a tattoo: but when released, it was a rich green wave of memories, flaming seams and flaming seals. And at that point I hadn't seen her, nor Harry, for something like six years. I was thirty now – over six years – although nonetheless of course I remembered it all forensically.

I was going just then to meet my husband of four months – less than four months – but found my footsteps slowed, which was strange, since typically I hurried everywhere. And there was a general slowness then, after I had seen the landlady – a distension, it was almost like horror – like everything in the environment was a sign.

I wasn't married long. Things had happened suddenly.

I was going at that moment to meet my husband.

I continued, pressed, on my way, against the crowd, as the cathedral bells erupted and the birds scattered and gulls opened, as supple as crossbows, looking for scraps from tourists on the grass. I wondered how much I had told my husband about the episode with Harry when I was twenty-three. Little, I reckoned; hardly anything. But it had happened, certainly, to me.

It seems funny to say I have never listed the facts. This is because they make me sound foolish.

When I was twenty-three, and studying in London, I met a man who was older than me – a married man, a writer – and fell in love. Things happened suddenly then as well. We left London, this man and I, and travelled to Ireland, where I am from. We had met in April, in the first bit of mild weather; we went to Ireland in August. We came to stay in a cottage at the bottom of a tubular lane, the type in Ireland called a *boreen*. The cottage was his; he rented it, he knew it well.

I have taken apart every panel of this, like an ornamental fan. But we stayed in the cottage for three weeks only, just three weeks, because it was cut short you see – cut short after just three weeks, when I'd left my entire life behind.

Afterwards, for years, things brought it back to me, the cottage, suddenly: dusty aubergines; a copse against a cold bloodletting sunset in Phoenix Park; the smell of burning timber, or of damp. Once in the film institute I was folding my coat under my chair and when I sat up I could smell it – the cottage – smell smoke, wood smoke, on someone's clothes, and I was seized with strange autonomous ecstatic grief.

I think of it in certain atmospheres. A species of spacious evening, in the countryside especially; the sky stretched and pillared, wet scents of land-water, wet dog, wet dock, steeped leaves, and earth rippled up by hooves or bicycles or boots. I remember standing in the lane barefoot, bath-time, the lustful chill and coming discomfort of nightfall – the slow rich reclamation of the fields and hills by dark-ness, threaded starlight, night coming on like someone filling a bucket with dark sand.

I could stay here forever! I thought. I could live on here, forever! I was young back then. I was always so wound up.

But when I saw her, the landlady, in Cow Lane, when I had been married for four months and six years had passed

9

since it all, it was not that things came flowing back to me. In fact it had been with me, close to me, sewn into decisions like signatures, for years: redrafted, redesigned, streamlined, all confusion corrected, all forgotten details simulated, supplemented, quantified.

And so the sight of the landlady in a marvellous moss-green coat – the kind woven in Donegal and treasured for a lifetime – looking no older, looking more beautiful really, the sight of this was a source of grace or abrupt unasked-for glee. Like I had been waiting all this time to be rediscovered.

Really they are always with me, always near to hand, these memories. Image and gist maybe. Distilled.

A morning in the cottage, say. Outside the cottage: there, in the steeping lane. On this morning – I cannot capture it intact – the landlady came upon me peeing in a copse with a woollen rug on my shoulders. When I saw her I cried out to excuse myself and stood up straight. Harry was back in the bedroom, asleep.

She said, Oh dear, oh dear, the dog has run off, and I answered, I'm sure he'll come back, and she paused at a slant as if hanging from something, her face a half-rictus of pain, so that I imagined her to be judging me, although now on reflection I think she was only distraught.

Very early. And here she was running about after the dog. As I gathered myself up I felt the sensational field of my body, and especially my fingers, expand, spreading like filaments to the broken grin of the tree trunks and growing things, the liquor-smelling richness of decay, the path churned to peaks and troughs. I felt she had brought other people with her and they were watching me. But there was nobody around.

I went back to the bedroom of the cottage then. I don't understand how a man can sleep like that. Don't they worry what you will do, unsupervised?

I have watched my husband, asleep, similarly: so vulnerable, so trusting, or unthinking. You could be a Judith sawing the head from Holofernes; this could be Molly's Chamber, a girl filling a pistol up with water and inviting the magistrate in. All of these being idle thoughts of course. Free-flowing from below.

Later that same day, when Harry was once again elsewhere – working, of course – I sat on the steps as the evening fell and anxiously tried to absorb it, the lane of trees, the sounds of the breeze sifting dryly through the trees, the spokes of rowan with red berries, or to find meaning in it, to compose a deathless sentence that would explain it all to me.

I remember now that I'd felt helpless in the face of this task because I did not, for the most part, know the names of the trees.

I remember the giddiness that was a kind of declawed trauma when Harry told me, You are a complicated girl.

This is how I picture myself: as a girl, awaiting instructions, her knees drawn to her chest. A sense of aggravated static or of glittering anticipation, blackly glittering anticipation, and in such imaginings I was painfully alone. Much, much harder was the task of conjuring the man – Harry – from a distance, on *mature recollection*, and trying to wonder what he was thinking, if he thought about it at all, if he whipped my interest and discarded me accidentally, or without malice, without sufficient empathy – or if, really, I'd wounded him with what I'd said on that final day.

What I had said: I will not join your – *chaste harem!* You won't put me back in a box like a toy.

Snottily, it must be said. Insubordinately.

On Dame Street, after I had come ashore, I turned, I walked; I watched for the landlady from the corner of my eye. My gaze alighted on the faces of people coming towards me in case I saw someone else or something else significant, in case the day was about to become a theatre of synchronicity, as days can become at times I think when fate is accelerated. I even paused and gave the street time to unfold or loosen something – I walked slowly, I thought slowly – but there were no more disclosures.

I thought, then, that I had been waiting, I *had* been waiting to be rediscovered – I had been waiting for him to return – for a long time, that this had been an unspoken hope and a wishful vigilance but that, since I'd met my husband, it had receded. So much so that I saw the impulse abstracted before me and felt sorry for the person who had waited, and I thought with some pleasant condescension, how does a person waste her twenties like that? The answer of course being easily indeed. As easy as can be.

Passing Essex Street I also thought of how boring life could be and of how boring people were, how inhibited, and that it was natural to conceive of wild aspirations to cope with this.

For the rest of the way I slipped into the notion that my husband might have gotten to the bus stop before me, might be waiting for me, but judged myself at the top of Parliament Street to be idiotic because he was never waiting for me. As I walked the sheer rain began to fall again, lightly, so I pulled up the hood of my coat, the coat with the tartan pattern like a picnic blanket that I became sick of suddenly and which made me feel plain. My husband was always late. He proposed to me, really, to get out of being held accountable, one evening, for being late – to get out of being held accountable for this and other things.

On the quays rain ruffled the river as the evening came on. When a bus pulled in I let it come and go, watching it lurch off and join the stalled traffic, and wondered if, one day, I would jump on a bus anyway, without my husband: if, one day, I would lose patience entirely. I saw him coming in the dark blue coat, the satchel swinging by his side, and smiling ruefully. His complexion was weathered from working, for many years, in hot weather – from living in Spain. The effect of his heavy lids was a languid expression I found restful to observe. When I saw him my irritation lifted.

Little kit, he greeted. This was the nickname he had given me. Because I am slight and I bite. Seven minutes, he said, looking at the LED screen, that's not bad, is it?

There is power in a past, I thought, and liability too.

How was work? I asked.

My kid, he grinned, is going to win the chess tournament. He referred to the boy he had been coaching at the school where he taught history.

Oh my, I teased, you will be so fulfilled.

He can even beat me now, he said.

The grin was real; the excitement was real. He was like a child about teaching, about guiding and being seen as a guide. I always slightly disdained this since I taught third level and didn't give a rat's ass about it. I see now this was obvious and unhelpful.

You should come to the tournament, my husband said.

I don't understand the rules, I retorted, because I went to *state school*. But then I laughed: Yes, I'll go, I said, I'll watch. It would be nice to see the place.

You might need to get Garda vetted.

They'd want to vet me all right, state school and all of that.

I knew that he wouldn't ask me again. I'd have to ask, and by then it would be too late to arrange anything. Because we hardly knew each other, our interdepend-ence sometimes took the form of wary bluff and games of chicken; challenges, withholdings. But we didn't talk much about our marriage, about the decision we'd made. We behaved as though it had always existed.

Are you all right? was something he asked me a lot. He would say this and watch me from the side of his eye. And I would pretend I did not know I was being watched.

Harry watched me, similarly, from the side of his eye.

Harry was in my mind now and weaving between my thoughts disruptively.

I remembered, standing at the bus stop I recalled, our first meal together – our first meal, Harry and I – and that it was famine food, it was cockles and mussels in broth; there were candles burning on pale pine tables, and he watched everything that I ate – tracked it, it seemed, from bowl to lips – and looked stiffly at the wineglass every time I lifted it. We were in Borough Market on a summer night. I was reading *Little Dorrit* at the time and I talked about how boring I was finding it. I was aware that my petulance made me look childish and guileless and attractive.

These tactics, I thought: you are tactical. The thought made me ashamed.

Standing at the bus stop, my husband placed an idle hand on the small of my back. Always this hardly calculated gesture of proprietorship has felt authentically, absorbingly, erotic to me.

I remembered Harry, spontaneously, grabbing my calf. Before me on the motorbike. Geyser of gratitude and passion at the grabbing of my calf. I knew absolutely nothing about men then, at twenty-three, but I'd learned a little since.

These two men, as I placed them alongside each other now, were not the same. My husband you see was wild with love for me, or not *love* for me, but a dependence that predated me and had no doubt attached itself to other women, earlier women, with a tenacity so burning it eventually burned out. Harry on the other hand had never needed me, but for in fits-and-stops of anger orchestrated by my body and the way I used my body, leaving bits of it lying about, such as a leg cast out under a table outside a restaurant in Borough Market, heedless and scantily furred at the thigh where the razor had stopped. A leg thrown wide denoting hipbones open as a jaw in shock.

Harry had been a figure of awe to me. My husband, increasingly, was not: his love was a gauche and floundering type – or seemed so – full of hunger and puppyish need. To this end, the end of preserving things, my husband was also dishonest, or could be. Harry was never dishonest with me. He was smooth and contained – an image of him: the door to his office locked against me – and a canvas for huge projections, at the time, on my behalf. But I can't, I thought then, at the bus stop, blame him for that, really.

How was the library? My husband asked me now.

Oh, fine, I said. Still on the lesser Gombrichs. I was reading, then, about illusion. I have always been interested in that.

The bus drew up. As we travelled through the city the rain began to weaken and a surprising final show of sunlight swept across the evening, leaving a red residue, so I said, We need to walk this evening – straight away, when we get home. We need to just drop all our stuff and go straight out. Before it starts raining again.

There were no free seats on the bus, only standing room swinging from poles as it dawdled north.

The old trees of the suburbs were copper and abundant. The trees at the Bishop's palace spilled over the walls and littered the pavement with gem-coloured mulch. The landlady and her sudden exact apparition was everywhere, though nowhere substantial, and I started to wonder with application what, in fact, she might be doing now, and did she still live in the old Georgian farmhouse, and did she still rent to Harry, and did she remember me. And where *he* might be. I'd assumed he had gone, was in London, or somewhere else. I'd never before thought of Dublin as somewhere that Harry would manifest. I'd considered it a planet apart.

My husband sent messages from his phone, one-handed, fluently and with concentration. I looked at him. He was good-looking. His eyes were extraordinary; his hair was still blonde, floppy if it wasn't cut, even though he was forty now, and it all made me breathless sometimes, his body, its largeness, its mindlessly entitled occupation of space; his lips, which were full for a man, like a matinee idol, and his skin that was so weather-beaten it betrayed, after everything, his age. A large part of my marrying him was, I reflected familiarly, for sex. He made love without skill, rutting and frank and violent, as if he'd gone without it a lot in his life, something which didn't make sense to me. As if he hadn't used his looks to get by or seduce. As if he hadn't noticed them.

I first met my husband on the platform at Connolly Station, on a dry morning, at nine o'clock. I was returning from staying with my friends in Monkstown; it was a still day, the steam from the sea and the slobland at Booters-town heady. The hulk of Howth like a slab of beef. I wore the long woollen coat like a picnic blanket – the very same coat I was wearing now – and my green fingerless gloves. I sat barefaced and indifferent to the action of the morning until my train began to creep in, with a series of short faint screeches like the scraping of a plate, and at this point, abruptly, with a movement that seemed both sudden and utterly natural, a man with large pale eyes sat into the bucket-seat next to me and said, This will sound weird, but can I have your number?

I was charmed, and I was rather charming at the time. You could tell from a distance that I was somewhat under-occupied. I smiled as if I had expected him to swoop into my life like that and wrote my number on a ticket with my name, Alannah, and I said, Here's my train, I have to run!

I swept into my carriage like a girl in a film. I didn't turn to watch him wave or read the number and my name as it drew off because I felt bashful; I went into the bathroom, allowing the slow sucker-door to seal behind me, and looked at myself in the mirror instead. He didn't call until the following day, and in the interim I became concerned that he had forgotten me, when I had already begun to grow fond of the origin story – of the station, the train, the great icy frightening eyes – which sounds even now like something I made up.

When he did call I rode my bike to Botanic Avenue to meet him from work, cockily apprehensive, and for a few minutes we couldn't speak. After two more coffee dates in quiet rhapsody the ceiling began to recede.

I loved. It is simple. There was nothing to stop me. I really didn't have anything else on.

When I was in London, years before – when I met Harry – I was a little similarly idle, bored – I had lots to do, but I felt disconnected from these obligations – and this is probably not a coincidence. There was no one to stop me falling in either case because no one was watching me. Because I was quite typically and ardently alone most of the time. As I have always been.

The man from the platform and I walked, on our third date, to the botanical gardens. We strolled through the palm house, by the blue fins of succulents, the cacti like torture implements. We were careful and cool and witty with one another. Or I was. At length I said, Well now, what is it that you have to say to me? Why weren't you free on Friday night?

A little longer, he replied.

Outside the sun was bright, the trees in high relief. As we walked under an avenue of trees, past grandparents with prams and toddlers, he put his arms around me for the first time, drawing me close to him with emphasis, gripping my hip.

Tell me, I commanded. Are you married? On the run from the law? OK, it isn't funny now.

He pushed his face into my hair. For a moment or two we hung there, before he asked if we could sit, and we found a bench overlooking a slant of silver birches spaced apart.

I think that when I tell you this, he said, you will get up and run. He was clinging to me and looking ahead.

Jesus. I tried to lighten him. What are you, an assassin?

He said nothing but planted a kiss on my temple. We had not gone to bed yet and this was the closest, physically, we'd been. He was pressing fingers softly on the bars and hollows of my ribs – pressing ribs, glaring bleakly ahead – and I thought with a spike of surprise about Harry's hands, pressing and counting the very same bars and hollows of my ribs. This thought, like a ghost in daylight, faded out. Faded out of sight only, that is; remained, otherwise, in a kind of waiting way.

Tell me, I commanded, because I am starting to think that you are married. I thought, oh God. There is nothing new under the sun.

I'm not married, he said. Then quietly, shutting his eyes, I am father to a little girl. She is less than a year old.

Are you living with her mother? I asked at once.

No.

But you know each other?

We've been involved, on and off, for years.

But not now.

We hardly speak without arguing. But. He looked around. If one of her brothers came by and saw me now, he would break out the hurley, if you know what I mean.

She is not, he added, my only child. When I was at college, he said, my girlfriend got pregnant. I have another daughter, she's a teenager, and she grew up abroad.

Well you're older than me, I said slowly, in shock. I suppose history is inevitable. I have history, I said. I thought, privately, that my history just then looked less substantial, less fleshy, than partners, children, and duties; than the exotic word *abroad*. My history was, rather, an emotional undulation without a name. I found this thought unpleasantly humbling.

Close to us a ride-on mower was grinding and blowing shards of grass to the air; the birches trembled delicately; the sky was clear. He was holding fast to me now and asking, Do you want to run? Do you want to leave now?

But of course I did not want to run because I was intrigued. I saw myself even then as the very flower of generosity, petals aching open in reception, affection, and grace; we had passed through the palm house, clammy and airtight and safe; I saw complexity and delicacy under a bell jar. Also I thought, well, none of this is really *my* problem, is it?

Well I'll have to think, I said. Do you want to walk me to my bike?

At this, the man laughed with relief, shaking his head and looking at me; repeating, *Walk you to your bike*, saying, But won't you stay a bit longer?

I've got to go, I told him. It's late enough.

I rode into town as the evening approached. Spring was coming, and it would be a beautiful one.

Harry, I reasoned on our bus home from the city, married months, had been *worldly*. Harry had been all over.

He worked for television and theatre companies; he worked for the BBC. Harry would go anywhere really. Strange places you don't go, like Ottawa or Iran. But it wasn't only that – Harry was a man of the world, half-feral and adaptable in the way of the truly rootless, mildly amoral cosmopolitan.

My husband, by contrast, gave an impression of naivete. That day on the bench, against the snarl of the mower, he'd asked *Do you want to run?* Sensing I wouldn't run and hoping I wouldn't run.

At the same time – I watched him now, texting away on our bus from the city home – my husband could double down if he wanted something. He had, in the evenings, a comical way of groaning and clicking over test papers. He came from the Castle Catholic class: those who were doing well always, even under occupation and even after recession; slumlords and tightwads with occasional ersatz knighthoods, that kind of thing, and, although I was vaguely rough-trade in my roots and spiritedness, he liked the glaze of grandeur education gave to me. In theory at least.

My husband liked to be admired. He struggled if the world did not reserve enough praise and validation for him. In exchange he performed the patrician manners of a man with a lot more ready cash than he actually had, and played at being a hero to the boys he taught – being boyish himself, having wit. In between, he was mischievous. So much between us was mischievousness.

I have to hold this up, to point to it, when I try to explain why it is we got married. It was just kind of *bold* or *naughty* you see.

That evening, we arrived home to the trees of the garden, reptilian palms and gingko, dripping needles of rain so softly it was as if the sound were happening in my head. The apartment was pressed into the basement of a Victorian villa and belonged to my husband's parents. Which is to say it did not belong to me.

The first time I came to this apartment we were drunk, both of us drunk, acquainted about a month and crashing up the avenue with the tendrils of our phone chargers catching in privet and escallonia. The night was still and otherworldly, smelling strongly of the sea, the several smells of the sea heaped or stepped and distinct – canine, decaying, bodily – as we swept into the garden, tripping over pots, and through the door, and at once even though I was drunk I was taken aback at the mess, at the two cliffs of junk crushed onto either side of the corridor.

It was so indistinct to me. Two walls of savage clutter, books and boxes and furniture, which had formed a coa-lescence like a mesa or a prehistoric cave.

After I married him and moved in I came to believe that the walls of clutter would never be shifted now, that they couldn't be disturbed. Grit-rings of dust or dried topsoil where certain foothills of junk had been disrupted declared the presence of something sedimentary and permanent. If I rose in the night to use the bathroom I had to pass through it in darkness and, in these moments, its force turned it into the first corridor in the world. It became the alleyway between our house and the neighbours' in childhood, the alleyway where I looked up at cruising clouds and seabirds in the channel of sky, where I was lonely and ill-at-ease.

It became the corridor of leaf-splashed Perspex in Harry's cottage and the still older, still more lost, galley of wicker furniture tacked to my grandparents' house. It became the eye of the needle and the birth canal.

In comparison, I owned little at the time of my marriage. All I brought into the apartment were some clothes and my books, my boxes of notebooks, but other than this I hardly occupied the place in any material way. I became the prey that may or may not still be there when my husband returned from work. Strands of my hair gathered in the teeth of the drain, of the bathroom sink, and strands like handwriting adhered in places to upholstery. I moved through the house naked, for the most part, even during the day, feeling like a spar of tree that has been peeled. Free of my own history.

Indeed I felt no ownership whatsoever over the place for the first few weeks. There came a time when this changed – when the term began and I caught a sinus infection, and I became cold and intermittently miserable. I had started to work at the university, signing off the dole, and I began to fantasise day-long about crawling back into bed, about the dusty silence of the apartment, and to wish at times that I lived by myself.

But when I met my husband in the evenings, I was always happy to see him. Before dark we would walk on the shingle beach, sometimes as far as Bull Island, as the flashing of the chimney-stacks at Poolbeg strobed and stained the bay. Clusters of light on the coast suggested a world of people, huddling against whatever suggestion or vengeance brooded offshore, in desperate gestures of self-belief. Passing walkers in sibilant anoraks glanced at our faces with interest because, I suppose, we were happy-looking.

On this day, the day of the landlady, the apartment met me with the odour of the last meal I had made and I said again: Quick, let's go walking before it rains.

It was darker and the coast road lined with springs of streetlight. A ferry slid from the bay miles away, lit with lunatic richness. We walked the wooden bridge in cross-winds. My husband said, here, hold my hand, then banded me to him by the waist; we progressed awkwardly, in step. Eventually I said, It's too wet for this route – waves jack-knifing – let's do the coast path. On the seafront there were restaurants and glowing terraces.

We stopped into the chipper and my husband kept asking, are you sure that's all you want?

On a bench I remembered endless winter evenings in adolescence, in the village in Fingal where I grew up, sitting under the viaduct, eating chips and freezing in parka jackets and passing around vials of vodka, the harbour low and a shopping trolley like a wreck wretched in the silt of the harbour. Dripping arcades of the viaduct. I described this to my husband on the bench. I explained how glad I was that I had, eventually, grown up. How glad I was that now I could do whatever I liked.

I don't think, I said, that Anna drinks vodka under a viaduct. Anna was his eldest daughter, a teenager. I had wanted to turn the conversation to this.

I wouldn't know, my husband replied.

I am nervous, I continued, about meeting her tomorrow. It's a shame she couldn't come to the wedding.

That was never going to happen, he said.

I knew from photos that the girl was exceptionally pretty, far more so than I was at her age, and ensconced in the most expensive boarding school in town. From this she deigned sometimes to descend and meet her father – as he saw it – and once, he said, he had spotted her with a gang of giggling girls, bunched together and crossing Camden Street, streaks in their hair and bags from Mac. I thought: she must have wonderful poise and self-control, this child. I never kept the man dangling as elegantly as that.

Her father had raised her alone, still a student, until she was four; it was, he explained, much like an animal raising a cub, without a clue. When she was four her mother's family arrived and commandeered her forcefully and now the trauma of this incident had become a reticence between them that was agony and jocular at once. Her mother had always been so unwell. Or indifferent. I could never quite be sure.

He told me the details some weeks into our courtship as we lay on the green before the gates of the cemetery, where there was a pub and a ring of quiet cottages. There were crowds around because it was mild. He had been drinking the night before and as he told me there were tears welling and slipping on his cheeks though he was not sobbing, it was some strange reaction, symptomatic. His head was on my belly and I stroked the soft fair hair. I thought, I can take it, I have room.

On that night of the landlady I did not, in the face of my husband's reluctance, discuss Anna any further; I knew from experience and from previous experience, with Harry mostly, that one must muster patience on a quasi-Daoist level when dealing with men. It is something they really should teach you at school. Instead of talking about Anna we left the bench and the sea-wind to return home, scrunching our paper bags of chips into a neighbour's bin. We descended the outdoor steps, softened by grass and dandelions, to the door of the apartment, stepping over pots of fierce geraniums.

Inside I switched on the electric fire, which smelled of scorching dust, and took a shower. When I emerged my husband had turned on the television and was following the coverage of budget day. The footage showed politicians in the Dáil making a point, one by one, of performing monologues feigning shock and dismay at the conservatism of the budget, which would, they said, do nothing to address the housing shortage, the single most pressing and shameful issue for the state.

Instead of seeing to this, I pointed out dryly as I wrung my hair with a towel, the reigning minister for finance had followed protocol in heaping endless gratification on the elderly, ensuring pensions and fuel allowances, medical cards, bus passes, television licenses, regardless of income level. Medical cards to rich people like your parents, I continued archly, sitting on multiple properties just like this. Very well for them. Morally speaking, such money could be put into homeless services, but it won't be, because homeless people do not vote. The grey edifice, I said, of the upholstered old – they vote. So there is this parallel ideological commitment to believing that the old are worthy indeed.

You think so? My husband asked.

They haven't compensated the Magdalenes, I conceded. Not all old are created equally. And you Celtic Tiger boom brats torpedoed the economy to begin with.

My husband was ten years older than me. Harry had been over twenty years older than me. I considered these men to be the blameworthy custodians of the world.

Oh jargon, my husband now remarked.

He had pulled off his jumper before the electric fire. This movement caught his t-shirt slightly and, before it fell softly into place, I saw the broad flash of his back.

Nothing will change, he continued, until all the young people and those other groups you talk about – single mothers, squeezed middle, working class – come out and vote in their own interests.

Yes, that's true.

I was at Trinity, he said, with half of those junior ministers.

The newscaster turned to his screen and exchanged opinions with a journalist dispatched to the midlands, to a one-horse town, who was speaking to representative citizens underneath the amplified chatter of rain on a golf umbrella.

You, said the journalist to a middle-aged man, as a father and worker, what do you think?

As a father of five, as a father of five, I jeered. As a dacent Irishman, what do you think?

The journalist then addressed a girl of twenty-three, and

this girl reported that her generation didn't care about the budget at all. It mattered little to them because most of them would go abroad to work anyway, she said. There was no point in even getting upset about it or protesting any more.

That's what I thought, I said, when I went to London.

London is where I was, I said, when I was twenty-three.

Where were you, I asked, when I was twenty-three?

My husband counted back and said, Madrid. Calle de Campomanes. With Canadians: one of them, the girl, she wrote me emails for years afterwards. One day we got drunk and woke up in Santiago so hungover we couldn't believe we were still alive.

The girl, the Canadian, I said. She was probably in love with you.

Oh yes?

You never notice these things, I said. Or else you pretend not to notice. I looked at him from beneath my eyelashes. You pretend not to notice the effect you have on women.

No effect! He blew out his cheeks. Never. The tide wouldn't take me out.

Oh, jargon, I said.

Poor girl, I said, sending love-letters into the waste.

When I summon my eldest stepdaughter to mind now I see a selfie, a distillation, an expression of joy that makes her look so like her father I am haunted at the thought of her inner life. She seems a more exquisite thing than I, better formed and more protected.

The following night, in a bar above traffic, my husband drained his pint of beer and looked out the window.

She's really beautiful, he told me absently. You'll see. I'll get her now. I'll take her to the restaurant and meet you there.

All right. I felt nervous. I tilted my face for a kiss.

I knew that I was plainer than the girl's mother had been, just as I had been plainer than Harry's wife. If I were their age, I thought, these men would want nothing from me – it was a cruel thought, and I wondered if I should be so hard on myself, sitting here in the window and finishing my gin.

I had felt this shadow of inferiority before. I had felt it on the day the landlady took me to see the big house. The day of the haystacks and mist, the day when I piled blankets over myself and lay awake. This was years ago. So clear, however, in my mind.

I had walked through Cow Lane, consciously, once again today: I did not see the landlady.

Waiting a little bit longer in the bar, in my unease, I tried to return to my book, but I could not concentrate. I set off early for the restaurant. Darkness was coming. It was a new place that had opened on the quays, and from without I looked in huge windows, warm with light and the avidity of people, and a banquette with rushes and milk jugs suspended over it. The evening was cold with a bolt of black cloud over the dome of the courts. Inside, a maître d' approached. He led me to a high marble table with several stools and a can of light on a chain.

Thank you, I said. I'm waiting for two more.

They were already late. I wondered if the robust twists of bread stacked in a basket to my left were real or fake. I didn't see anybody that I knew. The food was expensive but I would not be paying for it. At times like this I simply felt too large. I am not a large person but I felt too large, as if I'd bloated, as if I were rangier and wider and more ungainly than other people.

At last my husband appeared with a girl in a gabardine mac and I didn't wave him down at once, I waited to watch him with her, to watch him interact with her. She was seventeen. Her hair was blonde and lay between her shoulders like a blade. They were sharing a joke, and she seemed shy, and his expression even from where I was sitting looked so roguish, handsomely so, that I felt what I often felt on observing my husband: pride, some arousal, and an after-pang of panic at myself.

I was young, I thought, when I met Harry, not that young but still *young*, still empty-headed in a way I could not appreciate at the time, in a way I could condescend to now. I was not well-connected or remotely protected at all. I thought of myself arriving at the landlady's house on a cold morning, in the leaking dawn, a pale thing with cropped hair and black-soled feet, no idea of her sublime universal irrelevance, scared: I wondered if, on that morning, she'd felt any sense of protectiveness towards me. I wondered now why she didn't call my mother or something like that. It was not a thing I would have suggested, ever, but she was a grown woman – she was an adult – and, perhaps, she should have known.

I don't know. You look just like an adult, at twenty-three, I suppose.

My husband smiled when he spotted me and waved. His daughter nodded and moved with small steps, looking at her feet. Her demureness was surprising.

It is lovely to meet you, I said.

When she bobbed her head and smiled a little, her hair swung slimly from her shoulders, where she caught it like a comfort blanket, raking fingers through.

My husband introduced me with a beam and took me, as was his habit, by the hip. He dug a kiss into my lips, and I knew that he was nervous then. He interrogated his daughter somewhat blandly about school and grades as we waited to order. I had lamb mint salad and my husband crab omelette. The girl, to my delight, wanted fish and chips. I was too afraid to talk to her and she was quite frightened of me. We had nothing in common of course but this man and I registered with some surprise, belatedly, that I was her stepmother now: it seemed an intense and outlandish imposition on her, a presumption or a liberty. I had a stepmother too somewhere. I was also terrified of her.

That woman! Being shown to an undressed bunkbed in a box room, no bedclothes. Sleep where you like, she said. The house was a new-build in a half-finished estate and the window looked out on the ruin of an abbey church, bare grass and burial markers.

My husband's daughter warmed to the topic when she began to speak freely about her friends: they had been on a school trip to Florence together, there had been ructions in the *pensione*, and as she progressed it became racier: so-and-so and such-and-such a nightclub, gossip and hilarity, filth hinted at before she returned tight-lipped (actually pursing her lips in pleasure) to the food, before asking if she could have just one tiny glass of sparkling wine.

That's funny, I told her, because, when I was your age, I went on a school trip to Italy too. I was studying art and I loved it so much: I worked all summer as a waitress to save the money.

She looked at me and nodded but didn't speak. I realised she had not addressed me so far, that she had addressed everything to him.

I still have all the photographs, I said. I smiled as if this were a pleasant memory. Really, and I remembered it now, I had set the alarm on my Nokia thirty-two-ten to wake up at five and crossed the wind-bawling green of the housing estate, to wait at the edge of the housing estate and opposite the skeletal frames and snagging tarp of the latest housing estate, until my uncle who worked at the airport pulled up and gave me a lift. At the airport the other schoolgirls had been delivered there by their mothers, mothers who now held their faces and teared up and said, be good, be safe, have you got everything? I remembered feeling repulsed by their babyish need and mildly alarmed at my abject and conspicuous independence. The art teacher was crabby and acted as if I were an apport. How did you get here? She asked. How long have you been standing there?

And the landlady, of course, in the cold light: *London?* She asked. Harry had gone back to London, yes. I was alone. I had walked, in the wind, up the green boreen.

I loved art, I said warmly now, when I was at school.

Before we had a chance to order coffee, Anna turned to her father and said, I can't be late getting back.

You're not late.

I'm going to be. I got in trouble last time.

He, I pointed out, should be the one who gets in trouble if you're late. He should have to explain himself.

She did not laugh; she looked at him firmly, holding her coat.

When we had put her on a bus we walked along the quays, crossing the river to Blackhall Place, falling into step with the tramline. It was cold but still and good for thinking.

What do you think, he asked, of the history thing?

His daughter was doing well at school in every subject except history, which was the subject my husband taught at Gonzaga.

I think she doesn't like History, I offered chipperly and dishonestly as I thought, I will not be drawn into conspiracies.

But it's the only thing, my husband persisted.

He interpreted her failure as designed, and as a gesture against him, much like her refusal to accept work experience in a school during her transition year. This I felt was an example of my husband's astonishing intermittent childishness and lack of comprehension as to how women, or anybody, worked.

Has it occurred to you, I asked, that she is failing history on purpose so that you will offer to help her?

I offered, he shot hotly. She refused.

I was, I will admit, a little taken aback at this. I thought on it.

Well, offer again. Over and over. She has to see that you mean it. It's likely that it means a lot to her.

My husband, now, began to rehearse again the many things he'd done over the course of his twenties and thirties to remain clinging to the raft of his eldest daughter's life. When she was born she had been tumbled into his arms at once, while her mother left. I just had, he told me again, this travel cot at the end of my bed. He shaped it, little empty space, before him with his hands.

He said, she doesn't remember any of this.

When her grandparents took her to Spain, on their retirement, my husband followed them and taught English, precariously and peripatetically, for many years. They would make him wait at the gate to take his daughter for the day because the family wouldn't speak to him, they sounded like the very worst of Irish arrivistes, but also terribly glamorous – the sick mother, the college girlfriend, a gymkhana champion, blonde.

In my life I am frequently doubled and undone by blondes.

He said, again: But she doesn't *remember* it: she doesn't remember that it was me who looked after her.

Why don't you explain it to her?

You've got to be so careful, he said, with these people, meaning her relatives. You have to be careful not to antagonise them. And they have lots of money. They had a house on Waterloo Road that they sold in the boom for two million or something like that.

Rich people, I remarked, are unnatural.

Oh, the rich, Harry had sighed once: I will tell you someday.

This history, my husband's life, had been flattened and dried out like a flower head. I couldn't pick even at the edges of it, it was held away from me. At times such as this I tried for scraps. I was flattering the crow to drop its cheese. I offered cold-cuts of my own life – everything, really, but the finer details of Harry – and my husband hardly noticed these but at another time would accuse me again of never explaining why I was estranged from my father's family, and why I was so hard on my father, whom my husband, like practically every man I've ever been with, and for reasons that mystify me, appeared, with ease, to identify with.

Sure enough, as we walked, he asked again, Why don't you speak to *your* father?

He abandoned me, I said simply. Over and over again.

Maybe it just looks like that to you.

No, I was a teenager by then, I remember it all. Anna was only a baby so she doesn't remember a thing. It's different.

Whenever I said her name my husband looked uncomfortable, as if her name was a taboo, and not mine to say. Or maybe this was just how I felt. Like my husband and his family had not only material wealth but symbolic richness and symbolic worth, tragedy and dignity and callousness, above and beyond as I saw it the prosaic everyday gloom of my childhood dysfunction, which was the same dysfunction as every other house on the street. Pregnancy and madness in mansions and Latin was more interesting.

Night-walking in the city was something we liked to do. It was early and there were crowds but there was something vagabondish to it too, a ruthlessness and a root-lessness. It cleared the head.

In doorways, shopfronts, alleyways, there lay the year-round dispossessed. Some sat in couples, two men or a man and woman, or with patient terriers they stroked or cradled in their arms. To look at them was to feel a gulf open, a lake of guilt. I thought of it now but did not say anything because I figured that to do so was pious; I do not like how people do this, drawing on the unknown hypothetical or reified misery of other people, dwelling on it pleasurably, scrunching their face up in lust, shaking their heads, saying *Isn't it terrible.* I didn't comment on the homeless – they were not begging, we didn't shake our coat-pockets for coins – because it was so obvious.

We picked our way to Abbey Street to catch a bus. We sat on the top deck. We sailed through streets scrubbed white with light. Neither of us drove and we spent half our life doing this, riding buses through the city of Dublin, watching from above.

I think that went well, my husband said at last.

Me too, I answered. She's beautiful and smart, and quite like you. I feel like an imposter or a fraud. I mean that I'm nothing like a mother in the least.

I think, my husband told me loyally, you'd be a great mother. I think our kid would be so weird. Imagine it.

It would be great, I agreed. It would be a genius, and the best-looking child in the world. It would be a boy, tall like you, with my black hair and your blue eyes and some amalgamation of our mouths, and I'd force him to be a piano virtuoso.

Why?

I regret that nobody did that to me. I would have a trade and I could make money and travel the world with orchestras.

After a moment I asked, And will we have our own children some day?

Oh yes, he said. As many as you want.

I did not want many. I wanted one. I worried for it even then, before it had been called for or thought of, since the strength of my affection could be animalistic and all-devouring and so intense I felt my life would end when I got pregnant, I would become something else, something feral and so fulfilled there would never be any need for writing, for studying, for art, ever, after that. Writing for instance was sometimes what I did instead of eating. It was alien and demanding and godly, dissolving time, depositing me half-insane on peaks and city streets, at kitchen tables, in cafés, dazedly post-coital and amazed.

Riding the bus, I laid my head on my husband's shoulder and took in the smell of his skin and sweat strained through other, intrusive smells, deodorant and damp, the cheaply optimistic florals of shampoo. We passed a barrage of villas and then the beaches scooped out blackly in the coast were visible and it was home, I realised with excitement, for real, my home, I had a right to it, my life. I could not believe it. And I mean that I *could not in fact* believe it, not even when it was right before me, because I did not feel entitled to it, not really, even though I wanted to feel – pretended to feel – entitled to it.

I had never really thought I would get married. A part

of me presumed I was too broken-open or strange or resistant for something so customary, so conservative, to happen to me. I mean, like all women, I'd had to think about the *possibility* of getting married and having children, it had been part of the cat's cradle arching around my life since I was small, but I came of age during the economic boom, and I watched all my cousins throw extraordinary weddings with pearls and spitted pigs and yoke themselves to mortgages on semi-detached houses and wind up hollowed-out by debt and what I interpreted as dangerous boredom in a succession of dormitory suburbs. Their children to me smelled of margarine and seemed raised by the boom of great monster TVs and since I was priggish and bookish and highly strung I cultivated a defensive hauteur. I did this from the dark mahogany dining room table of my grandmother's house, over my homework.

When I got married it was not for laky mahogany tables or for children smelling of margarine. I did it because it went against these things.

I also did it because I needed *something to happen to me*: I had imprisoned myself amidst chilly achievements, and because I loved my husband with honeymoon love – because I curled into my husband's chest in bed and chanted, passionately, stay with me let us go away together somewhere live together only you and me and you and me and you and me only. I said out loud certain things I would have wished to say to Harry, all those years ago, but could not say, because – at that time – I was not entitled to anything.

All day, this being just a day after the landlady, I'd had intermittent memories. Light and dry as the brushing of drums, these were in the third person, false memories or

symbolic memories or instructive memories. In Drogheda, at twenty-three. But most of all in the cottage, alone,
engulfed by the still and stout and absolutely appropriate
things of a life, of his life, which is to say of Harry's life – the
lamp and the books and the bed and the loveseat, content
to disclose themselves frankly, like family members, all
reposing and ripening into a realisation of vulnerability.
His vulnerability, I mean. His chairs and plates and books
and cat. And I couldn't believe, at twenty-three, that I
was among it like that; that I was allowed to play house in
this place, I hardly dared to believe it, I almost wanted I
think to destroy it quickly and get this over-fragile sense of
safety, of belonging, finished with. I knew I was unworthy
and there was something truly dreadful about that.

Truly dreadful. Oh God I thought, on the bus with
my husband now, how ashamed and strange I was back
then – it can't happen again. It can't happen again.

We returned to the basement apartment.

And in the hallway of my home, dark, I stood, striking
out against wallpaper, third-person perspective again: legs
crossed at the knee, handbag in hand, sleek and ready to
run, run, run into the night – into annihilation, I'd always
thought; into the sea, I'd once assumed – at the first sight
of danger, and I must oppose this, I thought, I must fight it
and find myself here, with my feet on the floor of my own
apartment. I am in the world and in my body. I am not an
idea, I am real. I am not a mistress, I am a wife.

My husband had closed the bathroom door. There were
so many things he would never tell me, and a significant
portion of my power lay in my patience and graciousness
in the face of this and, concomitantly, in my quiet but
abiding weaponising of those aspects of my own life which

lay outside of my husband's influence. Sometimes I exaggerated the life I had left outside of him, even though, increasingly, I had no life outside him.

It is something I must look back on baldly now, squint into from a distance. The divide, that is, between my thoughts and my behaviour; the hysterical independence I had built and the simultaneous, deeply urgent, desire for immolation but also, on top of these, a faltering or aspirant sense of sanity – images of a household and a family, my rights and status, the things I could ask for and the things I would need to secure by strategy. Things that would make me legible to the world so that I would no longer feel so poor and obscure and misunderstood. It is all quite simple in the end. I knew in short that I was *on to something* then. It made me feel unstable because I could not trust.

I'd trusted once. I'd jumped into a happy helplessness with Harry. It had backfired spectacularly.

As my husband and I drew back the duvet in unison I said, I saw someone the other day, from years ago – I got this shock, it was hilarious. I used to call her the landlady.

Now it was my property, like copy.

Part Two

In Drogheda, at twenty-three.

I sat in the church on the main street and I looked into the face of the relic's head. I knew the head quite well, but I hadn't seen it for years. I had landed in Dublin and jumped on a dusty bus through the hayfield seething of the country, old coach roads, a horizon cut and pummelled by short shots of the sea. All the way I worried about meeting someone who would recognise me. Now I was here and nobody had recognised me.

Even the country looked different – even the country looked as though it had changed. Whenever I came home from London to visit, I would be collected at the airport, but this time I got straight and white-faced on a coach, like a tourist or, as I was, like a girl on a secret mission.

The head had suffered much. The expression on its face was a continuing suffering, a look of concentrated tolerance towards something which was either unpleasant or so pleasant it passed beyond the bounds of decency; it became dangerous, and painful, especially for a holy man.

Mortality! I hardly thought of that.

The head was alive, in one sense, I thought. Selfhood

is only as real as the action of muscles on the face in a given situation, and even a mask is an action of the face. This selfhood of the head – frozen, lipless, nose blunted cutely by decay – went on and on, like a sanctuary lamp, facilitating further selfhoods in the people who came and went from the altar rail.

Shut eyes imply privacy but it is only the privacy of the sleeper exposed, the privacy of the lover asleep, the stranger asleep in your bed. Only the privacy of the skull. I thought these mordant thoughts but not of my own personal mortality. At the time I read a little in philosophy but mostly I thought it was arid and weird, this insane unending hypothetical conversation.

I'd brought hardly any books from London, actually.

I had entered through the gable hood of the church, folds fountaining vaginally to the tympanum, and taken a seat, perhaps obnoxiously, close to the shrine. The head forbore from a velvet cushion in a display case, like a lizard on a rock, below the ridiculous fretted steeple rising to the ceiling of the church. The martyr was canonised in nineteen-twenty, a second miracle waived, and his obligation to forbear was only as old as the state.

An old woman – there is always an old woman – rose from her spell of prayer and scudded towards a side-door. On the altar a priest was fussing irreverently. It was a hot blue day outside.

When I was a child, I was thrilled by the head.

I had been a good child here: we used to come to Drogheda for schoolbooks and school shoes. It was the nearest town, then, to the village at the edge of Dublin where I grew up. People hardly went as far as Dublin city until the motorway was laid down. Always as children we would ask to visit the head before home. Then, it was the same, to me, as a shrunken head or scalped Apache, a witchdoctor's familiar, or the head of the horse that says to the goose-girl, *If this your mother knew, her heart would break in two.*

One night, on a swing-set in a garden after a children's party, alone, I convinced myself that the bloodied rags of setting sun were the wrappings of the head of Saint Oliver Plunkett and that, soon, I would see the head itself scream-ing into being like a new planet, soon this would crest from the rags, and every time I swung high enough to see over the wall I came closer and closer to being subject to this scene. When I imagined the screaming head now, I wondered if it was in fact the Icarus painted vividly in the toilet stall of Macari's Italian, or a cartoon of the fleeing apostle in *The Taking of Christ*, which we crayoned in at school. It was certainly not this quiet, withered, strangely feminine thing behind its glass.

The priest left and the church was empty but for the eternal old woman shambling at the back with donation baskets. God, I thought suddenly, indulgently, why are we here? I should have never left Borough, I thought, but then an acute hallucination of myself, cycling into a steam of poison in the Square Mile past people in suits and spike-heels eating devolved foreign food from plastic tubs, that unglamorous effluence of project managers and telephone girls I worked with, winging month-to-month and sometimes week-to-week to temping positions, ethe-realised, and I felt I never wanted to go back to London – I wanted, in fact, to be precisely *no-where*, to be in *no-place*, *nobody*.

The martyr's remains, by the way, are also present in

Rome and Walsingham. Some saints have a proliferation of flanges and teeth; others slip easefully into waxy sleep.

I told Harry in a soft moment once, There is a song in Irish, *a chinn duibh dhílis, dhílis, dhílis*, which means my black-headed sweet, sweet, sweet. And God help me, because that's how I feel about you, jinxed out of syntax: *sweet, sweet, sweet.*

It was because of this impulse, I guess, that I left London.

I left in a hurry, really, but I dealt with everything, I dealt with every white-hot requirement, I made sure the roots were singed, closed off, so that there would be no returning to my former life, or my former self. I packed a suitcase and threw out all the things I no longer needed and sat in my bedroom, waiting for the moment I could escape.

I went to Drogheda to be reunited with the relic's head.

And oh I was filled with such excitement in that church, on that first day! It was so *different*: my life as a woman, not a child. This was my life as a woman played out in a town entirely, stonily, indifferent to me; a town of stone, a town with a terrible tower, a town of plywood windows and stinking silt when the river is low, a town of water-suicide.

I was filled with dark excitement. This is why I put it off.

But at last, of course, I told him, I am here.

Marvellous! He replied. It was such a flare of rare generosity I almost gasped. I am in the church, I added, with the relic.

What are you doing there?

Praying for my soul, of course.

Have you been bad?

Well, let's see.

I waited for him. I cantered down the steps of the church. I looked about to make sure people could see me climbing onto the motorbike. I found that I couldn't look at Harry yet. I looked everywhere else, overcome by frightening delight.

It took some time. It was some time away. I looked out through my visor at everything, at the countryside, rich and twitchily northern at times, nearing the border.

At first I didn't even see the cottage coming. Harry said, do you remember? Yes, I answered diligently: Me first, then you.

Or else?

Or else it will fall over.

When we had dismounted from the bike he looked sternly at me, as if trying to make up his mind.

Birds called everywhere – it was early evening. How beautiful, I observed, though the cottage was ugly, actually, from the road: the cottage was an ancient thing gummed to new wings. It was not much to look at, from the road. Harry had shown me a photograph in London – it was a picture of the front door, the blockish concrete steps, but he said, This door is locked all the time. I walk around the side. A small wooden cabin, the office, had been built next to it, close enough to duck between these easily in rain.

The place had once belonged, Harry explained, to an old bachelor whose whittled crucifixes still littered the mantelpiece. On taking it, Harry discovered a kippered *Fiesta* slid beneath a floorboard, lovingly preserved, and filled with girls who were the old man's patient harem throughout many lonely years. When the bachelor died the younger man arrived to put a wing of wood and Perspex on the house, to insulate it; to build relationships with local quality, to construct bookshelves from breezeblocks and board up one superfluous door. The door the ghosts would process through when they returned.

I know the area, I had told him as we looked at the picture; it's near the Colpe. It's on the headland. It's kind of near the estuary. You know, I said, I grew up not far from there, over in the border just, in Dublin – weird coincidence, isn't it?

Entering the cottage for the first time, I became nervous and hovered by the door, considering a long mirror – some former pier-glass, from a public house – behind the door, which was not just dusty but marked with half-handprints as if fingers had drifted over it, leaving rills of dust. Shoes and those unforgivable sandals he wore all softening in a heap. There was a smell of ginger, timber, and something animal.

I looked in the mirror: I looked at myself. At twenty-three it might be said that I had singular looks. My face was either coarse or attractive depending on the time of day, the light, the context, and my mood, but never anything between these two extremes. My complexion was tan at the time, and my hair was very dark, usually piled at the top of my head; I had and have a high-planed face that is almost Tatar but then, out of nowhere, peasant-thick. I had the pertly pokerfaced physique of all young girls, slight swivel-handed wrists, a stomach or a *tummy* – untouched, untorn, intact; a thing to blow raspberries on – swelling slightly over cereal-bowl hips, except for first thing in the morning, when it was flinching and concave.

I chewed my fingernails so that they were grubby, and my nailbeds cracked to wicks, but one day I got a short prosthetic manicure and waited until he had drifted off to tear abruptly at his back, neck to buttocks, leaving eight delicious welts, saying Isn't that nice, do you like that?

Come in, Harry called, and let's have a look at you. He was in such a gentle mood. I could hardly believe it was real. Working here must have been lonely, I thought, but now he had company in me: my power dawned upon me once again. When he'd dismounted from the bike at the church to receive me, as I cantered down in my travelling trapeze dress, he seemed so pleased, and spoke so quietly to me, in a way which was sacred and not a performance and my absolute favourite tone.

To begin with, Harry and I were shy.

After a time, I came towards him slowly in contrition. He rubbed my arms and shoulders, smiled at me, with creases in his eyes, so high a smile.

I bet you're the talk of the parish, I said.

The postman has seen my last film, Harry conceded. I think I have arrived.

What did he think of it?

Deadly.

He did not say that!

You say that. Harry moved off, laughing. Alannah says that. He seized a saucepan playfully. I am going to cook, he announced, or at least I am thinking of it. The more I think of it the less I feel – well, you have just arrived, it is your inaugural night, isn't it?

55

I'm a native, I said.

And so, I think we should have oysters. But. For this, I think, we will have to go out.

My heart, at this, rose and settled and sifted like a disturbance of birds. We could go out? Go out, go out, go out!

Some minutes later I stood in the pier-glass once more, this time shucked out of my travelling dress, a dress of anaemic candy-stripes, grey and pink, city colours, and nothing against the riot of green and the glazed brown of the river and Colpe as we buzzed by it – nothing to the countryside, frenzied and fetid at once, the blue of the sky and the sea and the mountains heaped like stacks of smoke, toothsome catastrophe of caravans on a slope, the sour fields of blazing rape. Without the dress my clavicles, rosy with sun, were on display, my ribs like two canoes, my poor pale legs, and my bare feet battered and pink.

I want you, I instructed, to tear me in two. Harry's tobacco-brown fingers rooted at me, his teeth sinking into my neck, the root of an erection at the sweet spot right between my buttock cheeks. He was not tall but stocky, and dark, with bushy hair cut close or neglected to become slightly wild. His body was fighting age in some places and losing the struggle in other places; there is nothing, I now know, that can be done for a man's behind. They are betrayed from the lower back. But he was muscular. I would catch sight of a bicep and go weak at the knees.

It really was that ridiculous. And I had been such a stern, scholarly girl before, you see. My last boyfriend was ice-blond and shy, and would sit playing music through his noise-cancelling headphones, skinny and flinty in baggy clothes, in a little ball of sunlight that came through the front window of the clean apartment. As he sat in the ball of sunlight, as I watched him from the couch, reading a book, I would see slight expressions pass across his face until it eased eventually into fallow indifference. Then I might suggest we go out for dinner somewhere and the boy would take ages, *forever*, considering options and scrutinising.

But Harry was one of those men who regrets his appetites. Could not look me in the eye. Imagine what abjection. Imagine how much hatred is bent up in that. It was all terribly exciting.

Oysters, he repeated firmly.

I shook out my first-night dress from the suitcase: a long denim shirt with a belt. For punishment. The kind of dress you wear on the morning after a summer wedding if you get invited to that sort of thing. When I moved to London I changed the way I dressed, I began to wear those watercolour city clothes, riverbed-fawn for autumn and ice-blue for winter, indifferent duck-eggs and paste-pink, cut like sandwich boards or pinafores with no ruches, no florals or frills. Seashells. Dresses like the cell of the anchoress.

Can I go barefoot, do you think?

You can do, Harry sighed theatrically, whatever you want, I'm sure.

I did not go barefoot at first but made a pantomime of wearing his bad sandals: too big, every step was a boom making present the leather and tyre-rubber soles, and we had to watch the dancing action of my feet all the way from the motorbike to the coast. The sandals were ultimately too cumbersome. I removed them and flinched barefoot over shingle and dunes to the pier.

Racing yachts were scraped against the bay. There were people everywhere – holidaymakers, local kids, blow-ins from Dublin – dangling feet over the silted bed of the low harbour or drinking outside bars on the seafront.

Harry and I progressed separately, or rather I walked behind him, lifting my knees, to the fish-shop, which was closing: a woman packed away zodiac wheels of sardines. She knew Harry, and we were able to take the final table on the deck. The sky was pink.

I am going to tell them I'm a bigshot, Harry explained to me, so they will let me go out on the boat to land shellfish with them. Someday soon. The woman set two heavy platters of oysters and lemon before us. This, Harry said, is the best thing about the place.

Irish people don't eat oysters much, I said. I was always chanting cheap cuts of wisdom about the Irish, mostly their failings, which as I saw it compromised me.

They should, Harry replied.

I ate shyly. I have a problem with oysters; the flesh does not detach exactly and seawater, lemon juice, stings my throat. My tongue extended to force the bitterness, a muscle like a dorsal fin, the sound of empty shells like ring boxes.

Melancholy.

Here I am, I said.

Here you are. He smiled.

When we had finished eating and our cutlery lay crossed in apology I said, Watch this. I stood and walked to the unguarded edge of the slipway, where lazy water matted with sea-wrack slapped.

Are you going to jump in? he asked.

No.

I had only just thought of it, or rather it had come whining into my head like a saw, a burning filament, some mechanical and violent but rational thing, and I want to explain to you the way I was thinking just then – the way I thought, at the time – but it's hard, or embarrassing, or ridiculous. I had only just thought of what I was going to do. To break the tension and melancholy. This melancholy I had fallen into, right then, eating oysters by the pier, in this moment of quiet after all the excitement of the day, the excitement of leaving London and coming here.

I think now that something was flagging, then; something was flagging and nagging at me. In this quiet moment. The impossibility of the enterprise. I had given the room away – the room in SE1 – and all my things were in boxes, in storage with friends, and I would go back for them, or maybe I would never go back for them. Harry didn't know this because I hadn't said a word to him.

I knew that to say it would cause a rupture in the atmosphere between us, the atmosphere like a dream, and looking back I can't blame him for all that happened afterwards, not for this moment of quiet in which the appalling possibility of abandonment settled into me and made me want to jump up and pace or scream and which instead made me walk along the pier, forming a plan in my mind instantaneously, taking my phone from my pocket and snapping at the grubby compact shell to unhinge it and slip the flake of the sim card out of it. I put the sim in a dress-pocket.

I retraced my steps along the broad arm of the pier until I felt sure that there was a steep drop to the sandy floor, and then produced my mobile phone, holding it up to him before tossing it candidly into the sea. It sank at once. It was as if nothing had happened. Shallow guilt sprang in my chest. I breathed deeply to diffuse it. Some yards away, two boys with meshwork nets on rods of wire looked at me.

What did you throw? piped one of them.

Evidence, I called back. Evidence of a crime. I laughed to show I was not serious.

What was that? Harry demanded as I sat.

My phone.

Your phone? He seemed genuinely incredulous. Do you really mean that, your phone?

I don't want it. I tried to look disinterested. I sucked a lemon slice. Melancholy. I said, I hate phones anyway.

But surely, he insisted, it is a waste of money to throw it into the sea? They are expensive, are they not?

This prudent point irritated me.

It's only a phone, I said. I kept the sim. I can get another. It's not a big deal.

All right, all right. Harry held up his hands.

I don't want it here. I don't want to be distracted. You are always, I pointed out, complaining about phones and *distraction*.

Later we crossed the stubble field in twilight to reach the landlady's house. She had been an actress in London and could not stop laughing when she met me: fine hands with one sapphire ring and one wedding band gripping her slender knees as she laughed and laughed.

What larks, she said. Oh, Harry, you bad old thing.

Since I sensed she was jealous I made a point of admiring every painting in the room, moving from wall to wall, to show my figure in the dress. I wondered if they had slept together. After all, it was years he was coming here. But she seemed, or wanted to seem, devoted to her husband.

The walk back was hazy with wine, and the cottage

comradelier by its light: tasselled lamps lit it up like a grotto as we made tea and Harry looked at me with a glow in his eyes and I realised again that age really bothered these people, it was the dragon they couldn't slay. I was over twenty years younger than Harry, twenty years younger than the landlady, and consequently a queen.

Harry had cleared a desk for me in one of the upper rooms, a room with yellow wallpaper half-scraped from the walls by time so that its sun-blanched garlands rose and sank unevenly. I opened an accordion file that had fallen behind and discovered lace-top stockings at seven dollars, never opened, never worn: I put them on, and Harry dragged his tongue up either seam. I used a broken riding crop, decayed and soft, against his hide. A scarf was tied to the bars of the bed. I indulged myself. Always he smelled so good, but more so in the countryside it seemed, fungal but spicy and leather-like.

In London when we met, as the summer came on, it seemed like the whole place smelled chemical, and one day we wandered into a fever, viciously, in the sex-and-sebum air: a chronic smog from Africa hung over the sun, and he came to get me from the British Library, and buzzed to Shoreditch, accelerating whenever the traffic broke. At the studio he rented I screamed, actually screamed, *Oh oh oh oh!* pushing fingers under armpits and so oiled, so wildly dialled-up that I did not notice the concrete crunching beneath me until it was done.

Ordinary things that ordinary people did to distract from passion didn't work for me. I hardly read after I met Harry and I never watched television. Harry, so quickly, had taken the east and the west from me, taken my faith. I don't exaggerate.

He was talented. After we met I looked for his first book in the British Library. There was no story, only movement and broken sentences, in an austerely swaggering style. The reading room was as bright and cold as a wedding cake. I thought of a fountain, speaking to itself, and the marvellous spill of water on wasting stone. I thought of my love, hot, lonesome in brilliance, or drinking too much, or fucking a woman not-me, young and hungry and angry and *pounding* her, not-me, I imagined a cowboy fuck beneath the ruined ranch, I remembered the various unwashed smells of men, and I decided I never wanted to sit in a library again.

He was unfulfilled. There was no second book.

He was simply huge. Smooth and tumescent and bright as a feverish child. Little slick of semen at the end. Dull and friendly in mouth like a curious animal.

His first play debuted in the year of my birth. So, you must imagine eighties Dublin and the pigeon-coloured living room of my parents' house, headscarfed women, driving rain, a column of coins as a Christmas gift, a baby reposing on rock-roses: a world without ambition, which was what my parents chose to build instead of raking hell.

He was married. But I didn't think about it much.

I sometimes felt he hated me. Because a thing that had begun to happen by the time we came to Ireland. To make love he bound me to him from behind, or pushed my face to the side, or pulled his fingers through my hair, which was all right except that he no longer looked me in the eye. It was lonely as the moon. But perfectly OK in its way. You see, it restored my religion, or *a* religion, to me. My lover was a god.

As I lay in the dark next to my husband, all that time

later, I thought that, really, I should laugh at myself – at my younger self – for her simplicity. But it didn't seem pretty from this distance. It seemed sad, the saddest possible thing. An aching even now.

After my first night in the cottage I slept late. When I woke up Harry was absent – locked into his office at work, as he'd warned me he would be – and there was a cat in a room, a rather basic cat, a cat with white and black fur, like a Friesian cow.

It climbed into the bed while shouting at me. It continued to cry, even though I was rubbing it; it threw its head up and rolled into the curve of my hand. I knew where I was and why I was there but still I felt somewhat anxious, as though I had woken up sober in a stranger's room. The animal wanted to be doted on energetically and this gave me time to plan my next move. Nobody had mentioned a cat.

I dressed and moved to the desk Harry had cleared for me in the other upstairs room. It had been cleared in advance of my coming, he explained, since he'd spent the whole afternoon getting food in and tidying up and other things, and I felt flattered by all of this, I didn't think I required pomp at all – I mean, at that point in my life I hardly ate anything. I ate crackers and popcorn and cereal in my rented kitchenette, pasta tubes with tuna and mayonnaise, but I didn't like cooking or possess any talent in that area and still as an adult I hate to cook, actually; I hate to see people eat my mediocre fare and look depressed, it makes me angry, I think, for God's sake, it's only bloody food.

On that day in the cottage I tried to work, but I was bored. At eleven I heard the front door bang. I scampered down the ladder, pausing at the bottom to watch the considered descent of the cat.

You have a cat! I said.

He's half-mine. Harry had swung immediately into the kitchen. The landlady feeds him most of the time. I come back after a long absence and find him roughed up, with somebody else's blood on his shirt, but I never ask. He bent to scratch the animal's chin. Are you hungry, thug? The cat meowed as if it understood.

How's the work? he asked briskly, standing up. You slept in.

It's OK. I toured the kitchen again. I looked at everything: all of the pictures and tchotchkes, the bachelor's bundle of crucifixes, the death-stare of a dresser fronted with glass. Harry took some cheese from the fridge. He explained how good it was, how properly made, while slivering the block itself with a knife and feeding these stingingly rich slivers to me – feeding me with his fingers, straight to my lips, quite out of nowhere and still monologuing levelly. And then, for the first time that morning, he looked me in the eyes.

Hello, he said.

Hello, I replied, and I smiled.

I was getting good at this. I was getting good at integrating his strange turns of mood and mischief, a dialectic of detachment and intense interest, as these occurred. It was like learning dance moves, or a script. But you should know I was always slightly terrified. I never knew what he was thinking. I mean, I projected, fulsomely – it was clear from the start that I would have *very little else to do* in this place – but every projection was also scrutinised and second-guessed in a hall-of-mirrors kind of way and really a person could go insane, and in fact I did go, in a way, insane.

Would you like, he asked awkwardly now, to do anything?

I'm happy here, I said. And I was. He returned to work and I went into the garden, where the heat was building nicely, with sunblock and a bath towel. The garden was more of an accidental yard: there was wood beneath tarpaulin and a bike beneath tarpaulin, a collection of dried-out iceboxes and the mummified leavings of what might have been an attempt at home cultivation – starved and cracking plastic plant pots, nursery pots – and a sealed prefab, in which Harry kept car parts and motorbike parts and other things he didn't use. All of this was ringed by trees, some of them cotoneaster, which is to say some of them deliberate. Some of it was wild and some of it deliberate and some of it deliberate but styled to look wild.

Much like the man. In fact I think that describes him quite accurately. I mean I have never known anyone like Harry since, but I suppose I have a better grasp now of middle-aged men. Of the extreme melancholy and longing which overtakes them and which they always believe to be original. I was seeing it, at forty, in my husband. My husband had said my name one morning, when we were drinking tea in our bed: he'd said, Alannah, I don't want it on my headstone, like, he lived and he taught at a school and he died and that's that. The strange elective emphasis *Alannah* stayed with me – it was needless, there was nobody else in the room, it went beyond the conversation we'd been having about work or daughters and stepdaughters and so on – because it suggested a plea, it singled out a certain symbolic audience, the woman who would witness the man as a man on behalf of mankind.

They get tired of that audience in the end. In the end you can say, you are wonderful, talented, I believe in you, and it will mean nothing, they won't care what you think. Or perhaps they'll retreat to a cottage with a twenty-three-year-old girl.

Harry, as Harry explained more than once, had been a prodigy, bursting onto a scene that was niche and electric in the first years of Thatcherism: I was a prodigy too, I enthused, winning prizes and being the only girl in the convent actually reading the free *Irish Times*. Oh yes? he asked (side-eye). Harry was a prodigy and an *enfant terrible* and ultimately an affluent sell-out ('Yes, sell-out') writing scripts and copy, writing films, keeping a Mayfair townhouse stocked with the spoils of Empire, marrying into a Grand Family. Or at least that is how I imagined it. I certainly knew he was rich. I pictured an elephant's foot of umbrellas by the door and a pimped sound system playing Miles Davis; cocaine hoovered from the dust-jackets of books on Weimar-era porn.

Or rather I picture it like this now. At the time itself I was green and beguiled.

In spite of all this, however – nonetheless – Harry did not consider himself a success, or enough of one. That he was emphatically a success from a financial and reputational point of view didn't alleviate the fine angst, the angst like a patina, I sometimes saw on his face. I myself of course was only starting out, with the bluestocking ingénue thing going on, and nothing like an immediate threat as a mind or an artist or social presence or anything else, but still. I remember his face. A look on his face. Sitting outside a café in London. I don't recall what exactly was said – a dismissal of something, a script he had done, a curl of the lip, a look of contempt, for himself and, by extension, for me, the one who was – now I remember – praising it. Sometimes he was gracious of course. He had an English way of intoning *That is kind of you to say*. He had been an actor in London years and years ago, with the landlady. There were no videos of this on YouTube.

I will write another novel, he said. Someday I will run away from everything, I'll go somewhere with grapes, and I'll write a novel that will be serious, not commissioned. On a typewriter.

You don't need to use a typewriter, I chided. That is a–ffec–ted.

In early courtship, Harry had sent me an internet link to reports of a new planet suspected to be travelling mutely, and thus far incognito, just outside our solar system. Imagine, he said, the peace and ease of being that planet. Harry had also been to some lunar place in Israel and made wry enquiries about becoming an Orthodox monk.

Your bravery, I often told him honestly, is what I like. It is your courage that I admire. I told him that I sometimes felt I came from the most cowardly generation under the sun.

Everyone thinks that, he advised. But yes, I really don't get young people now. Frightened by everything.

There are more things to be frightened of.

Are there? He had lost interest: I remember this now: a scrap of conversation, snagged. Very little interest. But then again the side-eye, watching me.

Now he came out of the office and into the garden – time had passed – and put his hands on my bare shoulders. I thought of saying something explicit and vulgar because I knew that it unnerved him, but I did not. I was hot. My thighs were clammy with crushed grass.

I'm a little bored, I said, and I might go into the village.

Into the village? I was going to make some lunch.

I'll eat and go in. Did you say there was a bike?

We had bread and butter. This was all I wanted. In fact I craved it, something plain; we ate standing at the marble slab in the centre of the kitchen. How is it going? I asked.

Well, Harry said at once. And I'd like you to take a look at it later, if you would oblige.

Oh I would, I said brightly, but are you sure? I have no expertise.

Of course you do. It's just a treatment. It's supposed to be funny. So if you don't laugh, well, I'm in trouble, aren't I?

After lunch I took the bike into the scrappy village – really a townland, a planed-over market square – which was nearest, to the north. It was a ride of twenty minutes or so, in-and-out of fuming tunnels of hedgerow and arcaded hawthorn trees, and didn't feel dangerous. At the edge of the village there was a salvage yard with a flowerbed cultivated in county colours and a sign reading SLEEPERS FOR SALE. There was a library like a bunker in the village and a huge cool newsagent, a sandwich deli and the scream of milk steamers, but this was still deep country – tractors parked at angles everywhere. I could sense the boredom that would pervade the place all year. I supposed that, to Harry, it was maybe quaint. To me it was overfamiliar.

But I felt better than it now. I felt singled out.

I tried to spend time, and then I cycled back. I felt the gentle emptiness of the cottage, and washed under the faucet for a while, and soon Harry reappeared and called for me and said, While you were out I had a delivery. It was milk – untouched milk, straight from the cow, and chilled – in pure unlabelled bottles. Have you ever tasted it, he asked, like this?

Funnily enough, I said, I had it in Borough Market once. I mean, I went all the way to London for unpasteurised milk.

He peeled back the foil and I took a mouthful of cream and when I had swallowed I said, honestly and with shock, Oh God, that's *fucking* incredible! It tasted – it really did taste – like life itself, and his face – a sudden and open picture of joy – took me aback, in the most delightful way. All that dairy, I think now, to fatten me up.

Have more, he said. Have as much of it as you like.

Later I stood in the office, trying to train my gaze on the screen and not on the shelves of books, the shelves of records, the frank decanted matter of Harry's interior life – of his mind – as I read, anxiously, aware of his eyes on me. After a while he relaxed and lay on his back, on the long limp surplus couch, with his hands behind his head. This pose made him look like a younger man.

It's very good, I said carefully, as I read. It's written kind of to a template, isn't it?

Well it has to be, it's television, Harry said. He sat up and rubbed his eyes. Never write for money, he advised.

To infiltrate the house, I began to secrete hairpins into bookspines. I knew I was not the first woman here and the thought made me vengeful and aroused; his wife rarely, he said, condescended to come down, even though her family home was close by.

In London, when he had finally said, *My wife is Irish*; described the area she came from, I had laughed, replied *No fucking way*. I suspected him quite genuinely. We were in the gin bar of the St Pancras Hotel. I squinted and cocked my head to one side, turning it all the way, like a bird of prey, I said: It cannot be, you are joking me. I had come to London to study, to get away from Ireland.

I sent long emails diagnosing my neuroses and, soon enough, Harry's neuroses too.

Your wife, I said gravely, is cruel.

I saw Harry's wife once, in a crowd incidentally.

I saw Harry's wife once in a crowd and she looked apprehensive, probably because there were so many people there. She had a screen of yellow hair to her shoulders almost, a rather lemon shade of blonde. On one of the campuses there were two ornate staircases poured into a kind of marble pool, and events tended to culminate there with wine. I was standing at the stairs being bored, as I was often bored, by the other doctoral students, when this woman swept in with a halo of lemon and a private look of apprehension – you could tell she was nervous, like a horse – I am sure nobody noticed but me, sweeping in because (and I felt this was the cause) she had never been taught to enter a room any other way.

And one day I made a fierce speech to Harry against her cruelty and I think he laughed at it, since I was fiercely serious as a child, although he waited until I had left to laugh at me; laughing against my proper ferocity. I *could* be ridiculous, but it is the risk you must take to be listened to, especially when there are odds against you, when you must be resourceful or entertain.

Another time, in my bed like a tenement bed in Borough, wide and iron-framed and depressed at the dead centre, I toed Harry in the spine and remarked, You're frightened of me, aren't you?

In Ireland I was a little more reticent, to begin with.

An afternoon – the following day, perhaps: the second day – we broke from our work at three and sat in sagging deckchairs on the grass. We spoke lazily, taking the sun. Harry said, When I was your age, I was in an acting troupe, and we really called ourselves a *troupe*, and I lived with my girl in a squat in Hackney before, you understand, Hackney was – in. Cool. It hardly had a roof. There was a rant-poet underneath us: do you know rant-poetry? He really did *rant*, you know. You would hear him in the night. And then, he would be coming upstairs and tapping on the door for sugar, or a teabag; Harry laughed. I can hear it, he was so – posh, really: you are *ever* so kind.

Harry said, We used to pack into this Buick GNX, seven or eight of us. Go to some jazz club; it was called Slim Gaillard's. He looked at me as if I would have the first clue what that meant. Well, he said, in pursuit, of course, of girls.

Oh but you had a girl.

I had several. I was young and really *very* handsome you see.

When he spoke like this he lit up. He began to hum songs he remembered and, if possible, to dab at the keys of a large keyboard in the dining room. He would ask me if I knew such-and-such a song or musician and I would know nobody, I would know nothing, and I would feel self-conscious and plain. But I hardly think Harry noticed this kind of thing now: I think now that he was in some sweeter ether of his own.

In London, when it began, I used to send jpegs instead of messages, in response to some emails. I sent *Judith* by Caravaggio, just the face, wearing an expression of gentle objection I found hilarious: this jpeg indicated scepticism about some point he had made. If we were arranging to see one another and he took his time about it, holding off on telling me when and where, I would send him Poynter's *Orpheus and Eurydice*, in their boiling bedsheets, her eyes closed and the skulking serpents at his feet. If he wanted to be left alone to work in the studio for a time I sent one of several John in the wildernesses, to which there would be no reply – no reply nor acknowledgement. But best of all was Holman Hunt's moronically literal *Awakening Conscience*: the girl's expression and the

luminous wallpaper, the carriage clock. This was in response to any roguish remark about my innocence. The
song they are playing is Irish, I pointed out, in parenthesis
– the song they are playing is 'Oft in the Stilly Night'.
One day Harry retorted with *Lady Jane*, ready for the
chop, and I said, You don't get the game, you are doing
it wrong.

Now I remained in the sagging deckchair, with herbal
tea, as he rose to tinker about the motorbike and do something, fix something, though I didn't pay much heed to
his running commentary – I returned, instead, increasingly
searing smiles. To watch him do anything made me feel
thrillingly *present* and it was always like that: it was like that
from the start.

I got this bike for Ireland, really, he said. You understand why. There are so many narrow roads – those, what
are they, *boreens*?

Cow-roads, I chanted then. Boreen, I said importantly,
means *cow road*.

At times, he said, there will be cows on it too. In the
lane outside. Proper, actual, shitting cows. Look out.

I got the bike for Ireland, he continued, and then, you
know, I became so fond of it! I brought it to London
with me. So, typical middle-aged man, you know; typical
midlife crisis: a motorbike.

And a mistress, I piped.

Goodness, he said without missing a beat, is that
what you are? Are there conditions? Will you require a
pied-à-terre?

Perhaps. And to be kept in lingerie.

My dear, if I thought you would *wear* lingerie I would
fear less for your welfare. He looked at my breasts, which

were loose beneath my dress. I dug a bare and calloused heel into the earth. I winked. But I felt dizzy at such times: he could be frank, but he was mostly so occult about everything sexual. I can't explain.

Or perhaps I can. Now, that is: perhaps, now, I can explain.

It took a long time, you know, to get Harry into bed. Several dinners and strolls on the Heath. And when I finally did, I had to go circus-style: after wine, standing on my own bed in Borough and kicking off my shoes. Then came my shirt, then came my skirt. Then came underwear shimmied out of and tossed out-of-frame. I stood in swagger-pose with my tailbone jutting out and ran my hands over myself – music playing away – and he stood in the doorway, looking everywhere, and finally at me, and I said – bravely, playing – Come on now, amn't I the greatest thing you've ever seen?

For which I felt embarrassed afterwards.

As I serviced him the first time he lay poker-straight and staring at the ceiling, so I slid up from beneath the sheets and asked, Are you enjoying this?

I think it's quite clear I'm enjoying it.

But still he remained still, inert and erect, and completely silent; that is, until he came suddenly, right out of nowhere really, and I got such a fright I jumped back and squeaked and said, Oh wow, you startled me, at which Harry began to laugh with relief – saying Officer, I was minding my own business, and he startled me!

And then I lay on his chest and he stroked my hair and he said nothing, but his fingers wound around it and drifted over my temples to trace my eye-sockets, my cheekbones, and my lips; moved down to my collarbones and my ribs.

What are you doing? I breathed.

Getting a sense of your contours, he replied. When he said this my insides felt oleaginous, as if something might come pooling out of me. This was not an active or avid state of desire but something timeless and sublimely poised as the air in a spirit level.

Now, in Ireland, he crouched before me in the deck-chair on the grass and dried his hand on a scrap of fabric. I swung a toe in the air as if I intended to catch him under the chin. He stood up and walked behind me, out of my sight, until he was suddenly there, leaning over the frame of the deckchair gamely, squeezing me quite fluently – squeezing one of my breasts. Just a touch. And then sprang up again and jogged carelessly into the house.

After a moment I followed. He was reading messages he had tacked to a notice board. Lots to do, he said. Always lots of repairing to do. Lots of work, when I come back.

At a loss for any other way of seizing his attention, I came behind him and embraced. Still half-involved he dipped and when he stood up straight I was on his back, hanging with my arms around his neck; I dragged my knees up, snagging one thigh painfully on a belt-buckle, to grip at the waist.

Giddy up, I said flatly.

A slipped disc, Harry declared, is how this ends.

He shunted me carefully to the floor. He turned around and looked at me. It's nice, he said quietly, having you here.

And this made me blush – this made me glow, I was terrified. He really didn't touch me all that often in daylight.

Hardly at all. He just watched me a lot. And what else can you do, being watched, but perform?

We worked for that first week. Or he worked and I read and wrote and snacked and napped and began the project of drawing Harry – in his absence, at the kitchen table, mostly – on a large piece of lovely woven paper that was tinctured with damp because it was bought with a discounted ream from a fire sale. I drew in charcoal, brittle wands of charcoal, as was my preference. These allowed for a moody *sprezzatura* to mask the humility of my skills. I have always been better at describing pictures than drawing them.

On the third afternoon books arrived in a package from Amazon. I said, Can I read this first, can I read this after you? I put down a collection of Raymond Carver stories and said, You can have that, I'm not interested in that.

Not Carver? Harry asked.

I read it at college. The boys all loved it. That and *On the Road*.

The boys?

The boys were idiots, I shrugged.

Well, naturally, Harry said. He asked: But have you

finished that other one you've been holding on to?

Nearly. This was a book about the influence of Saint Paul on the Western imagination. He'd given it to me because he knew that I was writing about church furnishings. Or rather he mistook this for theology. Angels, he had speculated mildly, dancing on pins.

So then. He thumped down a book in performance. You did not like *On the Road*?

No. I don't like machismo. This made him laugh. Except for you, I said. But you, I said, are also so refined: aristocratic manners.

Aristocratic?

In Ireland we have a word for your type. I was emboldened: That word is *squireen*.

I have heard it, he said.

And in France they have a word for women like me, I continued. That word is *coquette*.

I felt weirdly drunk on my guff. When he departed for the office I went upstairs to my desk in the upper room. I found myself able to focus, suddenly. My mind at such times was a grand hall of busts and buttresses without too many people in it – only the pleasant glowing echoes of things I had read, fading out with oily ease, like the sound of gongs – and I felt content, working there, on a hot day at the end of summertime, a rim of hardened purple in the sky towards the east. I made notes in neat hand and saw myself doing this, regular and approved behaviour, less a coquette than a clever young woman in a world that was not, or not always, hostile to her. In such instances I suppose that I almost liked myself. Or I saw myself as something other people might understand. Not a strange thing different from everyone, tasked with turning this painful difference into a system of quirks.

I was surprised and froze when I heard the door and his steps on the ladder again. It was not yet three o'clock. He appeared to the waist and looked at me. I turned to him. My face must have appeared surprised. My eyebrows likely raised.

Harry stared at me. This stare lasted mere milliseconds. And yet with time it has been distended. It has become one of my dearest personal legends. It is an image I dare to recall, an indulgence, and I hope – I still hope, sincerely – it is not the case that I am fabricating or doctoring, that it never happened at all. Because I want to take it to my grave. It was a look of supreme awkwardness. He had been going to say something, but forgot about it.

He was going to say something, but thought better of it.

He looked so – what is it? Embarrassed?

Vulnerable.

Is everything, I asked, all right?

He looked at me with his dark eyes. And all at once the spell was broken – there is no other way to say it – the spell quite *snapped*, we were returned to our public selves, our strategies, and he raised his hands and brought them down on a step of the ladder theatrically. The gesture echoed the way he had planked the book down earlier.

I am thinking, he said, pausing for effect. I am thinking, perhaps we could go out?

Right now? I asked.

To the beach. Get some air. It is hot. We could walk. He frowned: I don't think, he said, I can go back to it, the work, today.

83

It occurred to me in a splash of disloyalty that he had not thought, he would not consider, the possibility that I in fact wanted to work and would not want to stop. That also I was working on something. Namely my doctorate. But of course I did not give a damn about that actually.

I'd really like to walk, I said.

We'll take the bike.

Yes. Sounds good.

Sounds good? He looked at me as if he did not believe me.

Of course. I was surprised again: Of course, Harry.

I never called him *baby* or *love* or *sweetheart* because I knew I was not allowed to be openly affectionate – not even in bed – but privately I called him *darling* and *prince* and *death wish*.

We travelled on the bike. He sped up on the suspension bridge, as I liked, which made me whoop – my bare arms cooled, then burned, by generated air – but when we hit a pothole I shuddered severely and bounced on the seat and, in an instant, unthinking, his hand travelled around to squeeze me on the calf. This was one of few spontaneous gestures of open affection, without calculation, Harry made in our time together. And even recalling it now I want to close my eyes and die. Oh-my-oh-my.

At the beach he pointed to the sky.

This is what I love most about this country, he said. The skies. You always know you are on an island; it is always changing, it never stops. Because the landmass is small and the weather, you know, is big. There is so much. Drama. Look at that.

84

There were curling clouds, gold-foiled, but on the sea the purple strip of sky had grown severe and the breeze was dying. There was different weather in the west, in Westmeath; there was different weather in Newry and Carlingford, different weather over the Isle of Man. Mourne was becoming blurred by the tension on the sea. It indicated, I explained, storms. There was a summer storm coming. Spiny lightning and thunder bolts.

Is that it? He looked quickly at me.

I think so. You know. The heat.

The beach was bulbous with dunes and every dune sharpened by seams of strafing grass, tough grass, coastal grass; the rubble piers of the estuary were brutal incursions of human concern.

On a rock offshore were cormorants folded like funeral umbrellas. Look at them, I instructed. Harry obeyed with interest.

They are eerie, he said.

I was happy. It came to me boldly and mixed with longing. I thought, if I could become the sea, the sand, the air, the rocks, the cormorants, the steely sky, the pier an arm extended frankly into blue, I would, I would, I would, I do.

I think standing here that I never want to go back, I said.

Harry swept down to pick up a stick of driftwood. Flotsam–jetsam, sukham–dukham. He pushed a ponderous tip into the wet sand, drew a line behind us both. Air fresh and virtuous. The sky a metal swell. The thought of leaving oppressed me; the thought, even, of returning to the cottage oppressed me.

When I was little, I remembered suddenly, I thought *flotsam and jetsam* was *wantsome* and *getsome* – you know, like, wants–some, gets–some. I was disappointed, to tell the truth, when I found out that I was wrong.

Very poetic, Harry said. We had fallen into step.

Sometimes I write poetry. I used to. Not so much any more. I realised I wasn't good enough to be *brilliant*, so I stopped. I laughed. The boys, I remembered. God the boys. We were in a writing group. I was good but they didn't include me in anything. I wasn't allowed to be a *poet*, really, because I was a girl.

They would not include you for being a girl?

Well no, they had to include me: I don't mean literally. I mean culturally.

Surely nobody could stop you?

I felt hot. I felt irritated suddenly.

I mean that there was an unspoken assumption, an unspoken *indifference*. I paused. A strategic indifference.

Yes, I know what you mean.

If you know what I mean, I asked huffily, why did you ask me that – why did you say *nobody could stop you*? You knew I wasn't speaking literally.

He had made me feel foolish, but he did not respond to this. Instead, after a moment, he asked, do you like it here?

I love it, I answered quietly.

You would not rather, for instance, be with your friends?

I did not tell him, then, that I had given up my room. I had gotten my deposit back and passed it on to a girl I knew from UCL. I could have told him then but I didn't because it was the absolute last thing I wanted to do.

Well, I tried to be light-hearted, you are my friend.

Glad to hear it, he said.

When we returned to the cottage, and despite what he had said earlier in the day, Harry went back to work.

Part Three

Part Three

If you could dive into an old life – something you never protected when it was happening, something you believed to be a prelude at the time – if you could dive like one dives into love, or fall slowly over a precipice into it, enthralled, would you do this?

Sometimes it seems like this is all I do. Like my past is a residue riming the world of the present, lying over everything. I've been living at speed because I know I can revisit the edited version.

When I was with Harry, for example, I took notes. In the three weeks that I stayed with him in the cottage I took many, many notes. And at that point I was only twenty-three. But I knew I was going to need the notes because something important was happening to me. The notes were not to record so much as to create a future out of notes. I suppose this was calculating. It was not even the case that this love was the first or the last love, but it was the first I was fully conscious of and fully conscious for: I saw the seeds, the brilliant engine of complexity, latent in the first eidetic flashes of our acquaintance.

I still couldn't explain this, years later, because it lay on me like an inexplicable given, like a primal memory.

I read a poem aloud to my husband after dinner. I'd found it among papers from that time. A gate skidding in the wind, it said; tearing home with rabbits in a bag. A poem about men.

Very good, he said.

Isn't it good, I pressed, for a young one?

What is it about?

I don't remember. I pointed to a paper bag of notebooks, old notebooks from my studies, many of which had been scuffed and softened by age. Some of the notebooks dated back to Harry too. I am, I said, going to do something with these. It seems such a waste of writing to have put it all away when I finished my PhD. I took them out today to look at them.

Certain of the notebooks, from the earlier stages of London, when I was beginning my doctorate, were breezy and optimistic, even when formal – were blue or pink, decorated with postcards of *Cupid and Psyche* or *The Ambassadors* or the stickers from Pink Lady apples. Within these notebooks there were faded but neat passages about draughtsmanship and imagination aligned consciously or adequated to produce beauty. There was something cloying to these notebooks because they had a self-regarding eye on the future and knew that, one day, they would be dug out as little missives, charming missives, from a charming time of life. Later notebooks grew smaller and started to become diaries.

I used to write so much, I told my husband. Like, to nobody.

This had been my life in London, before everything: writing, writing, writing.

The day I met Harry I wrote three pages of Thomist aesthetics in pencil. The pencil meant that I was writing in the British Library, where you couldn't use pens. I would have stepped out to the roaring cliff of the atrium; I would have used the hot-water machine. I would have drunk an Earl Grey and tried to look pensive. Frail rain would be drying rapidly from the tiles of the piazza. There is no indication that this was the day I met Harry, but I can remember; I can look at any piece of handwriting and tell you where I was: Gatwick, Senate House, the Seven Bells, or the dearly-loved deal table in my room of bracelets, brushes, child-of-Prague – slight housemate singing – bunting bleaching on the public house below. That was near the old Marshalsea.

When my husband first met me I was still writing a lot, writing towards something. I don't know what.

When my husband first met me I didn't have a job, and I was yielding – lilting – sonorous – usually semi-dressed. Towards the end of this period I had gotten bored and restless, even paranoid; my husband sometimes said such things to me as *not all of us have it as easy as you*, but I was idealistic enough to let that slide, although I should not have let it slide.

I suppose I was simple and self-absorbed and I saw to my own appetites mostly, meaning that I never asked for very much, and with men honestly what I've seen whether it is nice to say it or not is that they can't imagine you elsewhere, they cannot imagine what you do or what your life is like outside of their sphere of perception, if you are not in the room with them you have etherealised, you have become an idea. You are surfing seething galaxies, riding on zephyrs, all the rest of it. Until the lamp is rubbed and here you emerge in the room, or on the city street, or in the bar, or in the bed, to grant wishes again.

There are uses to this. You can do what you damn well like. You will not be asked about it in any committed sense. You can get away with all kinds of things if you are so inclined.

But when I went back to work, as a researcher and teacher at the university, I was no longer surfing galaxies, I was doing something concretely oppressive, something which closed my charmed life in a kind of vice, and I was happy, I was so happy – I was grateful – but I was worried, also worried, for the state of my soul.

It seems pertinent to add here, in my defence, that I'd had many jobs before, some of these deeply demoralising: I mean that I had scraped rind into a churning waste unit and scanned death certificates. But these were always temporary and ended.

The churning waste unit was my first job, when I was fifteen. I cleaned tables and swept ashtrays and put out the small fires ignited in bins by improperly swept ashtrays, and on my first day washed a ballroom floor with glycerine and cold water because nobody – nobody – would tell me where the hot faucet was, and I was fifteen and had simply zero fucking sense. I would drop forks into the waste unit and cause it to back up or leak catastrophically.

I asked my husband now, after dinner, what his first job had been, and he said, When I was eighteen I spent a summer in London travelling between relevant newsagents and manually checking that a certain brand of cola was the only product displayed in the relevant fridge. If any other soft drink was displayed in the sponsored fridge, the fridge advertising this cola, it would be a breach of contract with the cola suppliers, who were my employers.

You were a guerrilla shopper, I hooted. To imagine my serious and pompous man at this work made me laugh. I don't think, on reflection, that my husband ever told me he, with all the boys and girls hired to look at innumerable fridges, was also wearing rollerblades at the time; this seems an unlikely detail I have added by myself. And yet how much pleasure it gives me to picture him, young and lovely, rollerblading through the sticky streets of summer London, bent to the mission of looking at fridges and safeguarding the advertisement rights of this cola, so many corner shops manned by youngest sons, from Parsons Green to Stamford Hill, and nights lost to nineties clubbing and the mushroom-mood of e-tabs and the fresh aggressive mornings of London, the rollerblades, the anarchy.

At that time he would have considered himself on a pleasant detour to a good adulthood, to a profession. Just as I did when swatting wasps and washing dancefloors and dropping forks into a mechanical compressor. I was such a burningly ambitious girl, but my husband, I thought now, could be described not as *ambitious* but *entitled*, a totally different mantle of effortless authority that was never more threatened than in this daily life we shared. I, for all of my casualness, was doing well.

Now, after dinner, my husband had said, You should write more poetry.

Oh God I don't have the patience, I said.

That other stuff you do, I mean, people won't read it – it only reaches this tiny number of people.

Nobody reads poetry either you know.

But it's lasting. It lasts. People will still read it in ten years.

Shortly after we met he had bought me an expensive copy of *The Aeneid*, which of course I hadn't read.

We'll see, I said.

I think you could write faster, he insisted, and write more. He looked at me straight when he said this and appeared to be sincere, but in response I raised my eyebrow and chanted a line I sometimes used for him, coquette-tart: Your unasked-for opinion is noted and will be placed under review.

Oh yes? my husband cried. It broke the tension. He crossed the kitchen to me. Cheeky kitten, he said.

It was that weekend, the weekend after budget day, the weekend after I had met Anna, that my husband proposed something brave and simple to me: he wanted to enter politics, to begin working from the inside, to resume a former intention, a former dream.

And when he proposed this I felt, acutely, that I did not believe in him. This realisation came swiftly and left a wound. I am sure my husband saw me flinch. There was always something so provoking and chaotic to my husband's way of life.

A dominant image of my husband, my husband-and-I, then: heavy rain, crackling like fat, as we run hand-in-hand and impractically for a bus or a cab and a late appointment; we are not sure what day it is – neither of us – because of that trance we went into, together, and always it was I who had to break it.

One thousand days in office, my husband explained in excitement then, is all you need to make a lasting difference. One thousand days.

But of course, I said, you do not just *get there*.

It was one of those heartbreaking afternoons in autumn,

so sadly lit and still. We were standing outside his parents' large house near the coast, at the top of the curt doorsteps, where the rockery crawled with coral shrubs. My husband could become mildly manic on a sudden gust of whim. I sometimes think he married me in a similar mood. Struck bell of Harry onto something – let's go out, go out! – but then flaking, deflating, openly, visibly, when it doesn't live up to the ardent urge of an earlier mood.

But you've never worked in politics before, I told my husband.

I was almost in it, he replied. Anyway, that's not important, is it?

I just feel if it's something that you wanted, you would have done it by now.

You know the situation, he said.

I did know the situation, and it answered everything: Anna, calamity, waking up in Santiago, Canadians.

My husband told me an anecdote, replayed a reminiscence, many times, without appearing to realise that he was repeating himself. He was twenty-two, it was the summer before he was due to begin a master's degree – a degree he would never finish – and from this degree would flow aptitude and scrutiny, and through this degree he would migrate from history to politics. He was twenty-two, it was summertime, and I have seen a photograph from this time, he is young and smug and beautiful; girlishly delicate then, tall, animated by conversation with another person holding a placard, on College Green: he is raising a hand and turning frankly into some kind of deposition, some kind of instruction, knowledgeably and unselfconsciously. He is the kind of boy I never would have dated when I was at university.

But I would have wanted a boy like him, certainly.

This I said: All kinds of crazy wild things I would do. Except that I was twelve, technically, the year you were twenty-two.

I was still a good little Jesuit then, he said.

You weren't good enough, I leered.

He was twenty-two, and that summer went driving through Europe with a friend, a diplomat's son, in a car – passing borders and vineyards and chateaux and the Ardennes – passing through Amsterdam, staying in a stained room with vibrating beds and a brochure of handcuffs and torture devices rentable from reception, blasting parallel to the Camino without walking it, which *says it all*, really: which tells you everything you need to know. On a highway in France, en route to the Channel Tunnel and to London, some red road as I picture it, they became confined behind a slow-moving freight truck for an hour.

And we were going insane, he explained, because we only had one album in the car, which we had been playing over and over again, and it was U2's *All That You Can't Leave Behind*.

Any single song from *All That You Can't Leave Behind*, febrile or fragrantly issuing from a radio in any given circumstance day-to-day, was a trigger, ultimately, for the anecdote.

So my friend looks at me, he said, Like, will we overtake? It was a two-lane country road, no room to overtake. We couldn't see past the truck. It was all we could see. And I remember those seconds, our looking at one another, asking without asking, Will we risk it, will we overtake? I can still see his face. He was just about to pull out. And right then, this car comes speeding by – doing ninety at least – at the other side, some Alfa Romeo or shit like that, some *playboy*, he laughed, you know? And we knew in that millisecond that, if we had pulled out, we would have been killed. That would have been the end of everything.

It seemed really amazing at the time, he said.

Afterwards we felt *high*.

And then at the end of the summer I went home and she was pregnant, and I had the baby in a travel cot at the end of my bed.

And I think about it still, he said.

You think about it, I added sagely – feeding him the line – every time you hear *All That You Can't Leave Behind*.

On the steps, a day in autumn, he looked at me solemnly. And I could only say, Yes, I guess, if that is what you want, as I observed him with puzzlement or with concealed pity. There was a family dinner unravelling inside. I knew that at least some of his relatives were watching us, in boredom or idle malice, from the window of the living room.

You see, with you, my husband continued, I feel like I could do anything.

That's sweet, I said. Within reason.

As I started to think about it in the coming days, I gradually pathologised my husband's ambition as follows. He was sent to boarding school, away from errant parents, and a lay brother took such a shine to him he would give him books of poetry – books my husband kept, the seeds of a life spent reading, the origin of his attachment to me – and much encouragement; this I thought faintly scented of pederasty though I never said it; he'd conceived, in his teens, a sense of solid and aspirant selfhood, a self that was sedate and authoritative, and wished to embody this selfhood properly, in a way that could not be threatened by errant parents or illicit children or batshit women or economic exigency. I considered my husband's ambition a symptom of parental neglect and Jesuits, a symptom of wealth and unpreparedness, which allowed him to remain so charmingly naïve, so vulnerable to tantrums when the world ran up against him, as he saw it, unreasonably. To think of my husband as such made me sad for him, and queasily ashamed.

A little bit of pity is inevitable between us, is it not? *The painful condition*, as my sister once said, with all the lapidary acidity of folk disenchantment, *of heterosexuality*.

When he disclosed the brave and simple intention to enter politics, I searched for things on the internet and found cached files indicating that he had also attempted to stand as TD when he was twenty-two – right before the baby, I suppose, and sometime after the near-death experience – and failed to be nominated: this was something he hadn't said. Something left out of the anecdote.

I thought of the near-death drive and of the Buick GNX.

My dearest wish as an adult was, really, to be quite simply a normal person, which is to say to exist as something other than a burning wisp of futile rage; to belong, to be loved, never ever abandoned again. Because I was aware of this and felt bad about it I existed, as I was beginning to see at that time – four months into my marriage, or thereabouts – in a state of quiet conflict. I sometimes felt I was standing beneath someone's window, lamenting, a dog or an unreconciled wraith.

And so when my husband told me he intended to enter politics, standing on the steps above the coral rockery, before the big house where he had been raised and spoiled quite garishly, I finally said Yes, tell me: tell me all your plans. Being needed in such a potentially practical way was like going back to school in September, with new shoes and pencil case and mission statement, with the way lighted by praise. But as he began to speak excitedly I realised that there were no plans, only august ideas, and I told myself that, really, he had been so thwarted in his life and so despairing – even idle – it was lucky that I had arrived.

It was October, which is to say a haunted month. I was invited to a party at Halloween and I said to my husband, I don't think you can come.

Why not? My husband was sharp.

Struck bell of Harry rather suddenly: *Are you bored of my singing?* One day at the keyboard. No – not daytime. It was night.

You will be babysitting, I told my husband. It's inevitable.

I may not be, he protested.

Anyway, I said. It's all arty people. You won't like it.

Spongers? he teased.

If you talk about spongers, I shot back, that pal of yours in the Dáil, you can look at him! What kind of salary does he have?

This was an aide, an old Trinity friend, who'd met my husband for drinks in Buswells the night after his revelation of ambition on the steps. My husband came home afterwards enigmatically happy and self-regarding, but would not give much away about what they had talked about, even though he was quite calamitously pissed.

I was hoping my husband would come to the party because I wanted to show off; at the same time, I knew that my husband would be lost among theatre and art people and I was partly concerned for him, partly taken with a vague sadistic wish to see him struggling with it. In the end he was babysitting, then not babysitting, then finally coming to the party for two hours before going off to babysit.

I painted my face in an unimpressive approximation of a Day of the Dead death's head and wore plastic flowers in my hair. We rode the tram to Smithfield and went looking for the party among quiet airy squares between artisan cottages, silent mews, and red-brick nineteenth-century streets. Fanlights, door knockers, and windows braced the pavement with candid unbroken stares. The sky was muffled, holding the ochre impression of city light like brass. My face caught the attention of a drifting pack of little girls, carrying bags of chips and rolling bicycles, who hollered, Are yous going to the Halloween party? We let them lead us through more streets towards the house with the clever crepe tacked to the door. A girl on a bike dragged a foot and asked my husband, several times, Why aren't you dressed up?

At the house I tried to give the girls a note from my wallet but they fell silent, exchanging glances, and refused.

The door to the party was opened by a slim and intensely intelligent conceptual artist I knew because, years before, I had conducted an interview with her for an arts magazine that didn't run and did not pay a kill fee and now whenever I encountered her I was embarrassed and looked everywhere else and could not explain myself.

You look great, you look great! I cried, introducing my

husband, who at once complimented her on the Halloween decorations, beautifully constructed clouds of cotton
wool spun whimsically but anchored sturdily to every
light fixture. He spoke in a manic gush and I was pleased,
relieved, to see him speak at all.

This is heaven, said the woman, meaning the living
room; the kitchen, you'll see, is hell.

I was alarmed to learn there were not many people in
the kitchen yet and consequently it would not be easy to
blend in. My husband stooped in the small space, and I
greeted my friends with hugs and air-kisses because my face
was pasted over with greasepaint. Nobody else had painted
their face. In the shallow dash of the window above the
sink I looked ridiculous, but soon enough I forgot about
this, telling a comedian I recognised that two years on I
still recalled some aspects of a routine he had delivered at a
festival I had enjoyed – this was true, it was so funny; the
comedian accepted my enthusiasm with a blush.

My husband, as I had anticipated, became shy. At
gatherings he often sought out the man who was most
like him, which is to say earthy or roguishly decent, but
there was no man like him at this party, only actors and
artists and journalists and practice-based PhDs. He stayed
at the party longer than he should have stayed. He always
overstayed at things when I was there; he felt at home in
my atmosphere, and I in his. This was a true thing about
us. My husband relaxed around me. Or at least he did at
the beginning. I rewarded him for remaining at the party
by sliding over, hips skimming breakfast bar, to kiss him
lusciously, refusing to ask him if he was OK, because this
I felt was an infantilising thing to ask. At this moment
however I also felt that I needed to pee and passing the

bannister bulb at the foot of the stairs I rummaged idly at the coats to find my own, to extract my phone from a deep pocket. There were a number of missed calls and a text from my mother and I knew before opening it what this was about, I would have known even if there hadn't been a more recent text from my sister cresting the other texts and saying AT HALLOWEEN.

We had been aware that my paternal grandmother was dying for a week. We were estranged from my father's family but for an aunt or two and unsure about going to the funeral; or at least I was unsure. My sister both frankly refused and then laughed at us in surprise at the very suggestion. My sister had two young children and gave less of a shit about everything. She would be abrasive about it anyway if anybody dared to feel a thing because we had defined ourselves in contradistinction to my father's baroque awfulness since we were teenagers.

I returned the phone to my coat pocket and climbed the stairs. A bedroom door was open. Some students were smoking weed. I love your makeup! one of them cried. In the bathroom I observed that the place was much cleaner and neater than mine, used the toilet and settled my hair, and asked myself with soft clarity, how did I feel? The answer was a rather blunt Nothing. It had been at least ten years since I'd seen my grandmother.

When I came back down the stairs my husband was rushing from the kitchen with a worried expression on his face, mid-way through a faintly frantic and apologetic *Christ I have to go*. I didn't see the time, he said. He never saw the time.

At such moments I played the role of the perfect girl with fluency. I put my arms around my husband and said,

I will miss you, but I know. You have to go. You have to see the baby. Give her a kiss from me. My husband told me as he always did that I was wonderful. He asked if I would wait with him outside until he flagged a cab.

You won't get a cab here, I replied. I did not add: we are in a fucking residential area.

My husband did not suggest that I stay at the party as a result nor did I particularly want to stay behind.

I was plumbing my chakras and solar plexus, those vague loci of emotion, to find if I felt anything beyond a barely present dryly luminescent sense of self-importance at the death of my grandmother. Consequently, we walked through several silent orange streets, my husband towing me behind him by the hand, to the North Circular, where the special branch squad car that often rested at the junction with Black Horse Avenue sat with lights extinguished, two guards chatting together in the front seats. We were close to the Park. The air was slippery and liquorice with trees.

I am sorting this, my husband said suddenly.

No, you're not, I replied.

I am, I am sorting it.

I rolled my eyes. I had not even said a thing.

Taxis streamed up from the Park gate but did not respond to my husband's outstretched arm, prompting my husband to mutter, Why do they have their lights on then? At such times my husband became distracted. I know now that his mind was fixed, with hurtful purpose, with guilt, on his tiny daughter, on her mother, and on the weight of expectation, something I imagine as a groaning bower of trees but instead of blossom there are faces, accusations, precedents; his mind was fixed on these things and at the same time struggling to repress them or appease them with such hoarse banalities as *I am sorting this*, a phrase my husband came out with frequently, like a mantra or a symptom or a tic. At the time I tended to assume my husband was paying more attention to me than, I realise in retrospect, he was capable of. Or else it is possible I knew, somewhere, that he was not attuned at all to me or my mood or my thoughts or my needs – it is possible I made great allowances for this, carved martyring space in my mind, reduced myself to a vapid apparition who *would not complain*; did that thing I blame on men but am in fact complicit in, certainly with Harry anyway. On the surface, now, I ignored it.

But I suddenly said as we stood in the street, I don't want to go back. Can I come with you? My husband jerked around as if some external force were acting on him.

Darling, you can't, he said at once. You know that.

Just as far, I looked around me, as the house. I'll get a taxi home.

On your own?

Well, I'd have to go home alone now anyway.

I warmed to this line of argument because my husband was brought up in an affluent suburb and educated by Jesuits and Dublin Seven represented a kind of ghetto to him.

I was thinking of the dining room table, the dining room table of my grandmother's house, and the years spent doing homework there, with the television on, before my father remarried. And then even after my father had remarried, because he would combine his visiting duties to my sister and I with his visiting duties to my grandparents and thus kill two birds with the same weekly stone. This was Wednesdays I think. I had hockey training. I still wanted to fit in at school. I had shinguards and kneesocks and a polyester miniskirt, and all the girls wore football shorts beneath the skirt in case it blew up with a breeze, since showing knickers was at that point unthinkable. I had a ghastly gum shield of plastic softened in boiling water, fitted to my teeth, and hardened to the consistency of burned bacon.

I was thinking, the night of my grandmother's death, of her dining room table, of a set of trigonometry questions open before me, of the television on. Of the galley my uncles had built between the kitchen and the shed, which smelled of potatoes, and where there were old kitchen pans for playing with, and where once I was slapped in the face for a reason I can't now recall.

I don't mean to suggest that I was physically abused. I quite deserved that slap, as I remember; I must have done or said something outrageous. It is quite likely that nobody else can remember either, because it took place many years ago, and all sorts of random and radical irruptions of drama, of melodrama, characterised my final years in that family.

I stood on a kerb in Dublin Seven and I thought, because I couldn't help myself, of the galley and the pans. How cats would plop onto the ceiling panels; you could see the pink pads of their paws and claws and brushed bellies. We monkey-swung from the wheeled scoreboard on the cricket pitch and played the-grass-is-lava, the-grass-is-piranhas, punched our hands into the sockets left by speeding cricket balls.

We were so bored. Oh Christ alive, we were bored. Nothing happened until everything happened and my father left, and because I had been brought up so obedient, reticent and polite, I could not scream or howl or fight against the sheer walls of indifference I faced from every adult in my life until I was an adult too, and turned around, and said several irreversible Fuck Yous. Something I repeated, later, with Harry.

This I was thinking as a cab finally drew up, as I climbed into the cab with my husband in the year I was thirty, when I had not seen my grandmother since I was nineteen at least, and she had died. I felt nothing and I was concerned, not by the notion that I might be somehow cold or unfeeling, or emotionally repressed, but by the knowledge that there would be other deaths – so many deaths – between now and my own and these would be much worse, so dreadful, inconceivably dreadful. Dreadful to a degree I could not honestly conjure as a proposition or hypothesis, comprised of connective tissues and triggers whose complexity, even from a distance, was alien to me. This meant that no matter how derelict I'd felt in my life so far and no matter how depressed, the real matter of human grief was still waiting for me. And I was unprepared for this grief because I still felt like a child. I felt as if my childhood had extended into adulthood and I was living in a liminal state without defence.

I was *becoming* but the vagaries of fate wouldn't wait for me to grow complete. They might strike at any time and all belonging to me could be torn away, a roof ripped off the world, it happened to someone every day of the week, of course it did.

There is an earlier Halloween I have not forgotten. I was about eight years of age. I went to a party in the house of one of my friends, whose mother was different to the other mothers, and whose house was different to our house. The woman was offbeat and artistic and single. There was a laughing Buddha with long earlobes on the mantelpiece, a vegetable plot in the small garden, and a menagerie of domestic animals each with unique personalities we children could appreciate. At one point a chicken I think, I swear to God, who would have nothing to do with us.

Other mothers for the most part on my street were ferocious, with children and kitchens that never stopped smelling of fat; with rampaging whippets and milkmen and egg-men and the vegetable man; with the cobbler's van, Rottweilers chained to the shellfish packing plant, rats clapped to death with coal scuttles. Several *umwelten* overlapping in that Irish way, like downloads buffering and shuddering: four television channels and a standardised value system, piled fires of pallets, tyres, mattresses, at Halloween.

On this Halloween, we came back to the house of my

friend's mother, this single woman, after we had been trick-or-treating. I can recall kneeling above a basin of apples and coins, cold water running from my chin, feeling averse to ducking again. Outside was an anarchy of fire and fireworks. In other parts of the house adults were talking and laughing, drinking Blue Nun, and at one point the front door snapped to and closed again and the little girl whose house it was rose in fear and said Mammy, that was my mammy, she went out. Where did she go?

Another woman came in to shush us. She played with us for a while. We stood around and tried to smile, awkwardly aware that she was unused to children and overcompensating and slightly drunk. My friend's mother returned. She spoke to the adults first. My memory of this is speckled; time may be crunched uncomfortably into itself. I don't know. I do know that at one point she came, this woman, to sit with us and told us softly that a friend of hers, a grown woman, had tried to kill herself that night.

At this we fell into a dazed silence, lusting for more information but conscious that we had to pretend to be respectful now, since a question posed wrong in that world could mean a wallop on the behind. Now, said the woman, still softly, you see, while you are here having fun it is not like that for everyone. Some people are having a terrible time. Some people are very sad.

You must understand that the adults said things like this to us all the time, and teachers especially, and particularly about the starving children in Africa, who would love the cartons of lukewarm milk and egg sandwiches we tried in desperation to dispose of at breaktime. This woman, who was bohemian and kinder, did not in this moment draw on that lazy guilting gesture like other mothers and teachers would have done: she meant to be honest with us and not manipulative. Anyone else would have added *Now let's say a prayer for the lady* but this woman never said such idiotic things.

I thought for a long time after of the other woman, the one who had tried to die. I knew that she was beautiful but distraught and would have eyes that did not recognise you, or anything, and perhaps she lay poisoned on a Persian rug, and perhaps there were candles in pumpkins burning solemnly around. That perhaps she regarded herself in an enchanted mirror, clasped her hands theatrically, and smashed it with her fist.

My husband and I sat in a taxi under streetlight stripes, travelling the North Circular.

We'll drop you off at home, my husband said.

No, I'm coming to Castleknock, I replied. I said to the driver: Castleknock.

Now lads. The driver drummed his steering wheel affably: What's it to be?

My husband protested but I said, Castleknock, thank you, you can go by the Navan Road.

The driver looked at me in the rear-view mirror and said, I know that.

To my husband before he could protest again I announced, My grandmother has died.

Oh. He fell silent and took my hand. After a moment. Oh, love.

He crushed my hand close and I recoiled: I said, I do not feel a thing.

My husband, by way of consolation, searched for my face in the gloom and said, Well, she was sick. I was amazed and turned to him.

It isn't that, I said.

As we drove, the driver asked about my face, and because I had completely forgotten the greasepaint I turned to my reflection in the window and laughed hollowly. There were fireworks frying in the sky, and when these whooped and dropped the driver sometimes cried *Ho-hey!*

We reached Castleknock in less than twenty minutes. My husband asked, can you wait for a bit? He was looking up at the apartment block. Some children ran by, capes and shopping bags cackling, trick-or-treating a little, although it was getting late.

I dug my hands into my pockets and walked towards the canal bridge, where there was a pharmacist and betting shop and restaurant and a bar with a terrace that fronted onto the water, rebounding on the water's static skin, with grills overhead and fat plastic ashtrays. I pushed into the bar, which was crowded, and in which everybody was wearing costumes – several more elaborate death's-heads, vampires and ghosts and a morose-looking loner, at the bar, in a biohazard suit. Tilted mirrors on the walls and ceiling made the place look bigger than it was. I ordered gin and sat alone primly, placing my phone face-up on the table so that I could see him phoning or texting.

Time passed of course. The DJ played 'The Monster Mash'. Two devils in bandeau dresses, together with a man who had an axe protruding from his head, asked if they could take the rest of the table and, when I nodded yes, began at once to try to identify people in the room. They were from the country.

I knew it was foolish of me to have come and I struggled to define precisely why I had come, things had been on my mind – overlapping things, Harry and Anna and the landlady – but you know, it didn't seem terrifically unusual to me, it didn't seem ridiculous or degrading or even anomalous to be nursing gin and looking at my own cartoonish face in tilted mirrors, listening to the devils and axe-man talk about whether or not to go into town and go dancing at Coppers or Dice Bar or Q-Bar – this situation was, to me, lamentable and entirely boring, but not, just then, absurd. To be married and shredding beermats in a suburban bar on Halloween night, alone, like a single girl, like a dog tied up outside.

After an hour I phoned my husband and he did not pick up, but messaged, *just a minute, little kit*. He phoned a moment later and the baby was crying away in the background.

I should just go home, I said.

You know, he said, that I would prefer you here. I wish that I could be with you.

My husband wanted us to abscond to the South of France or Spain. We lost none of our illusions because we were safely tethered to our life in Dublin now. There was no risk of abscondence and no reality to intrude.

It took me a long time to hail a cab, so long I was close to tears when at last one shuddered suddenly around one of the quiet street corners – everything was apartments, the silhouettes of public swings – and I could ride home. I do not like to arrive back home alone. There is a line from *King Lear* that I think of, *Go to thy cold bed and warm thee, Go to thy cold bed and warm thee*, and I chanted this in my head to soothe myself as I curled up, shivering, against the sheets. It was in fact too cold to sleep for a time. Fireworks continued to sound like artillery rounds in the distance, becoming a natural sound, a source of comfort. I dropped into sleep and dreamt of packing for a journey with my father, packing sweets with cackling wrappers, until something woke me; movement, some interruption in the moonlight glowing from a moon set in a nest of shell-shaped clouds, an oyster seed. It was my husband undressing.

And the minute I figured this out, I felt love. Love indistinguishable from the gasp of an infant, from early panic. Deeply unsafe love. The theft of sleep, and breathlessness. I said my husband's name, and again. He looked down at me curiously.

Little kit, he whispered. When he lay in the bed the mattress thrust me upwards and I put my legs around him, gripping stiffly at the thighs, feeling the harsh down of his legs.

My husband, you see, had not wanted to leave the mother of his youngest child until he could be sure I was onside.

This, as I later realised, was one of the reasons we became engaged so quickly – we became engaged in two months.

Even though it had only been weeks, I said yes because I felt I could make a difference to his life. I would no longer be a child. And he would look at me with such gratitude that – well! There would be no more abandonment. I would be Juliet looking down into the grave-wells of his pleading eyes forever. The Pre-Raphaelite lady rising and stretching, moaning and waning. A fist thrust into a mirror, an end to all lethargic afternoons. Escape from Phibsborough.

What else, I asked my mother, do you propose I do?

You wait, she said. You see how things turn out.

I'd rather take my chances. I have plans. I am clever and very competent.

Yes we all know that, Alannah. We are well aware of that.

My husband proposed to me during an argument in Glasnevin Cemetery. I had waited all day for him to surface and when I met him in the evening I was in a rage.

What is wrong with you, what is wrong with you? I demanded. I've been waiting for you. You said you would come. Where have you been? It's been ages now.

I told her, he replied.

Well good, I began to chatter nervously. That's good, that's good to hear, because now we can stop pussy-footing around. Now we can stop walking at opposite sides of the street.

She came over this morning with the child.

Did she try to get back with you? I asked.

When he didn't answer I shouted, Did she try to get back?

He told me it was a huge mess, a chaos. He was pale and slurring and staring deadly into space, and I accused him of being drunk, but he insisted he was not drunk. Hours and hours, I complained, I was waiting to hear from you. I am this close, I swear.

We walked together, in silence, to the terrible island of tombs, its steep moat dried to red by the drought, and the iron doors to the family crypts. We crossed to the island and looked at the Plunketts and Counts and castle officials; these were the old and forgotten graves of the aristocracy. As we walked, in the sweet evening with its spangling of sour flower-scents, a helicopter rose and clattered over Finglas. I was shaking but then I felt calm. We didn't speak. We had taken this route through the graves many times before.

Just a minute, he said, and darted into the moat. Gravel shifted and skidded at his feet. After a moment I cried, you can't do that! You can't pee in here! He zipped up and returned.

Not a big deal, he said.

I laughed with shock and put my arms around him. And there it was: the irreverence, the boyishness, breaking through, promising something about the life I could have with him. Taking instead of asking for instance, no longer feeling ashamed. In play, he took me to another table-tomb, lifted me onto it, and pushed a finger into my underwear; through laboured breath, I knocked my head back; I gasped, Careful, we'll be seen.

When I die, he told me, I want to be buried here.

I will make sure of it, I said. I held back. I was quiet. I held myself back. He knew I was doing this and that he would need to do something wild to loosen it.

We loafed slowly to the huge mock-Norman tower and sat down, at last, next to the beribboned stillbirths plot. It stretched on flatly, covered with dappled grass and small spontaneous plaques. We were quiet. He kneaded my hand.

The plot was upsetting. None of the infants, I pointed out a little pedantically, had names, until a revisionist move in the twenty-first century to record them. People had had to measure the site of their family burial in steps from the rim of the plot, seventeen steps or twenty-eight steps, after they'd buried the unbaptised stillbirths in the night. Many of the names were simply Baby. People used to believe their souls were fluttering in limbo like butterflies. I could hear my voice in the dusk and the faint slash of passing cars on the faraway road.

On the bench he put his face in his hands and said, So much trouble is going to come out of this.

So long as we are all honest, I said.

Can we, he asked, just get married, in a couple of weeks?

At the time I assumed he was attempting to distract me or keep me sweet. But afterwards I realised that he believed getting married to me would stop everyone – everyone in his life, including his family and friends – from trying with alternate slyness and vigour to persuade him that he ought to stop fucking about and go back, go back and marry and live with, the mother of his youngest child.

He was desperate to escape, but hadn't thought on it further than that.

That night we stayed in my rented room in Phibsborough. I asked, over and again, in different formulations, Why in God's name and why in the name of all things would I marry you now?

But my mind was twitching and ticking and my future was thickening.

We should wait, I said.

No, he ground. He meant soon. Within weeks. He was firmly resolved, in that mood shot through with mania, with demonic certainty, like a line had been crossed and could not be reneged upon. Something had been struck and the logic of our lives was being engineered and entwined.

That morning, the morning after the proposal in Glasnevin, I rose as he slept and went downstairs and wrote in my notebook: dream of an archipelago.

I still have the notebook and I remember the tilting kitchen, the magpies on the spin-line in the yard of blue concrete. Archipelago: a petri dish of immaculate blackness combed on closer look by locks of shredded water – waves building – infinitesimal increments of prehistoric geology – sliding whale-size staves of ice, a world before sound that is nonetheless dimly roaring, dimly dreadful, dimly immanent – dusting of islands, dandruff perhaps, white, rather like stars – I dreamt of church refurbishment and underneath the altar there were several emaciated effigies, each holding Veronica veils: they looked like people lost in a desert.

Sometimes I tried to break these rocklike dreams, these mad banal chimeras, up; they read like Revelations staled to something automatic and mundane.

That morning I read back what I'd written and thought, it has nothing to tell me. It has no meaning at all. I am merely a geyser of old feelings and, moreover, of old failings. And I decided, then, sitting at the kitchen table in Phibsborough, to stop recording my dreams. Less dreams and more action, I thought. Less dreams and more leaping into the breach.

I returned to bed, where he lay beside me. He hadn't noticed me leave. I watched him and wondered if he would still want to marry me when he woke up. I knew that I would say, quietly but ferociously, I do.

He had two children, two orbiting women. In the weeks leading up to our wedding, this fact made everybody warn me about him in severe tones, and stress obvious cautions, as if the complications of the match had not occurred to me. They did this with sad smiles, at kitchen tables and across hearthrugs plaqued with fire-sparks.

But of course I did it anyway. Marry him I mean.

I hired my wedding dress, a dove-grey glove to the floor with a sash of satin at the waist, and I wore a beaded band in my hair from which fell a sheet of frosty gauze. I wore old shoes with encrusted buckles. My husband and I woke up together and travelled to the registry office, and afterwards hosted a buffet in the basement of Fallon and Byrne. The food was exclusively snack-based because money was rather a thing.

At the party I was so terrified that I could not inhabit myself; I could not inhabit the reality. I wanted the day to end as quickly as possible so that we would be alone with this thing we had done. We made love for hours, twisting together like surgical implements. I didn't believe it was real.

My mother had said, You know, you really do not need to jump; I replied, Well, maybe we see the world differently.

When I first dropped the gauze over my face, standing in the dress-shop weeks before, I saw the world shiver in silver like a dream and my mother said, You know that you can still change your mind any time.

Who knows, I cried waggishly then, what the future holds?

In the run-up to my wedding, however, I was not always brave. At a bus stop that same evening, having picked up my veil, I began to panic and cry; at an appointment, just ahead of posting the bans, I thought the registrar was speaking ironically to me, that her marked-in brows were darting upwards in hysteria.

But also I thought: You, Alannah, have always been like this. You have always been like a cat that cannot come to a decision. Have you seen this in cats? They look, bewildered, from one door to another: it is a risk, because their pride is compromised by mistakes.

You must, in life, come to a decision. And since I had returned to Dublin it had all been so dead. It had all been the same day stretched over weeks and months and finally years; it had been the adolescent afterglow, and I was bored again. Getting married was like pressing buttons on a mystery machine to see what would happen next.

And for a long time afterwards I believed that my marriage was my husband's fault. This was easy – the belief came naturally to me. After all it seemed like I had done nothing to encourage his attention and love and that I had, if anything, been aloof. I was tolerant and hospitable, like a blank sheet, or not quite blank but certainly uninhabited.

One day when the mother of his youngest child arrived for handover and waited in her car, refusing to come in, stepping finally onto the pavement because it was a hot day, I watched her. I watched from the window, Pollyanna tolerant, sympathetic and squalidly self-regarding; I saw the woman, tall and rangy, stalking the pavement, through a fume of flowering trees.

I watched her covertly. I felt confident in my dominion.

And so although it was undertaken in madness (what larks!) there was calculation – latent – in the whole thing.

There was the bare-forked greed of a dream about effigies, torn free and scrabbling, zombies in a desert of need.

I see me sitting at the window in Phibsborough, before I was married, blithe and blank-eyed as a debutante. I see me standing in the window of my husband's apartment, watching the other woman, and I look in this scene to be as avid and uncanny as a witch.

I see my husband – I observe certain siftings, I catch the reflection of action behind his eyes – realise by degrees that our marriage has been my creation, serving me.

We woke up, the morning after Halloween, to All Souls' Day.

I didn't go in to work. I worked from bed, without getting dressed. As the day passed I explored with courage and curiosity the staler odours of myself. And while I was not watching the government fell. Or rather the elderly Taoiseach, despite being at the helm of the reigning party, resigned. This had been imminent for some time. Mutterings in the ranks, and a failed coup years earlier: I remembered seeing shockingly toothless countrymen, marshalled for the news camera as if by deliberate mischief, saying together, Dublin will try to take over the party, but Dublin *will not win!* Dublin being shorthand for progressive I suppose.

And then, when I was not looking, the Taoiseach – the old guard – had his authority tunnelled, as my husband later explained, from within; had the structures of support weakened, came around to a new coup, and was put out to seed, probably. Dublin won.

This opened a hole in the Party, still in charge, into which stepped a young and withering statesman who had waited in the wings for years and happened to know my husband personally since, long ago, they'd worked together in student politics. Right before that is the birth of my husband's eldest child and torpedoing of his career in politics, the point at which my husband experienced a moral ossification that preserved him mentally, emotionally and spiritually at about the age of twenty-two, and as it happens that year I made my Confirmation: firmly, resolutely, flat-chestedly, in buckled boots, like a streak of self-esteem.

I was welfare officer at Trinity, he said. We debated in The Phil once, him and me – I'm pretty sure I won. I was treasurer, he was auditor, something like that. We were very sincere.

Ego.

No, we had ideas. My husband did a double-take and laughed, with a shake in the laugh. Ego? He asked. What do you mean?

The student politicians at UCD were essentially all date rapists, I said. I said this gaily, as if it were a joke.

Oh, that's UCD, he teased. You can't expect better from the riff-raff. They were almost all gay at Trinity.

We read the papers; we read every paper. In cafés we read the papers we would not buy. My husband was excited but underneath this furious. He would have made a better Taoiseach – this I knew was how he thought, he would have made a better Taoiseach, and it should have been him, would have been him, had he not been cast into the role of provider prematurely.

You are like a dog with a bone, I remarked.

Imagine, though, the money I would make. Just a one-term thing. Then we could buy a house in Normandy – a *chateau*, I said.

– Then we could buy a house in Normandy, and you could write, and I could write.

We'll do that anyway. Someday. When your baby is older.

We had lunch with his father, and as they were discussing politics fervently I found myself appealed to and I shook my head. I said, You don't want to hear my opinion.

Oh, you are for the other side? his father asked.

I'm a socialist, I said. My father-in-law rolled his eyes.

My husband and I played a game, often, without our clothes: he was MI5, and trapped me as I tried to escape, asking Where is the semtex, where are the tunnels, while spanking my buttocks with increasing emphasis until I squealed for release.

On a weeknight I saw that a musician I worked with at the university was playing in an orchestral concert at a refitted warehouse off Little Britain Street. It was a cold night and the temperature was dropping, dropping, outlining the city in ice. Chairs – which, I noticed, were tethered together with plastic garrottes – were arranged in concentric circles around the orchestra, and it played excerpts from *Don Giovanni*, excerpts from *Tristan und Isolde*.

With Harry, I had once attended a concert given by a famous experimental jazz pianist in the Queen Elizabeth Hall. I squirmed throughout, dug my middle fingers into the webs of flesh between thumb and index to contain my frustration and boredom and bafflement, feeling convinced that the room was faking it, wondering how anyone could possibly follow the flights and rills. At times the audience moaned with pleasure, or one section of the audience would moan, and the other sections would take it up in undulations of appreciation, and even though the pianist had requested no photographs the audience spasmed and splashed with camera flashes throughout the show.

This is how obnoxious, I observed, Londoners are. Harry said that it would be much worse in New York.

I liked the Queen Elizabeth Hall. I liked the way the weather was always steady when you stepped out, as if the city were a function room, some gargantuan function room of furniture with dust-sheets and a tight micro-climate of windless suspense. The bright terraces forgot about the river. But there was always a doomy tomb-like darkness at Waterloo, pockets of bluish-black despair, and Harry asked, Will you be all right to get home from here? I had to be all right: my heart dropped, and the lights of the station were cruel, the atmosphere frank and dazzled, in aftermath.

Going home alone and shrunken, alone and meagre. Curling into sheets. This was something I had expected marriage to banish. Erroneously, apparently.

I sat now, in Dublin, in the well-lit ex-industrial space. As I was thinking and fading in and out of awareness of the music of the orchestra I grew gradually more irritated at the fact that my husband, next to me, was sending text messages and responses.

I turned to look at him, at which point he pocketed the phone, but soon he went to the bathroom and remained there for some time. During the interval I stuck my head into the corridor and there he was of course, texting like a philistine.

Has something happened? I asked.

Wait, he instructed. I'll tell you about it after.

Has somebody died?

What?

Some horns, without, were warming up.

Because, my pulse had accelerated, I think you should probably go home if you are going to make such a show of me.

What? My husband essayed – I had never before appreciated the accuracy of that verb, *essayed* – an expression of surprise. Do you want, he held up the phone, me to stop?

Yes, I do, I replied.

As we resumed our seats a dragging sensation came over me. The supreme irony, I thought self-righteously, is that my husband came from wealth and his parents, I felt, looked slightly down on me. And yet this was not the first time his pronounced lack of manners was made apparent.

But at the same time he could be gregarious, old-fashioned, and I never paid for a meal or a drink, I never paid for anything, I was not let, not even when I knew that his money was tight.

These are the things I mulled over, weighing and reasoning prudently, until the end of the concert, at which point we walked into the glassy chill of the night.

My husband was texting at once and I wondered if this was to provoke me, if my anger registered. I ignored him, looking over the shuttered shambles of Parnell Street, the Tesco glowing with a punch of festive yellow in the dark. Under the portico of the GPO they were doling out soup to the homeless again.

Well then, my husband said at last. I may have a job. Speech–writer. Get this.

No. I whipped around. Are you serious?

I have a meeting with him.

Fucking hell. My eyes were wide. You mean that for real? But when?

Next week. They are recruiting and they're going outside the old guard – they are looking, you know, to bring new people in. New loyalties. Just wait. My husband smiled. Let's see. I told you they wouldn't forget.

That's great.

You didn't believe me, he said impishly, with edge.

You didn't tell me much.

We were walking down Abbey Street again. The turn in tone made my heart ring hollowly for an airy instant; it made the sounds around me simplify. I was surprised to see a fight coming, a fight I hadn't sighted in advance, and the feeling was not unlike putting a foot out expecting solid ground and finding instead an unexpected recess, even nothing at all.

I tried to override my dread. We were going home. Those shocking moments, yes, when another person becomes substantial to the point of mystical malevolence, confusion, in your midst – when you realise you have been paying too little attention and now you'll be punished for this. I overrode. I took his hand.

When my husband said *one thousand days in office* I'd presumed he meant some agreed segment of time, a term or a probation period, including or perhaps not including weekends: a sublime space of development and decay given mathematical resonance, in which you could make a lasting difference. And I'd thought, for me that was three weeks in a cottage years ago. Emotionally open as a wound. A split bark with a stone driven into it.

At home, my husband grew more manic in his

self-belief, and began to chant plans and forecasts and judgements, asking for input and growing tense at my reticence, beginning abruptly to monologue forcefully on the issue of Irish education, and specifically third-level education, because institutions were *bloated* with workshy *ivory tower* academics, an area he had strayed into once when drunk. I'd presumed at that time he was threatened by it. I had known quite a few boys, over the years, to be threatened by it.

The Irish third-level education system should, he said, be *fairer*, be more *transparent*, institutions should not rest on their laurels and funding of the government. I ignored this and stewed tea until he demanded my opinion.

You don't want to hear my opinion, I said.

Darling. He was sitting on the sofa. The lights were all on, the kitchen window was a wet black hole. I stood at the breakfast bar. I still did not feel like I lived in the house. Darling, my husband said, I want to hear your opinion, it is important to me.

The highest-paid people in universities, I told him, are management and administrative staff. Academics are not workshy. They work sixty hours a week sometimes. Or at least they are expected to. I don't. That's why I won't be given a permanent job. I shrugged. All the cuts mean is that everyone has to do more with less. You suggest privatisation. That's a total disaster. I saw it in the UK, and the students become apathetic confused consumers, the postgraduates are forced to work for free, it's bullshit. I get paid—

But don't you think, my husband cut in, that it should be made competitive, that this would improve the quality of the teaching?

It won't. The quality is fine. The research is fine. None of these are *malfunctioning*.

I think that they are, to be honest. I think that they are.

Well I think, I stomped open the pedal-bin and launched a teabag into it, that I know more about the area in which I work than you.

This was I felt a fair point, but my husband was insulted.

You talk down to me, he said.

You're talking rubbish, I said.

You think you're better.

You know. I was trembling now. Everything I have I have worked for: everything that I am, I have done it myself.

And not me?

Fucking Clongowes? I baited. Fucking Trinity?

Oh for God's sake. He closed his eyes. Smallest – what is it – smallest violin. You are the stuck-up one. He spoke viciously then, in pig-Irish: with your *grantíocht móríocht*, big grant, to do research and look at pictures, to write *poetry*. You look down on me.

No I don't, I protested. Even though, at times, I did. I mean right at that moment I disdained him so acutely I could not look at him. I didn't want to think like this. I wanted to be compassionate.

He had said, *With you I feel like I can do anything*. I wanted to explain now: I grew up in the working class. People who believed in their personal limitlessness were considered sinister or insane. I can tell that a goodly portion of your essential success in professional life has stemmed from the laminated reference and handshake you were given by the board of your boarding school. I mean basically everyone can the minute you open your mouth.

Of course I did not say any of this. It didn't seem the right time.

But in spite of my muteness my husband was angry now, standing there angrily, saying *I know what I'm talking about*. Ranting.

Ivory tower, house of gold.

I began to feel something of the black-hearted panic, the same reflex of animal self-interest, which I would feel and quell and feel and quell in waves whenever my father or some volatile adult lost their temper with me as a child.

I saw myself from above, standing behind the breakfast bar, wondering how I could contain this but also desiring dirtily to strike my husband in the face, to tussle with him, feeling certain in that flaring instant that I could take him and restrain him and pin him down even, shovel handfuls of grass in his mouth, cry, Horsey, eat the grass! As we did as kids. As at least one cousin did to me.

Just leave it, I said.

When I walked into our bedroom I was still trembling, not because I felt myself to be in danger, but because the coldly lawful autonomous animus of my marriage had dawned on me. It stood like a monument, surfacing from the *tabula rasa* of the universe, a gravestone or an obelisk, and making material the metaphorical abdication of status I had accepted in getting married. I had as they say *made my bed*, and one cannot go running back to Mother at the first sign of trouble.

I had wanted this, but just then I felt trapped and relatively penniless, my thoughts swarming panicked into the night and taking in the rich streets and closed houses, locked gates and sealed lips, blind eyes, all the rest of it – this terrain that was new to me and which I could not command yet. I did not own the place, I could not clear the demonic corridor of junk and grit – much like the cottage, really, much like the cold and black-soled morning when I knew I would be evicted. A stronger stomach is what you need, I thought.

You can blank me if you want, my husband called in an ugly voice. I can't stop you.

I slept. I put it right out of my head. At some point in the night I felt his weight next to me in the bed, his arms encircling me.

I went to my grandmother's funeral without my husband, because it was a weekday and he couldn't get off work. I met my mother off the train. She had been divorced from my father since I was a teenager and now, as we saw his relatives on approach – recognised faces slightly steepened by the passage of time – my mother said things like, Jesus, she looks well and then, Oh, but Michael looks *haggard*, oh my God he's *aged*, and I tried to be measured or polite and insist, He's like eighty, I'm surprised he's alive.

I felt nothing for the church. I was disappointed by this, since as a child I had been quite devout. I realised that I might have used it too many times, as a symbol, freighted with implications about my childhood. On Friday nights there would be candles ducking and flinching in red jars – dimpled red jars – and the smell of wax, the Virgin in her niche of toilet tiles, the Sacred Heart with *ora pro nobis* in uncial script. I had told Harry: That church was the origin of my aesthetic sensibility. It wasn't the kind of thing I would tell my husband, who was no longer awed by religion, but followed its edicts in a weirdly cheerful and proprietorial way. His daughters were christened, he still had his old-school prayer books, and he had wanted, actually, to be married in the Gardiner Street church. And I had said, You must be crazy, baby, if you think that's ever going to happen.

But, I said coyly, you can get one of your old masters to bless us, *if you must*, taken it must be said with an image of myself in some sleek little vintage costume, bowing my head, then taking the priest out for dinner and saying things like, Would you like some more wine, Father? Can I fill up your glass for you, Father?

And of course my husband forgot about it and never looked into doing anything of the sort. Ceremonies and children and, now, political careers just sort of manifested before him, apparently.

The morning after the argument he had been penitent. You are right, he said, when I explained that he was wrong: you are right. He did not elaborate and I didn't dwell on it. But: I hope you don't expect me to fail at my life so that you will feel better.

Of course not, he said.

Well good, because I don't intend to fail at anything ever again.

This made him laugh.

Oh I mean that, I said, but I laughed along.

When Mass began I watched a young demi-cousin twist around and around in her seat, passing an even expression from face-to-face in the congregation, and observed no adult interrupt or correct her at all. She was a plain child, overweight, at that awkward age of eight or nine, with puppy-breasts already, and her look of curiosity consequently less cute than unnerving. I found myself hoping that she would learn not to do that soon. That she would learn to stop looking openly for trouble in the world.

The priest was new and didn't know my grandmother. He gave a kind of self-regarding spiel about death and faith, eyes glazed since he didn't consider these things – the threat of Hell, one presumes, or of hubris, or something – to apply to him, and I was disappointed for her, mildly affronted for her, although perhaps now she didn't care; perhaps now it was all the same to her.

My grandmother was born, of course, during the war. I used to think that was why she shrouded and choked all the windows of her house in curtains and blinds. She spent most of her day in the kitchen, which had a large window. There were runner blinds, a layer of synthetic net, and two columns of crisp velvet curtains that were lined with calico and trailed on the floor like something opulent or ecclesi-astical. I used to think, in my primly aspirant schoolchild way, she had grown up in the age of blackout curtains, something like *Carrie's War* or some other library paper-back. But later they told me that, in fact, in the sixties, a half-wit neighbour who was known to be a drinker would creep up to kitchen windows at night – kitchens contain-ing housewives – and spy on them. My grandmother was terrified of him.

I felt at first that the story was funny and poignant and of course absurd – why couldn't somebody run him, why didn't they *do* anything? – but, later still, the dry-heat seediness of it, the window crusted with fabric, the spoiled sofa of crochet throws like bladderwrack, became a kind of idle nightmare; became a teeming metaphor or a *mise en abyme* saying something while not saying anything about the condition of women, and repression, and soft furnish-ings, and sex.

My grandmother had been a hosier in her teens. She worked on the factory line. After she was married she made dresses, on commission, in her kitchen, for other women. She had her wedding reception, she once herself told me, in the parochial hall. They hired a huge Burco boiler to provide sufficient tea. She spent her wedding night on the mailboat to Wales, and had her first children – a young wife as I was a young wife now – in Whitechapel. The West Indian women in the council block would not talk to her, she said, and the whole of the block, she insisted, was West Indian.

I pictured the erect indignant woman with her funereal hooded pram, walking up-and-down and around-around Whitechapel, far from hen-wives and hosiery line, with two bonneted babies cooing out at her – two at least. Three years in she could not take the pea-soup post-war vibe any longer and took drastic action, in what I see, at this distance, to have been her combative, uncompromising style: she returned to Dublin, by herself, leaving the children with some other Irish wife – some other navvy-wife – and now, of course, I pictured the erect indignant woman with a silk scarf at her throat, a pillar-box hat, declining food and chat for the six hours it would have taken the ferry to get from Holyhead.

She returned to her father's house and waited there until her husband relented and followed her. They never left again.

Now this life, whose finer details were comic to me, had concluded, and no doubt she was all right with it really, being so old. I knew that I understood her as a kind of brand on history, a seal, a *fiery shorthand*; none of her sufferings were mine to inhabit, I had so many more freedoms; for her, I was *cast out*. In the otherworld she might look fully at my history and weep.

And yet. In the church, I remembered something else. I started and thought of the strangeness and fondness of the recollection. But as I turned it over in my mind I felt faintly ill.

All of these weird things that have become accepted: all of these coincidences, arranged and collected and pointing like clues.

I was not in Whitechapel when I met Harry, but I was also living in a council block – a post-war block – for crazy rent with four other girls. It smelled of bleach always. It smelled like it was trying to conceal some other smell, like a mortuary. A broken gutter caused a gourd of damp in one of the rooms. In the toilet, at night, the freezing tiles would twinkle here-and-there with silverfish. With time the smell of bleach became gentler and homely. This was, of course, in SE1. It was a room I gave away long before the lease had expired, because of Harry.

We met in Senate House, Harry and I, at a conference on censorship. I was wearing a short dress with duvet-blunt tea-roses and I remember this because I knew, as soon as I got to the conference, that I had chosen wrong, that it was too short and too cheap-looking. It was spring but there was a merry wind trundling through the courtyard, underneath the mausoleul hood of the entrance to Senate House, out through Bloomsbury, a cavalry.

Oh, and he followed me, I remembered – standing in Mass, standing for some Creed I could not fully remember, the crumbs of other people's muttering.

He followed me with the other students through Russell Square and to the Seven Bells or the Admiral or whatever it was; false chalkboards, cheeseburgers, thick steins and pints of beer, and when it got dark there were bars of heat and blue gaslight in the ribs of parasols outside. And by then, curiously, there was no wind. I must have changed the memory. And yet I see the square, its trees, in perfect stillness, like a frieze.

That night we rode the motorbike to my flat, to the flat in Borough that I shared with those four other girls.

Do you know the Tabard? I asked.

I think so, yes.

Well make like a bird for the Tabard. I laughed. I patted his shoulders decorously. Good man, away! You know, I added, it is the very beginning of the *Canterbury Tales*.

Behind the Tabard, amidst several sixties tenements, was the block where I lived. We sat on the floor of my room, on an acrylic carpet made to look Persian. All around were clothes and snapped CD cases, books, shoeboxes, junk jewellery. My bracelets and my brushes and my handless Child-of-Prague, a christening gift I took – with ironic fondness – to every digs I rented in.

We sat cross-legged in the very centre of that and talked about our lives and writing and I said afterwards to a friend, I know him, *I have known him:* I have known him in another life. Already how he smelled, shoe leather, brushbristles, hay-saving, hops – was everything. Then all at once he stood and said, It has been lovely, so lovely, you really cannot know how nice.

But you can't go, I cried.

I was I will admit something like three sheets to the wind, but still, my heart began to race: You cannot go, I said, what are you talking about? Stay here.

I can't stay here. He stood, silhouetted – I hadn't lit

a lamp, there was only the window and the city and the Shard half-finished, burning white.

To sleep, I corrected: I don't mean sex. Just sleep; we'll go to sleep.

I can't stay here, he said. I have to leave.

When I saw that he was serious, a certain vertiginous sense of loss came over me, so disproportionate, and so unbearably real.

Go then, go then, I answered rashly. You know where the door is. Go.

I'm sorry.

Go quickly. Just leave.

Is life just this – moments like hinges? And there it is: an image of her back, her pillar-box hat, descending erect and indignant down the scored stairwell of a post-war building. An image of his back, alert in the dark but no turning back, descending the scored stairwell of my post-war building. Like a tattoo or a pattern or an archetype you see. People leave.

I had said to my husband, after the argument, I won't stay where I'm not wanted. No, I won't. Although I wasn't really sure if this was true.

Harry had left, that night in London. On that night I had felt terrible, obscurely terrible, and gone to bed. Even though we had only just met, and he shouldn't have meant a thing to me: there was, you see, this kind of vertigo from the start.

The morning after we met I got up with a hangover and dressed as usual and went into the Maughan like a normal person but he had kept my number: he did not text me, he telephoned. As we spoke I sat in the little garden at the Maughan and sifted gravel with my feet.

143

By my mother in the church I thought, newly troubled: I have been so broken, so very desperate, in my time, haven't I?

Unmoored, you might say. Adventurous. Dangerous.

After the Mass I said, I'm not sure we have time for the burial, if you have to get back to work. Let me just say hi to Dad and we'll go to the car.

Whatever you like, she replied. She was looking indulgently about her. The dead woman had been unkind to her, after all. After my father had left, my grandmother came to my mother with her Eucharist kit. She said, Now you must ask for forgiveness.

There was something extremely strange about it all. About those weeks after I had seen the landlady in Dublin, on the cobblestones, when I had been married for just under four months. I don't wish to give you the impression that I found it anything but strange.

That one woman should come back into my life – the landlady – and another woman, my grandmother, leave, and that neither of these things should be related or twinned in significance, only random agitations of fate, made me feel as though I had suddenly come under intense scrutiny by some watchful force. By the universe. That Anna should come, blank-faced, trailing my mother and stepmother and myself at seventeen – myself, huddled at the edge of a building site, waiting as usual for something to happen to me.

And it just got stranger and stranger, you know: it just got faster and faster, the mechanisms.

I had a teacher given to sick leave and strange pronouncements at school. Over the blackboard she had pinned *Meallann muilte Dé go mall ach meallann siad go mín*: God's mill grinds slowly, but it grinds finely. It never left my head, of course. So many things I have forgotten – useful things – but there it is, and there it persists: *meallan muilte Dé*.

Not always slowly, mind. Sometimes it is plugged for a long time, blocked, and brims and streams forth through a rupture or a fracture in the moral universe – is what I started to think. It felt like none of it was within my control. That there were pistons and ear-splitting bells. Yet I woke up every day of those weeks by my husband, a man who hadn't noticed a thing.

Part Four

Part Four

An evening, early in the second week of the cottage.

Let me find it: dusk, and lamps.

Harry and I set to chopping vegetables as the light faded and I watched a window become a full-length mirror in the gloom. A sense of fretful bliss descended. I found that I could hardly speak.

I am quiet, I told him apologetically.

Oh, you couldn't be quieter than me, he laughed. Though you know, you are quieter than most Irish people.

He came behind me tentatively, placing his hands on my shoulders and running them down my arms. After a moment of this, hands came around and caught me by the abdomen, face pressed into my hair. In terror at breaking the spell that had led him to touch me I stayed still, hanging tensely, words surging in my heart like something drowned out by the sea, *o love, o love*. My thoughts spun to my lonely stomach and breasts, poor ribs, the curve of my hip. My body throbbed but his felt solid against me.

I remember that night – I see how it changed. I see the arc and know, for instance, that it rained. It rained later. It wasn't raining then, embracing in the kitchen. And yet in my memory, this moment in the kitchen, embracing, the tincture to the air of vegetables, was *glutinous*, that is the word, with latency: the latency of rain.

Newly married, recounting it at intervals in libraries and at my carrel in the research institute, in cafés, pondering it like a problem in those odd weeks after the landlady, I could see the overlay. I knew it hovered there, a nervous energy, a membrane full of nourishment and containing, you see, older impressions, older memories of rain. It was a *home*, a home of atmosphere – architectural – and a closeness: I was back in Ireland. My bones knew rain was coming because rain will always come in Ireland and I've spent my life anticipating rain.

I wondered if I had come home to Harry somehow.

I see the kitchen in dwindling light: I see us resuming our conversation. Lamps. But it was summer. Why the lamps?

Would things fare better for you, he asked as we ate, if you were to move into some other area, do something else, in London?

I realised that I had been complaining again, aloud and unthinkingly, about my doctorate.

I suppose so, I answered darkly.

The place is not what it used to be. When I was there and first married the place was a delightful shambles. East End especially. It is filled now with those people you mentioned.

Hipsters.

Yes. I remember a time when that word meant something else. We looked enquiringly at one another when his mobile phone sounded in the next room. I know what that is, Harry said, rising. It's the director. He goes on. I am sorry my dear, can you wait?

Oh yes, I'll wait, I said.

He was some time.

With the rain's latency, I think of the song I was listening to at the time, about the pain that flows through life like water.

I finished clearing up and sat down on the couch beside the window. I felt doleful, and remote.

When I came around it was cold, and I realised I had fallen asleep on the couch with my arms and my feet bare. Woken now by the chill, the radiantly rueful chill of summer nights – empty gardens, empty beaches, packed-up carnivals – and the pot of leftovers on the hob was also cold, the lamps were brassily cold.

I could see by the clock that about forty-five minutes had passed, not so long, not at all actually, but my head had begun to ache and I was cold and everything felt different then: a mirror-inverse of itself, uncanny. I hunted out a jumper of peach chenille. I was sitting on the couch again when Harry returned.

Are you all right? he asked, switching on the overhead light, a gesture which seemed somehow accusatory.

Yes, but I'm cold out of nowhere, I replied.

I think it might rain.

Really?

Come and see.

We stood in the doorway, where the air was milk, beneath the sensor light. A queen moth like a cigar stub was circling the bulb. The trees and boreen, pampas-grass and sky, everything was intense and condensed, silent, and without wind. It felt pregnant and prepared to rain all right, smelling almost chemically of silage, an odour that was cuttingly familiar to me although I hadn't encountered it since I was a child.

It's beautiful out, I said truthfully. It was shocking actually. You're upset, I said. I had not meant to say it and kindly surprised myself.

It's only work, Harry replied, but back inside he began to clean up the kitchen in complete and unpleasant silence. I stayed morbidly close to him, peeling an apple I then abandoned browning before me because I felt too anxious to eat it.

And there it was: latency.

I knew I had not done anything wrong and that he had probably fought with the director over the phone but my need was too terrible and compulsive. I had no hold, at twenty-three, on my own complexities.

I found myself speaking again.

Perhaps, I said, you shouldn't write for other people, you shouldn't write for TV. You have plenty of money and, now, you could write another book. You could write a novel. You could write what you liked, on your own terms. You could come and live in this cottage full-time. I remember – I began to enter into it, to feel authoritative – why I first came to art, and that was because I was sent to a storeroom at school, to get glue or something, and there was a print of a screaming pope by Francis Bacon, one of the screaming popes with the strokes like bars, like a cage, you know? And I wasn't expecting this, I was twelve, but I jumped when I saw it, it shocked me so much, it was thrilling and taboo or something, so weird, so I try to remember, sometimes, why I'm here, why I do it, which is partly for credit and grades and everything, but also because I am chasing that feeling, maybe, of shock, of coming across something real and repugnant and terrifying. That is the origin. It—

Stop, Harry said.

I not only stopped but lost my breath. I stared at him and was speechless because he had never spoken to me like that before.

I'm sorry, he said without sincerity, but when I'm deep in my own work I have to stay in my own work and not be distracted.

Oh, I said. OK. I waited for something more than this, but nothing came.

I, I said. And then I started to laugh even though I did not find it funny at all. I raked my hair to the top of my head and held it there, warm in my fingers, for comfort. OK, I finished thoughtfully. I went slowly upstairs so that he wouldn't think I wanted attention for going upstairs: it was not a tantrum but a tactical escape. In the bedroom I had nothing to do – it was even colder there – but the rain had begun, feathery and unfulfilling, on the thin old plates of glass.

I would experience this strange lonely panic again, of course, on the night that my husband mocked me and, newly married, I stepped into another room trembling, superior, enraged, also unable to escape. In Harry's cottage I tried to tolerate the silent scream leaking through me to become muscular, tension and adrenalin, until it subsided, and I could sit on the edge of the bed wishing suddenly, fulsomely, that I were drunk.

All right, I said, again, out loud. This time my tone was ironic and it felt as though I were breaking some kind of fourth wall.

Downstairs: I'll visit the farmhouse. I'll let you work.

Thank you. Harry was at the kitchen table with paper and pens. I'm sorry, he said, more authentically this time: this is the way, I'm afraid, I live my life.

Oh I know, I said. Or at least I'm discovering.

Do you want a raincoat?

Is there a raincoat?

There was. It was a lady's Barbour jacket and it had to belong to somebody but I didn't ask about that. I thought with an unwanted prickle of bitterness of that other woman, earlier in the summer. A woman with dark hair like mine and green eyes like mine who glanced at Harry singularly on the night of the Queen Elizabeth Hall; who crossed to speak to him but only when her friends were crossing too. I was pouring wine and saw everything, her anger and her Arthurian profile, but I knew if I asked he would dissemble – closed eyes, *oh that*, a sigh that crumbles to a smile. A finger to my chin or cheekbone. I didn't want to be a hypocrite. The jacket smelled only of wood smoke, like everything.

In the lane the last light showed the rain shivering, and the sound of the rain in the canopies was enchanting. It calmed me. It was by now about nine o'clock. In a more peaceful mood I rounded the back of the farmhouse, admitting myself by the kitchen door, as Harry had told me to do.

Oh hello! The landlady looked up from a ledger. She was sitting at her counter in a kimono, by a bowl of unyielding nectarines, and her fair hair was wet on her shoulders and neck.

You were out in the rain? I asked awkwardly.

I had a bath. She looked at me a moment. Has he sent you over?

I think that I am – I raised my hands in slapstick – under his feet.

Oh to hell with him. She sat back and looked around. Stephen is somewhere, she said. Will you have a drink?

That would be nice.

You are, she said, getting bored, I should think.

We sipped Talisker before a fire-screen even though the grate was cold and filled only with pretty twigs. The weather – which was insipid and not stormy, as I had thought – kept the air cool and moistened and enlivening. Stephen, her husband, was a tall and warm and donnishly bashful man who worked at Queen's, driving over the border three days a week. He spoke about his students, his history PhDs. They all sounded mystifyingly interested in parliaments from the eighteenth century. The landlady watched him ironically as he spoke but she was, I could tell, proud of him, and flirtatious with him. I liked both of them better after this. Before I left she said, You are a scholar too, are you not?

And are you good? Stephen teased.

Oh I'm brilliant!

I don't doubt it. He tipped his glass.

It's a pity, added the landlady, we do not have Harry tonight.

Oh he wouldn't, said Stephen, want alcohol anyway.

He is in the cave of creation, I explained proprietorially, with the *muses*.

Ha! Muses, she said. Harry was a rolling drunk once, you know.

He's mentioned it, I said. He had said nothing more but I didn't want her to realise I was interested; I didn't like that she had all this knowledge and wore it so chicly and vindictively.

Reformed by marriage? Stephen drained his glass and didn't look at me.

Put in his place by marriage, more likely, the landlady said. And look how well he's done. I remember the flat with the – what was it, rant poet? You grow up you see, Alannah, she turned to me: you come into your kingdom, in the end.

I am sure.

Do come and see us again, she said.

Another night. Certain nights bleed together but this one is pricked out for me, picked out, from the second week.

Let me find it for you: images.

Image of a man in a black mood, face unavailable. A blanket rough enough to spark. A young woman peeled like fruit, face ardent, lit by the smell of the bed – of peat and pelt and sweat – with hair cut in a pageboy shape she regrets.

What had been called *the cutest little cunt*, albeit by another man, a student actually, who lived with his grandparents so that there was a comical crooked crucifix over the bed. Cutest little cunt warm and tight and, to me, remarkable: I often drew the balls of my paws along it during the day. The student burrowed between my legs so deep I could feel the beam of his nose high up, underneath my navel.

This man – Harry – was so different.

He was, to begin with, still in an evil frame of mind. He had spent all evening playing keyboard by himself. I came back from the bathroom in stockings and he had slid to the keyboard stool; he was singing ragtime tunes.

Prior to this it had been going, slowly, where it should.

On the floor, on the ribbed rug, he had softened and come to me at last, he had slid one breast from the red lace halter-neck I wore. This wrapped around the ribs and tied at the nape of the neck. He sucked on one nipple so sweetly at first that it gave me a shock when he bit and I gasped and tensed under the hands that were kneading my stomach and pelvis. He might, I thought at once, actually want to hurt me, by tiny cuts instead of blows.

Now he only sat and sang compulsively, gruffly, as I curled by his feet like a patient pet.

Always it is perverse to realise that a man is afraid of you.

I could sure go for some whiskey, I said dryly, as if starring in a film he would watch afterwards.

Are you bored of my singing? he asked sharply, sounding like nothing so much as the *cigire*, the petty state inspector, at school.

I am never bored of anything you do.

He played.

Bed, I commanded at last.

In revenge he ignored me to begin with, where we lay in the attic room. It was always left purposefully coarse but I did make the bed and draw the eiderdown every day, and at some point in the day Harry would remake it and resettle the eiderdown, so that it was level and luminous. He seemed on that night slightly angered or frightened by me or by the litany of obligations my presence made necessary. Including sex. What could I say in response, to break the tension? Nothing nice this time; something cruel or obscene. Get hard and stay hard and satisfy me. If he lost it I knew I would not be able to prevent myself from giving him that look: the look of mother or wife in moments of disgust, the look of a mistress with the cutest tightest cunt that she has crossed the ocean to present to you. Put your hand in and draw out her organs like birds, like magic handkerchiefs.

Soon after it began he came abruptly as ever and silently, so that I could not see it coming, with a jagged buck of the knees and waist. Afterwards he held me tightly from behind and rested his hand on my abdomen.

Do you know what *cunt* is in Irish? I asked.

In the night it was not always easy to sleep next to Harry. I was afraid of him or afraid of the situation, or melancholy. He often slept in his clothes. Even if we made love he would get up and put something on – even though it was summertime – whereas I slept naked and emphatically so. This was part of my performance.

His clothes were expensive and abidingly Sloaney. He had slight sciatica at times and woke in the night, or half-woke, hissing, *fuck*, and I found this hilarious – I can tell you I found this utterly hilarious – although not for the reasons I put across. I laughed coyly at him one morning and said: You are adorable. Harry answered, Ah, it is like those wild animals with little faces you find appealing even though they are fierce. But really I laughed because it gave me scattered iridescent impulses of pleasure to see him look foolish for once, showing his age, when most of the time I lived and breathed in a shadow of awe, genuine awe, quite paralysing awe – I mean that I looked at Harry and thought, why amn't I you, and, why aren't we one? I should have had that life of adventure. I should have a life like that. So much time has been wasted, being good. I thought these things.

But in the night, if he cried out *fuck!*, not helplessly but in frustration at pain and its abruptness, I chuckled, I loved it, darkly loved it, and in the morning compartmentalised. For it made me quite guilty afterwards. I teased again, I said, you are so English, imitating: *fack!*

Sometimes, you know, I was not performing. Sometimes I was vulnerable. I was after all very young.

It is difficult to recall this now – oh I can recall it, certainly, but it is real, or have I doctored it? *Dotorossa*: the word he gave to me. You will have no more problems soon, he said, because you will be a bona-fide *dotorossa*.

This was the middle of the second week, when Harry was once again being nice to me. In continuing friable feathery rain.

We walked in the boreen, an uncultivated strait of tyre tracks like writhing spines. No county hunt had taken place that day: the foxes were safe, and no horses picked their way along the rims of carriageways. Here trees tittered and the puddles that we walked through were broken at the top with squalls of rain. Water rapped on his mackintosh and my raincoat, my two legs sheer in thin inconsequential hose and, underneath the raincoat, coltish. The landlady's dog sprang ahead to shit in the hedge. We were talking about me again, about my future, about my professional life. Or at least Harry was. This was an occasional favourite theme.

At this distance I wonder if he reverted to it – the paternalist concern – out of guilt or as some kind of distancing gesture, talking about the life I might have as if what I had now were a pit-stop or back-step, or convalescence;

referring always to those times in his youth when he himself was confused or without direction.

It was clear that he wouldn't be present in this future life being summoned for me. I chose, at least consciously, to interpret this rhetorical reticence as the sort of politeness one usually uses with lovers when one wants to be self-effacing or not presumptuous. After Harry, for instance, I did similarly on many dates: I told boys, Oh wow, you'll travel the world, when they spoke about studying languages or political theory or psychology or anthropology or information technology or basically anything really.

Now, with Harry, in the lane, it was not something I wanted to hear. My life was boring and broken, as I saw it. This was not a hiatus but a kind of Damascus moment, dilated. This was my – he was my – epiphany.

I never said as much; I waited for him to figure it out with me.

An old girlfriend of mine, he explained, became a professor of, I think, literature. I mean that she did well out of it. She is somewhere on the continent, in some university over there: Leuven, maybe. Is Leuven a university? Yes? I haven't seen her for years but I do know that.

I was silent for fury at first, then despair.

This is different.

It's different?

There are no jobs. It is very elitist. I cannot afford to be a jobbing tutor or work for free. I crunched fists together in the pockets of my coat. I feel sometimes that I might as well give up on everything and kill myself.

My goodness, said Harry. It is a little extreme, is it not?

But I am trapped.

Nobody is trapped. He looked at me. Especially not a young *dotorossa*. You are just afraid.

I have no means, I insisted.

You don't?

I don't have a bean. I kicked a pane of water to pieces at my feet, catching the attention of the dog, who stooped in enquiry. Let's not talk about this any more, I said, it's making me tense.

I just wanted to be helpful, he said.

At the end of the lane the old parkland was stubble. I tried to explain how well I knew it, this flatly saturated land with caravans and wind-chargers and complex aerials like gibbets rising over brown swatches ploughed straight as if machine-baled tight with string. Beaches glowing smooth and flesh-coloured: the flat and poisoned-looking fields much the same as in my childhood, silos rising solemnly.

In a few years, Harry told me as a blade of water passed between us, sending us to the sliding banks at either side, we will sell the house in London and move on. I might give up this place too.

You seem to love it so much, I said.

I have loved it. But there is not much out here.

Tranquillity? I teased.

Nonetheless a presence pounded in my chest. He said, But why not go somewhere where there is, for instance, sun?

Sun-and-grapes, I echoed.

On the return track, somewhat contritely, his step fell closer to mine. I jutted my chin out atremble, my long legs simply lovely to behold. He took a hose to our boots at the back of the house.

That afternoon, Harry said: Bad news I think.

You think?

London. I might have to go back.

What?

I did not let myself analyse it yet; I held my breath.

Over and back. The director, he wants to talk in person. It's that or bring him over here.

Bring him over. We can take him out and show him the holy head. I knew at once I had overstepped something with *we*: a *we* that was Harry-and-I and not Harry alone, or Harry-and-Harry's wife. He did not respond. Later, he said, Yes, tomorrow afternoon – I'll fly, I'll come and go. It might be Thursday, even Friday, when I'm back. You will be OK? Left to yourself?

I suppose. I'll let in the cat every day.

Oh, I don't worry about him. Don't let him boss you around. He looked pained. There is nothing to be done, he said aloud to himself. Over and back. I'll be very fast.

And then: These people, he said, they are so often like this. *Worried*. It is, oh I am worried that you are harming my vision! Artists, you see. Never write for money.

He packed the kitbag. Unpacked it, and repacked it again. He seemed agitated. I'm sorry, he said.

Are you worried, I asked, about the house? I won't burn it down.

I brought you over here, he said, and now I'm leaving again.

But you'll be back.

I will be back.

Harry. I was standing, then, behind an armchair. I was holding a fat little cushion, grazed chintz, between my hands, but I couldn't remember how it had come to be between my hands – it was there, robustly comforting, and

165

I was standing behind the armchair, as if the armchair were an altar. Harry. I looked at the cushion, at the teeth of its zipped cover, bared teeth.

Alannah?

Oh, I smiled. Say it again.

Alannah.

Harry. I am happy here.

It's nice, isn't it?

With you I mean. I am really happy, here with you.

It's just twenty-four hours.

Oh I know. It's OK, seriously. But I am happy. I wanted to say. With you.

I thought he might leave, but instead I felt his eyes on me, where I bowed my head. I put down the cushion and took hold of the wings of the armchair. I was standing as though I could push it on its coasters. Barricade the door.

I know I've been terribly busy, he apologised, but that is how it always is. It's how I live my life.

I was surprised. I looked up and frowned.

I know, it's OK, I can cope with that.

Are you sure? It's not much fun for you.

I don't mind at all. I don't mind at all. I mean – really, I don't! The sensation of something slipping from my grip.

The landlady is going to drive me to town, he said.

When he had left there was a wide and total silence for some seconds before, in the kitchen, the washing machine completed its cycle and sang out thinly – there were three notes, on a scale – and when we'd first arrived Harry had shown me this, caused it to sound, said, See, it sings out when it's done. Clever machine. In the kitchen the cat was also drinking from the dripping tap. He leaned a lovely paw against our porridge bowls.

166

I lay down on the loveseat and looked at the ceiling, at the vault of beams, for some time. I was shocked, after about a half-hour, by a knock on the door. It was the landlady. She said, Since you're alone, come over if you need anything.

Thank you, I answered carefully.

Good girl. She turned in her little boater hat. By the way, she added, the cat has killed a leveret. It's left it over there. She pointed to an upturned orange crate in the yard.

That was nice of him.

He's fiendish, she replied.

She did not stay away from me long. She returned the following day. She knocked on the door once again.

I will take you for a spin, she said.

We drove along the brown rim of the river to where the estuary began to break into sandbanks. A Norwegian ship was docked where cranes could swing pallets from its deck. The sky above was whistling clear, cloudless and cool.

Do you know where we are going? the landlady goaded.

I pretended not to have a clue.

We passed a hamlet and a tackle-shop reflected on the surface of the water. Evergreens above a drystone wall. A swan drifting beneath an information station indexing more unusual birds. The place became beautiful. The landlady's Land Rover rattled over a cattle grid that bridged an honest-to-God ha-ha and drew up the drive of a country house with a strange hipped roof like a mushroom. Many windows caught the light. A meadow, silvered by the morning mist, swept to the river below. There were extraordinary trees and grand steps to the dark doors and dozens of architectural features I couldn't name, like wildflowers, part of some knowledge lost to me or never obtained – I had never seen anything like it before. As the landlady parked to the side of the drive, a middle-aged woman emerged from the yard behind and waved her arms.

They are in London, she shouted.

I wonder if I can show this girl the hall for a moment. The landlady shut the door of the Rover and pulled her jacket around her. She is an art student.

I can't let anyone in. The woman shook her head and stood wide-hipped, with legs apart, as if guarding it. She wore overalls and a hat pulled low on her head.

I could see the tall gable of a chapel with a blue-faced clock on the front – worn down by time, now numberless – over a wall of ivy and withered trellises. The river shone as an arrow of geese rose against the sky and haystacks stood around in prehistoric mist.

The landlady argued, You know I'm Harry's good friend, but the woman in overalls would not be moved and we had to turn for home.

Just wait until I talk to Harry, the landlady swore. She had been embarrassed. But I knew she wouldn't believe me if I told her that I didn't care about the house, the house of his wife, anyway, didn't care for her or anyone; felt chilled by the deadness of the day, the thoughtless clock, the river-rot. The house in its elegance concealing a closed claw of money and the river sliding blankly by without comment.

Back at the cottage I pulled several blankets over myself and lay inert. She would say nothing to Harry of course. He might not think her stunt was funny at all.

Alone, for one day.

It got hot again. The rain receded. It remained wet, and hanging, and latent, and hot.

I rode my bike down heavy laneways, green and laden and white and alive, and loud with insect sounds. In the distance I could hear machines saving hay. The air was warping with midges around me, catching and coming apart. I stood on the pedals and pedalled slowly; I sort of *trudged*, rubbing against resistant gears. I was not wearing underwear. When I sat on the peak of the saddle this was such a strange feeling.

Nobody saw my shape sail through the bars of trees and under pools of cool canopy. I passed dusty mirrors in hedgerows. It was so hot I breathed heavily. I wore a long white smock, now pasted to my back with sweat and pasted to my chest. I felt a salty sliding in either eye, which made it hard to see, between this and the squinting in the bare sun of high summer, the nickel zip of light on car bonnets as these passed by.

I chafed against my brakes as far as the village again, where I rode over to the library, circling the small building twice around, around, singing; I turned, redoubled on the way I'd come, rode back to the cottage again. Always returning, a compulsion, after every hiatus from his atmosphere. I wore sandals with soles of old rubber.

This might be a cameo or boss of it really: a bike, a girl, the trees.

How is your wife? I asked Harry when he got back. I didn't even intend to ask it: it came out, meanly.

Quite well. He looked at me. Why do you ask?

Oh I don't know. Being polite.

I have something for you, he said. I got it in London.

How was London?

Ghastly, he smiled. He had bought me a mobile phone. It was much like an old one; I thought to say, *Let me give you money*, but then I thought better of it; I felt bad. I felt immensely unwell. I felt dizzy, but rooted to the spot.

Harry told me gently, You're a complicated girl.

But, he said, you know you should be careful with yourself.

He said, I like you a lot. Your complexity. I just hope that all of this is good for you. Is not, you know, harmful to you.

I want to get out of here, I said quickly. I want to get out of here, for a break, today. Just for a break. I felt savagely light-headed. Can we go into town?

I have work, but I will drop you if you like.

No, no, I'll take the bus; drop me to the village. I'll catch a bus. I felt that I needed to move, to agitate, even though the day was hot and stillness lay, listlessly almost, over everything. The rain had stopped but there was still a ripe weight to the air, something scum-rimmed and fecund at once.

This is a day I am trying to explain. This is a day I look back on, I looked back on — at thirty, trying to prise the fan apart, to isolate, to find something (moments like hinges): a *hook* — this is a hard day to put away: this is a hard day to explain to you. Very much like other days in the cottage. But not.

I felt kind of *caught*. I felt kind of *on display*.

There is a notebook entry for this day — a pink notebook, with a ribbon tongue — and the entry reads 13.05, 14.05. These are bus times. I must have looked them up on my laptop. I know that I was dropped to the village, on the motorbike, and caught the bus, and that the bus was stuffy and empty and swayed slapdash all the way, the driver completely heedless, the radio playing death notices. And when I dismounted in the bus station at Drogheda I thought for one burning moment that I was going, in fact, to be sick — I marched straight to the toilet, on which there was a sign reading PATRONS ONLY, so that I had to go to the man in his punch-proof booth for an old-fashioned key, clammy in my hand, to let myself in, to a cubicle of pickled spit-balls, where I did not throw up: where I panted and swore, for ten minutes, over the bowl. The light went out. I stayed in peaceful darkness for a while. I stirred and tripped the sensor once again.

I left. I'm all right now, I thought. The air smelled of

cooking oil. I went into the town I suppose. Some of it was familiar to me and some of it was new-seeming, like the Starbucks perhaps, and the art gallery. The old mall was the same, seedily lit and lined with try-your-luck vending machines. I thought I might go to the cinema. I thought that I might visit the relic's head. In fact I went into a large department store and drifted between aisles of summer clothes. I fingered synthetic lace g-strings. I bought myself one. It was, I recall, rolled up and secured in the centre like a shoelace or a dressmaker's measuring tape. I felt faint. I went into a café and began to fiddle about with the phone Harry had given me.

I want to say that there was no sound. That there was nothing but the underwater bulging of my pulse, steady and unending, in my ears. But of course this can't be true. It is a contortion of memory undergone for effect. It is a blurring or a burr or some other kind of opacity. A lull in courage. Because, I quite think, I had so much courage at twenty-three.

In Drogheda, at twenty-three.

I saw myself everywhere, as a teenager, looking for something to wear to get into a nightclub – something crunching with sequins, cutting me under the arms – or failing my driving theory test. The drama of the river and the tower, like a silver sandcastle, in which, we'd always been told, the prisoners of Cromwell were kept, outside of which there was the terrible Catholic massacre. I was a plain and heedless teenager, without any guile whatsoever, without any protector. The youthfulness I played up for Harry now was prosthetic and sometimes tiring, but also I wanted to curl up – only to curl up – like a child or an animal, cosily meagre, and be held.

I was there, that day, in Drogheda, because I suppose I wished for a little bit to escape scrutiny. To relax. I was so used to being ignored. It was strange and erotic to be watched but also fatiguing, frightening – a form of power that could oh so easily be lost. Womanhood generally had lately dawned on me as a source of extraordinary power, right out of nowhere, without virtue or labour at all. Weaponising it was so easy I sometimes stared at Harry and wondered if he was playing along, if this was simply some burlesque, only to see that it was *real*, the weakness and the hunger, the queer solipsism of man as *pioneer* beholding you, intervening angel, executioner, devouring trap; you are an archetype, a sign. Then when it's done they go deep into themselves. Or else they burrow into you, laying their head on your chest, like nothing so much as a little boy.

Harry did not do this – the burrowing: Harry lay stiff in the bed next to me and stared wildly at the tongue-and-groove ceiling. I would burrow into him, into his coarse curly hair.

This was how power slid back and forth between us.

I was in Drogheda to escape scrutiny – browsing now in a pharmacy, buying razors and shea butter – but why, when he'd only just come back from London, when I'd had twenty-four hours of invisibility? I was jealous, of course: I thought that he had stayed there with his wife. This was pain and not performance. It disturbed me.

And I knew then, in Drogheda, that I could run – I could leave, I could never get onto that bus and never switch on this brand new phone, into which I had not yet snapped the old sim card – I could disappear in a subtle huff, return to London, but this was bluff of course, or fantasy, because by the time I'd left London I was no longer living there at all.

I was living there materially but, in my mind and in my heart, I had departed, I was *finished with it*, even though I still had a year left at least to complete my dissertation.

I have always had friends who say, Oh, in London you can be anything, and I have always said that I am already anything and that we can be anything anywhere: if all you mean is making money, I say, well, probably. Yes. I never had any money in London. I was a student. Sometimes I went hungry and sat up watching my screen, hitting *refresh* until my stipend would appear in my account. Sometimes I temped. I worked at London Bridge for five psychiatrists. When I put out my hand to introduce myself to one he recoiled in disgust, really it was amazing, as if I were soiled: those men are so ignorant, really – tubby yoo-hoo types, half the time they couldn't change a lightbulb, they emerged from their office and say, Halloo reception-girl, yes, I'm terribly sorry I don't know your name, but my light has gone out!

It was also around this time that the helicopter came spiralling down over Vauxhall, like a boreal event – a blast that grew and shrank, the blooming of a rose in video. A spectacular crack. All at once the underground closed like a throat. There was, I suppose, what you call a *wartime air*, giddy and comradely: within hours of something the city healed over it, though, as if nothing happened at all, like the morning my friend emailed to say a pathologist's tent could be seen in Trafalgar Square and all day we watched headlines and search-engined it but found nothing, nothing to explain a pathologist's tent in Trafalgar Square.

I studied art history – I wrote about art. I was good at it. I thought hard about deeply abstract things. There is a painting, a painting by Patrick Swift, one of his Portuguese trees, and I gave a paper on it via Aquinas and Augustine: honestly, I told my husband later, I was permitted to do this and petted for it, at a lectern in one of the solemn salubrious rooms over Malet Street. I was twenty-two. The Portuguese tree is obscenely complex and sunned and salted, the more and more you stare the more details emerge, the more brushstrokes, which are interchangeable in the world of the painting with the seethes and knots and amplified aspirations of the tree; which represent proper bafflement and arrestment, as you would try to riddle out a mosaic or the face of someone you adored, willing to exchange places with them, finding yourself in their inflections – finding yourself in the fork of the tree's canopy.

Finding yourself in the blenching hands of Christ or the Virgin startled among her marrows and gladioli. Finding yourself in the corner of the image, an optical trick, a *memento mori* – finding yourself *otherwise*. Halfway metamorphosed.

Do you see what I mean?

And then, lying under trees. Hungover. Soho Square. The little gingerbread cabin in the centre of Soho Square. All the people, always, lying like victims in Soho Square.

Soho!

At the end of a party when everyone and the room itself were in pieces all, a fleshy editor sat next to me and asked, My dear, who did you come with? I gestured across the

178

room. My word, the editor nodded, how nice for him. I would like one of you.

You know, I said mock-severely, there is only *one* of me.

Well then, replied the editor mock-severely, I would like *some* of you.

I want to understand and I want to explain and I want to be unambiguous but I had such little information, so little, only the slight number of things I had been given and the speculative deductions I'd made about Harry, about his life, and the men I'd met afterwards, the types, in my twenties. My husband as he appeared thinly to me, almost phosphorescent, both an energy and a projection, both the real thing and something contrived.

Winding back as I can – all these images! Do I even want them? Can I sell them? Will they ever tremble out? – to London, always London. I go back now and it's not the city I knew. The city of my imagining, my collaboration, my libido. My misery.

What it was then: yes. Winding back. To the studio, which Harry kept in – where was it? It was not Bethnal Green, it was not Hackney: it was somewhere between. Shoreditch? I emerged from the underground and examined the map I'd printed out. I'd been to the studio, on the back of his bike, but never made it there, before, on my own. And it was hot. It was June. I was wearing flannel shorts and canvas flats.

The studio was always cool, because it was located in an old factory: there was a curling stairwell, a frightening coffin-like lift, and lots of doors along spartan corridors. Next to Harry was an artist who made, it seemed, exclusively big-bellied abstract sculptures usually had his door held open widely by a brick and he would wave, mindlessly and cheerfully, at me when I passed, because, I suspect, he thought I was somebody else.

All along the large window of Harry's studio there were cactus plants. On a nail on the wall there hung an ushanka-hat. He had pointed to this, once, and said, I got that in literal Siberia. There was very little else – a desk, a laptop, paper cards with points and plot-twists thumb-tacked to corkboards – but its austerity anticipated the cottage; its austerity was potential, not sterility. I found my way to the studio alone that day, tugging out my earphones as I climbed the curling stairs, and I was happy.

Yes, said Harry as I entered. He was finishing something on the computer. He made coffee in earthenware mugs, and, because there were no seats, we sat cross-legged on the floor.

Sometimes when I met Harry he was quiet, watchful, and horny in a writhingly reptilian way; sometimes when I met him he was briskly distant and paternal. This was a day of the latter.

Tell me about your Orpheus, he said.

The Poynter, I said, the painting – do you like it?

I do.

Orpheus, I said, is a story I love.

The lyre.

Yes. I stretched out my legs. Are you ready?

I am.

Orpheus is married to Eurydice, but she is bitten by a snake, and she dies. Orpheus travels down to the underworld to rescue her. In a Middle English version there are walls of ice – a kind of ice-tunnel, and people trapped in ice at the moment of their death, *glamoured* by fairy-ice. Anyway. Orpheus plays the lyre and persuades Persephone to let his wife go, to let Eurydice leave the underworld. There is just one condition, and it is that he cannot *look* at her. He needs to lead her by the hand from the underworld, from Hades, you know, without turning around. He can't turn around to look at Eurydice until they are safely back in, like, the world of the living.

But he looks?

He looks. He turns around and looks at her, halfway up. So she dies again. He takes one look at her, one glance, and she tumbles back into the underworld – I imagine, like *that*. I put my hands up in a pose of melodramatic horror. I tilted backwards. It was prayer-pose or surrender: it was the cowboy's *stick 'em up*.

She is lost.

She re-dies. She dies twice.

Why do you like it?

It fascinates me. I lifted my mug and drank my coffee. I reached over and stroked his hair, which was bushy curls, as dry as a shrub and seamed unevenly with grey. Because, I said, the question is always, why did he turn around? He had *one* job, you know?

And he failed.

But did he fail? I think. And this is my theory. I laughed to show self-deprecation. This is my *theory* of Orpheus: actually, a part of him wants Eurydice dead. The point of the story is Orpheus's grief, Orpheus as hero, as the one who brings Persephone round – he's so *brave*, that is the substance of the story. But really Eurydice can't come back. So he has to get rid of her. The urge to turn, to

181

basically kill her, is, I think, like the urge you have at the top of a tall building, on some height, to jump. The things you do to self-sabotage. The thing you say that is the one thing you *shouldn't* say. He wants her back but really he doesn't want her back so he kills her again. He can't really decide if he wants her or not.

Very interesting, Harry said.

The death of a beautiful woman is, unquestionably — and this, by the way, is Edgar Allen Poe — *the most poetical topic in the world*. I winked. I sipped. Orpheus is the proto-troubadour. The proto-breakup-album. Blood on the tracks and all that jazz. You know?

You, Harry told me then, are intelligent.

Of course I already knew I was intelligent. I had been called *precocious* and *little madam* since I was a child. But at this point it didn't seem compromising; in his eyes in that instant I did not feel smart-alecky. I suppose I felt *seen*. It was new and strange and it made the blood rush to my face. How ridiculous to reflect on this now but oh — how I held the man, such high esteem! My Elektra complex. Sexual electricity. I must have been easy quarry. Though I cannot so easily dismiss it, I cannot condemn him outright you know, because it was precious to me, this chemistry, this thing I could be for him, as I imagined it then — how proud I could make him feel. Giving him this share in my development.

Which is what I did, really. Great slices of myself.

And so I wouldn't run from Drogheda, from the cottage, from Harry, because I had nothing to run to and anyway anything I could run to would be boring: anything that I could run to would be death. I wanted to wait and see, I suppose, how it would turn out.

That evening I finished the charcoal portrait and presented it to Harry.

I look like a satyr, he complained.

You look like a mystic, I said. But I like you, immensely.

Part Five

Part Five

My husband rolled over in bed. He held his phone before him.

Who is it? I asked.

Anna.

What does she want?

Money.

I arched my body as I laughed. Funny, I said. My father called. I'd love to ask him for money.

What would he say?

What, what? I barked my father's voice. He'd have to ask my stepmother. She'd have to call to discuss it. She'd want to hear all of my news. She'd be round here and in your face before you knew it. She has people everywhere.

That night, when my husband was home, my father phoned again. This time I saw the call. In fact the phone rang twice, just twice, before stopping, and since the phone was old and oily and I am so butter-fingered I could not tell whether my father had hung up in haste or whether I had accidentally extinguished the call. If he had hung up, I thought, it was possible that he regretted it; if not, the onus was now on me to make good on what looked like a rejected call. I began to feel anxious and pre-emptively resentful.

I was lying on the bed by myself and the phone was plugged into the wall. The bulb in the sweet little lamp I had bought was blown and so the overhead light, in a shade of corny gold, the colour of living rooms in stark suburbs as viewed from motorways, fell over the chaos of my husband's possessions. I'd had a feeling this might happen. I'd had a feeling, after the funeral, he might try to call. I thought that I should not have gone. And yet – oh well. In some flat fluent way, low on affect or motivation, it seemed things were surfacing, people surfacing, everywhere, like a day-of-the-dead or a last fucking judgement, I thought, feeling anhedonically detached from it all suddenly.

When I phoned back, my father asked, Will I call you now, will I call you? Save your credit.

It's fine, I replied, I have a plan with, like, unlimited calls. It's fine. I think I hung up by mistake there.

That's all right.

My phone is. You know. Shit.

That's all right.

By now I was lying on my belly on the bed. In the garden outside the glass doors, where the draught glowed, there were trees – the climbing spinal columns of two maritime pines that must have been planted a hundred years ago.

My father began to express emphatic shock at the fact that he did not even know where I lived: *I don't even know where you live*, he said, in amazement, meaningfully, instructively, indicating that this was remiss of me. I did not say that the last communication I had received from him was six years earlier, when I was living in London, and took the form of a solicitor's letter to be signed-and-witnessed and returned, notifying me of the fact that I was no longer the imminent recipient of a share of the life assurance policy he and my mother had paid into since I was born. With the stroke of a pen the only inheritance I could ever expect was annulled, evaporated into air.

I've missed you these years, my father said.

Me too, I replied.

I felt embarrassed on the phone to my father because I was thinking that the girl he remembered or had brought up was dead. I, who knew her better than anyone, struggled now to recall what mattered to her, since that time of her – my – life invoked only a bass dread in my chest; a feeling reminiscent of childhood, waiting in bed to be yelled at for something.

That girl was also pre-Harry of course. For the first time perhaps the thought of this, of my father knowing of my involvement with a man almost the same age as him, struck me as absurd and embarrassing and strangely exposing.

The girl that was, long ago, even longer ago.

Let me find her.

A small girl in a school tunic, a wine-coloured tie on elastic at her throat, walking a circle in a linoleum kitchen, singing. To console herself. A small unremarkable early nineties kitchen with Formica countertops patterned like pale confetti, the cool of a stair rod at her feet where the linoleum meets a carpet the colour of mud on the other side of the room. Her father, whom she adores, is out of work just now and sleeping in the armchair. By his side is the cut glass ashtray on a spike of iron she is captivated by, at his feet an acrylic rug of rock-roses; the television ticks to itself like wicker, and on the television set is a box for charity change to Africa.

A small unremarkable girl, in a different Ireland. Even then.

When I began secondary school, when I was twelve, I began to be disturbed by things, by dreams and sensations and dread, and even though any interpretative plumb-lines that might once have linked me to it have been snarled by time I wonder if it reflected sub-currents of unpleasantness at home. I dreamt often of chambers and lakes underneath the school and I was fiercely sensually responsive to the world around me, although nobody knew, and nobody paid attention to me. There were just so many ways to transgress, at random and unknowingly, so many ways to trigger rage in adults inexplicably – they were always shouting, shouting, and I'd like to reach back through that receding cone of time and shout back at them or do violence – and for this reason I also shrank into myself. I thought, now, about mincing similarly around Harry's life. I thought about mincing around my husband's sensitivities and felt sour about that.

The call from my father was depressing and almost as soon as it had ended everything that we had said slid out of my head. Slid clean out of my head.

It planted a blankness in me, which would expand. This was what usually happened.

Shortly after his phone call, and once again over the phone, my father and I arranged to meet. I thought for a long time about what I should wear and met him in Phibsborough. I did not arrange to meet him anywhere near Dollymount or Raheny or Clontarf or Saint Anne's Park, anywhere near the apartment in which I now lived.

I stood in the teeth of the wind beneath the brutalist shopping centre in Phibsborough.

I had tried to think straight about everything and failed.

And then all at once I hailed him – this slight, ageing stranger – and brought him to an especially pretentious hipster café to disorient him. The staff there were always tardy and drawly but more than one said *I love your dress* as they passed, and I had to ask twice for coffee and sandwiches. I threw my coat up on a hanger on the wall instead of balling it at my feet. I sat straight and soon separated from my body, watching myself from above, from without, operating with calmness but babbling somewhat, presenting myself with the charm and defence of a job interviewee, of a guilty party overextending in her efforts to deflect.

Will I meet your husband? my father asked.

I'm sure you will, I replied, as if it had nothing to do with me.

Just as soon as he had the chance, my father began to hold forth about one of my stepsisters, of the trouble she was causing, getting involved with a young man, riding in a car with him at speed and crashing into a motorway barrier, lacerating her liver, and coming so close to death it was touching distance: had I not heard, he asked, about the car accident? I had not. My father seemed irritated. His voice grew louder, and he expounded upon it at length, lamenting medical negligence, talking severely into thin air in the same register as my stepmother – a register in which outrages mounted cumulatively, with breaks and deep recesses between them, to allow the listener time to recover or to shake their head or ask, are you joking me? So involving and absorbing was the endless volatility of his stepchildren, his wife, it occupied all his interest. He asked again if I was sure I had not heard about the car accident.

Well, I live in Dublin now.

And you are doing well, I see, my father said. You were always able to manage yourself.

Travelling into town afterwards, I felt obscurely angry. My father had listed all the people who would not receive my stepsister's boyfriend in their house on principle. He has made a fool, he said, of all of us. Time and again. A fool of us. But after that he backtracked and explained that the boy had seemed all right to begin with and that he, my father, had given him a chance.

Frequently during our meeting his mobile buzzed, and I stared forth with the glassy stare I once reserved for boring coffee-dates, for men whose conversation consisted of anecdotes in which they triumphed over a series of inexplicably antagonistic co-workers and car mechanics. I thought of my husband texting in the corridor, during the concert; texting on buses, in cafés, in our bed. Little portraits of absorption in a new vernacular.

I travelled into the city, quietly enraged.

But after I had eaten, in one of the Chinese buffets on Moore Street, my mood improved, and I could regard the reunion with my father without feeling fazed. This coolness made me feel proud of myself in a way that was also surprising to me. Surprising like the evening long ago in the cottage when, standing in his doorway in the breath of the rain, I had said to Harry, You are upset. An inspired incident of attunement and confidence, no waiting for instructions, no pandering, only outing things courageously: yes, I thought now, I'm unfazed, because what-else-did-you-expect? Behold, a man! I could have laughed. I knew my sister would be proud. Behold, the past! My father was frightened of me. He could not let me get a word in because what, in the world, might I say?

Funny, funny, I thought.

There was a smooth kind of condescension then because I was also late, and had noticed as much – because I had not had my period yet, a week in, and the quiet not-unkind shock of this realisation that morning had made me feel cosy and all at one with my life, suddenly, because I had not meant to get pregnant but I had not tried very hard to avoid pregnancy. Some species of known-unknown pragmatism, yes: some subcutaneous logic, I thought, operating autonomously, slowly, finely, and wilfully.

Although it had just been a week, then, I felt increasingly sure – increasingly so, as the evening passed. Increasingly, grindingly, excited. I thought of something like a prawn. My pelvis felt tenderly inflamed, as if a speculum had been inserted and forgotten in the hollow where I itched and smarted even though it was sunken within me, even though I didn't know what a speculum looked like. I never looked down during cervical smears. Was it something like a funnel, callipers, a vice? A cricket, a love-knot, a tuning key?

Nine months is all you need to change the world and everything. Nine months; three weeks; one thousand days. I mused on it. I have, I chanted, counted-out-my-life-in spoons, in funnels, callipers, a vice; in mystery and the most prosaically transcendent promotion one could get as a woman. I saw it only as a gift to my husband actually. Something infinitely more solid than a shot at statesmanship. My body as miracle machine.

There was a degree of one-upmanship to it, undoubtedly. I thought of our argument. I thought of *you look down on me*. Yes, and henceforth from the moral high ground, baby, for eternity!

If you say such things out loud the world pretends to be in shock but all the while the mill grinds gruesomely behind it all.

I was going out, that evening in town, with people from work. We met at the gates of Trinity, which were shut and signposted, and kids were coursing from the side-door slowly, compressed, looking, as I thought, like straining plasticine.

How is your research going? A colleague asked.

Oh, you know, I said. Getting there.

My efforts to compose something of structural integrity and academic relevance had thus far come to little more than a ragged mesh of arguments and insights that receded when I looked at them, like half-remembered dreams. Somewhere in this constellation there would be a thesis statement *eventually* but without this, now, I couldn't be calm. It was likely I knew that I was writing something creative instead of something scholarly and in resisting the indulgent trust one places in creative work out of abashment I was poorly compensating from a scholarly perspective and would end up as I knew with nothing much, with a dull piece of art or a weak academic work.

It is just, I reasoned with myself, it is just the research-reading is so goddamn *boring* to me now: I see the strings, I see the templates, and the jargon. I am never left surprised.

When I left the bar I walked through the pedestrianised streets for a little bit, the optimistic streets, feeling cosmopolitan, and I looked out for people with children – there were several, tourists and rich creatives living in cottages at the top of Synge Street, women with kerchiefs twisted thoughtfully in their hair — and looked into the solemn faces of little girls. I felt I had entered into something or ascended to a level above myself. I would grow a secret inside me and we — the child and I — would share the knowledge of that, preverbal lizard inferences, eternally, an entirely unspoken confederacy. I had known, I had known it was coming, surely — the night, I thought, of the dinner with Anna and the top-deck bus ride home. *As many as you want*, my husband said: I'd thought, I just want one. In this moment it must have been sticking gingerly to me somewhere, to some stalk or some organ, like cuckoo-spit froth on a twig; it must have been blending and remembering itself, its codes and destiny. Oh it all felt so lovely to think and to be, now, delivered to me. To my husband.

It might be a boy after all. He would look at me with tenderness — well! No more abandonment.

I was smug, crazy smug. I thought, I will not spend stupid money on bougie things. I will take all my sister's baby paraphernalia. I will be pure and clear-headed, and *come into my kingdom*, and it will be male so that we can argue prettily over Jesuit school.

It had gotten even colder by the time I let myself into the flat with my key. I knew this because the lock resisted me, contracted by the freeze. I had to catch it off its guard.

And as I undressed in the bathroom I saw, with astonishment, a bright bead of blood rolling soundlessly down my thigh.

It was followed by another and both curled with the surface of my leg and clung slightly in the pit of my knee. I felt as if someone had been scratching coins against the floor of my cervix. I could hardly believe it. I cleaned up and climbed into bed and it hurt, it went on grinding ghoulishly all night, and I watched the shape of my husband, sleeping next to me, and I thought: lucky for you, this time. Nothing to get in your way this time.

I lay in the afterglow of this petulance and was taken by surprise. A low moan rose through me, something from my entrails; I almost bent at the waist to accommodate it. The urge to cry was like rising bile and I let it happen, I leaned into the release.

My sobbing so throbbed the mattress my husband woke up. What's wrong, what's happening? he asked.

It's nothing, it's only that I am sad.

Sad? Has something happened? Did your dad say something?

No, no, no. I had forgotten my father entirely. Just, I said, let me cry; I pleaded, just let it burn out.

Alannah, you're worrying me.

Go back to sleep. Even as I said this I knew it was pathetic.

What's wrong?

I thought that I was pregnant, I said.

You're pregnant? His voice was whetted with slight terror.

No, no, no! I wanted to push him away. I'm not. It was a mistake. It hurts everywhere.

But you're not?

No! Shush.

It hurt everywhere. I imagined my organs corseted by tendons, twisted tight, like fists closing. Some tremendous surge of grief possessed me. I knew that I must look terrible. I pushed my face into a pillow. On the last night with Harry, after I had smashed the plate, I had felt a similar rush of rage and loss and I knew that this meant I'd been bested or rather I'd *failed*, I had lost, things like power and happiness swung out of me with a wrench and it would happen, of course, again and again.

Alannah, Alannah, my husband said. He began to hold me and to stroke my hair. It was hopeless and I was plummeting into adulthood and everything was my fault, I moved within these constrictions – the need, my need; the mesas of junk in the corridor closing into the first corridor in the world – but I was not up to them; I was not up to doing this.

What, my husband asked, are you talking about? Look, try to sleep. It will be better in the morning.

In the morning there was a bloodstain in the bed. The madwoman had been subdued and I moved bluntly, blankly, through the house, like an invalid. In the mirror I only saw the wincing face of a child who expects to be hit. I parted my hair when it was wet precisely to the left and right above the arch of my brow-bone, and as I did this I noted a thread of grey, the colour of lace.

It will happen, my husband said.

Will it?

I just need to get back into it. Make some phone calls.

I looked at him in astonishment.

I am not done, he added. He had been talking about himself. He had not got the job as a speechwriter; it had gone to a journalist from the *Sunday Business Post*.

I wanted to fold him into me, when he said that; wanted to cradle in Pietà on my lap. I thought how much it would disgust him to know I was thinking that.

Husband-child.

There is more than one way of looking at things.

When we first knew each other, he wasn't mine, he was another's – he was hers. Have you ever, he asked – this was four a.m., in Phibsborough, the window of my room pushed to, the warm rain soft on the shrubbery, the concrete, the canal, the air caviar, the air between us sharp as disinfectant – he asked, Have you ever cared for someone, known them so long, cared for them, but it is like you are speaking two different languages? It is like you are speaking English, you are both speaking English, but there is no understanding?

I said over and over, I don't want you.

I said over and over, I don't want half a person. But I was not honest or not honest all the time. I wanted to be – I knew that I could be – the woman who understood.

The streets that night, in Phibsborough, before we were married, were empty and silent but for the rain, the placid rain, a light summer rain that hardly leavened the air. But even though the streets were empty you could imagine sad oboes or the saddest love song, a dirge, carrying through the dark wet streets. You could imagine a single empty angel sweeping through the dark streets. You could imagine a knowing spirit, a grimy spirit, moving, you could imagine the rain running off its black feathers; you could imagine streets puddling and scrunching under streetlight like satin.

Are you going to leave me? I had asked then, in the dark. He gave me no reply. But in the end I didn't let the man leave, I was not going to let a man leave this time. I married him. It was not the moral thing to do and I suspect I brought down a hex on myself.

And now that we had married it seemed he had forgotten sad oboes, black angels, dirges, streetlight, steady rain. Or four o'clock in the morning, speaking under our breath, in the air like disinfectant, in the meat-air of ourselves.

When he didn't get the speechwriter's job he was angry and drank. And I said, on a weekday, Let's get out of here, and climb the hill of Howth, and get out of ourselves. It was early in the morning when I said this; dawn was breaking. We had made vigorous sudden love and my body was sore because my pelvis is too narrow and my hip is short, a step missed in the mist, but I got up to go to the bathroom and emptied my bladder and bowels and cleared

200

my sinuses, among the spotlit rubble of our ablutions, and I felt clean and winsome then – lighter and energised – and when he made noises about work I shook him, pleading, Let's just walk to the island and make up our minds, we can come back after that.

Don't you want to eat, he asked, little kit?

Just make me a coffee, I said.

We walked into the morning, which was flossy and mute, cold but close, down the fine avenue of burgher villas and ancient trees with roots knuckling up through paving slabs. It still gave me a spasm of glamour to think that I lived in this neighbourhood now. We walked to the coast road and the Irish Sea. I've known that water all my life. It's a filthy sea, a mutinously fuming sea of fungal colour and gull colonies; a trade sea, a snot-green sea. It is different to the Atlantic, an ocean of utopias: the Irish Sea exists to ship cargo and kill. Its coastline is the waste of Empire.

Amidst smashed public baths and piers, slipways and little castellated guest houses, smooth alcoves in harbour walls, one almost hears the phantom cranking of a music-box, the sailor's hornpipe, the departed carnival. England has eternally just pulled out of the place.

Great chunks of the coast, I observed, are Basically Margate.

I grew up on the east coast of Ireland, right against the sea, but I have always struggled to understand it, because, perhaps, it exists with a certain unthinking autonomy, it doesn't talk about itself. Dublin is a Georgian city, but its coast is emphatically Victorian, rendered and grandiose in a dimly populist kind of way – it evokes tattered bunting, cream sponge – and practically untouched since *Dubliners*, retaining a sooty and salty sort of genteel poverty swelled by slob-lands, sewage works, bird sanctuaries. Atavistic explosions of faecal content in the water are recorded on billboards between pampas-grass and dunes. Weather-stripped villas are banked against the elements. It behaves as though the climate is more clement.

There was a crepey copy of *Dubliners* in our house, on the bookshelf, and this was a cheap seventies *Dubliners*: it was yellow. It was not yellowed with age, it was just yellow. There were crowded pencil sketches accompanying every story and little or no para-textual information, so that I, as a precocious child, presumed *Dubliners* was a novel and read it as one. The text in its scrupulous meanness is so deceptively accessible. I waited for a long time to find the mystery of the death of the priest – with his snuff, his bicycle pump, his simony – to be reintroduced and solved and, when this did not happen, when the book continued apace and unconnected but for ghostly flares of inter-textual reference, I grew distressed; I abandoned *Dubliners*. My first experience of Joyce was so oblique, you see, as to approach sublime.

I can recall the bedroom, too, where I tried to read it – my bedroom in the semi-d where I grew up, downwind of the Irish Sea.

I dream houses, as I think everyone does, with cascades on the stairs and warm pools of water in the living room, and Butlin's mushrooms, and carpet foliage becoming sharks, or the villains from videogames. My boy-cousin and I leaping from one rock-rose to the next in peril and ecstasy. The houses and the town where I grew up remain, of course, but they are no longer the same houses, nor the same town: a quantal break has occurred. What I mean to say is that I once walked to school past the inland abattoir; I once disturbed a drunk underneath a tree at the weir, there were summer-night confessions and Corpus Christi processions. We were on the Dublin–Belfast trade corridor before the bypass and every year a small number of people would be killed by freight. People hit other people's children in the street. That kind of thing.

The very worst of the Celtic Tiger are two parallel petrol stations as you come-and-go into the town, thrown up like checkpoints in a mushroom field, with sliding billboards whose rotation sends a metronome echo as far as the Union pit.

I imagine myself at twelve, biking against a tarmac heap in the Black Hills, beyond my permitted boundary. An old man staggers from the trees, waving his hands as if to flag me down but only joking really, barking with laughter as he pretends to flag a twelve-year-old down. Now, there is a toll! he shouts merrily, trapping my wheel between his knees.

My family began in a house I dream about even now, it is a container for water-dreams. It is a two-up-two-down built for factory hands on the hosiery line, and it became the site of a murder in '98 actually. As a small child I was convinced that there was a severed ear on the stairs – a single ear, bloodless, laid on a carpet-tile. The ear had been deposited or overlooked, perhaps, by my great-grandfather, who was also (this cannot be true) the drunk at the weir, startled awake in a tweed cap and without any teeth. I hardly knew him, he died when I was young, though old enough to have conceived of the ear.

For certainly I invented the ear. I invented it to prevent myself from climbing the stairs.

As we walked, I talked to my husband about these things: I amused him, or I amused myself. I loved to hear stories from my husband's childhood. There weren't many because he didn't seem to think it had been important, childhood – he didn't seem to retain much of it at all. I asked once, And were you breastfed? I don't know, he replied, and I was scornful: nobody *doesn't know*.

I don't really care, my husband said, about the past.

This struck me as sensible suddenly.

You don't care, I spoofed, about all that you can't leave behind?

What. Oh. He laughed.

I will do it, he said. It will happen for me.

We walked into the morning, we crossed the wooden bridge. We walked arm-in-arm and pressed step-in-step in a way that was uncomfortable for me, since his stride was so much longer than mine. The island was like the moon or the Burren, sand scotched with rocks and black racks of seaweed, stiff weeds and thistles and stickleback; spiked wary salt-burned grass. The sea tumbled indifferently and slumped onto slants of smoothened stone. The Virgin watched from her chalk-white spike. There was no catching the quake of the water out – no matter how much like a death-rattle it sounded, it would not stop, it would never stop heaving and breathing in. Underneath a stone arch someone had written the entire 'The Lake Isle of Innisfree', and it never faded – it was never washed away. We went to visit it again.

The sun was stronger now. Crows squabbled and mobbed on the dunes. Gulls and egrets and pips and those screeching seabirds with their human cries gathered close to the edge. We saw joggers plodding in the morning mist.

We walked and walked until we got to Raheny, where we sat on the empty platform, and I asked for funny stories about the school where my husband worked.

At the summit of Howth Hill the day became hot, the sun coming in giddy peals through the windows of bars and restaurants. We ate and got drunk and stayed there until dark. We speculated about other patrons and walked, when it was dark, to the top of the hill, and saw all of the lights – the city lights quivering in clusters, the lights of the bay and the lighthouses sweeping, the slow lights of airplanes in totemic approach. From over the sea.

We can't go down, my husband said. His phone had been ringing all day. No we can't, I agreed, because, once we do, we will never be this happy again.

Don't, he said simply. He meant: don't be dramatic.

Some nights later, in Trinity.

Night of civil rain falling straight. The panes of the library as yellow lids of light. In the atrium of the Geography building, itself flowered and furbelowed, stood the standing silence, like standing water, generated by the suspended red elk skeletons; here, also, umbrellas popping like seedpods.

People who had gathered for the night lecture were speaking lowly, but when one or two laughed loudly the volume of their conversation crept up, then surged up, so that it became noisy, and a young student at the top of the stairs, at the atomic clock, had to shout over everyone, Doors open! Thank you for coming! I was by myself and I shook my coat out. It had been raining all evening. It was a clean rejuvenating kind of rain. When it stopped the world would be gurgling and fetid and green, rotting in places and blooming and swarming in other places.

We filed into the lecture theatre, where our substantiality was decanted into old-fashioned fold-out desks. The kind of people who went to night lectures at Trinity were old and rich, smelling of the steeping damp native to sash-windowed villas in Blackrock Bay, windows with protection orders – smelling of that halitotic aristocratic world, a world of retired judges and government aides, that I had, incidentally, married into.

That night, my husband was babysitting.

I saw Stephen, the landlady's husband, left of the lectern, preparing to give the guest lecture I'd seen advertised on the walls all week. His name had leapt out at me – it was the first time I'd seen him visit – and I thought, of course, another coincidence, although really that makes it sound more mystic than it is. This is Ireland, I also thought. Small. Still it would be silly not to step into a fateful situation. She might be there, mightn't she?

I had been eating a stale croissant from the college café, it had been wilting under a glass cloche all day, and there was golden spray and flakes of pastry on the sleeves of my jumper. Flakes of pastry tacky with chapstick. After the student had introduced him, Stephen began to deliver a lecture on the suicide of the eighteenth-century Anglo-Irish statesman Castlereagh: *It is done, I have opened my neck*, all the rest of it. I had come to see Stephen but also I had or I have I suppose some mischievous curiosity about Castlereagh and especially the ghost. Castlereagh you see was a marked and haunted man. Despite this, to my disappointment, Stephen didn't mention the ghost. Throughout the duration I longed for ghosts.

Castlereagh, he explained, had been confusingly accused of *la vice anglais* but there is no reason to believe this influenced his decision to commit suicide behind a dressing screen; people were routinely accused, wandering through those pleasure-gardens of the eighteenth-century, with *trompe l'oeil* strumpets and boy-actors and so on;

Castlereagh may actually have simply gone insane. Been *quite insane*. He slit his throat. The servants raised a wail.

Hunting in Ireland in his youth, Stephen did not explain, Castlereagh got lost; pressing through freezing fens to a hunting lodge, he was put into a room of animal pelts, with a roaring fireplace. Everyone in the eighteenth century was basically drunk all the time, by the way – drunk all the time, or most of the time, with no knowledge whatsoever of consequence. To Harry I read aloud, with astonishment, once: One of the lord mayors of Dublin was dyed with jaundice and dead at thirty *from drink!*

Anyway Castlereagh, a dour and humourless man who may or may not have been drunk, had a vision that night of a blue-white boy leaking luminously into position over him, set in the air, and this was called the *radiant boy*, a ghost foretelling violent death. I had told Harry that story. Stephen didn't mention it.

Harry had repeated: Radiant boy.

When the lecture had concluded there were questions, and every question pertained not to Castlereagh but to a don who had lately died, and the questions weren't questions but freighted reminiscences of same, and I thought, old people, and I thought of texting my husband: old people.

Thank you for this lecture, concluded the student – a graduate stripling, forelock-tugging type – which has raised a lot of interesting questions, and I am sure lots of you will want to continue the conversation in The Duke.

I had felt electrically victorious when the landlady arrived; when the landlady slipped, late but fluently, into a fold-out chair, some seconds into the lecture. It seemed a bounty too impossible to bear. For the length of the lecture I had not been able to incline my head and look at her, lest she disappear, or become someone else. But I knew it was her at once, her shape hit the side of my face like a roll of water, like someone joining me in the bath, and I had waited for this grace to diffuse through me, I had saved up the excitement, I had practised gratitude.

Now I found myself sliding towards her, in a ring of conversation with some staff and with Stephen, after the lecture had concluded and the room was buzzing with conversation again.

I remember when I was a student we were brought to The Duke by the English Department, I said, and they gave someone a book of raffle tickets, worth a drink each – what we did, I said, was use this to buy the guy with the book of tickets like six whiskeys, then take the book and drink the raffle tickets dry.

A grey professor looked at me through heavy spectacles.

Do you remember me? I asked the landlady.

Did you go here? the professor asked.

Of course, Alannah. Yes. The landlady began to laugh. Stephen: Alannah, remember?

Yes. Her husband smiled at me.

Stephen, said the old man over me.

I'm married now, I blurted out. I'm thirty.

Doesn't seem that long ago, she said.

Does Harry still come to the cottage?

She looked at me, smiling faintly, for a moment – looked away – raised her eyebrows as if expressing something, burning something off, suffering some internal strain – returned to me.

Oh sometimes, yes. He's divorced now.

No way.

Stephen, the professor said over me. He looked at me finally: looked at my lapels, and at my face.

I don't remember you, he said firmly at last.

I have no idea, I told him, who you are. I didn't come over here to speak to you.

Turning to the landlady again, I said, It was nice to see you both.

Will you come to the pub? Stephen asked.

The professor had begun to say something to me, to try and say something to me, but he, as I'd intended, had been taken by surprise. I felt a blush creep cruelly over my face.

Oh no, I said, thank you. But it was nice. Goodbye, goodbye!

Goodbye, goodbye!

Outside, the rain still fell, but slightly more slackly. All the windows now were backlit, candle-yellow, anciently. Front Square was empty as a church.

I knew that if I'd stayed, if I had gone along to the pub and talked, I would learn worse things. In her hands, in his, the whole thing would become the everyday embarrassing vanity of the girl who thinks she is the first – the first to what? Trade on her youth, mistake a game for love? Oh all my high ideals. Oh earnest faith. Oh jargon.

Couldn't laugh though. Wasn't funny. Walked slowly, wounded: the rain pitter-pattering, the columns of the old bank like bared teeth. A ravaged woman on the steps of Thomas Moore with a plastic bag. Jaws open, maws open: this is what it is to skirt along the side of a grand passion. I had to catch myself, and calm down before I went home. I couldn't tell if I was devastated or enraged. The feeling cooled to cynicism finally.

Rain under the streetlights, like a swarm.

You were easy to find, she wrote, *and congratulations on your career! It was very nice to see you the other night.* (Well, quite.)

You too, I replied.

Strikes me, have you seen this? she asked. (*Attached*)

I never studied drama, Harry told me once, I only tried my hand at it – I liked to act, and play, and *party* I suppose – so I banged things out, plays and set-pieces, but I knew nothing about Brecht or Beckett or any of that: most of the time, really, I was trying to impress some girl. And it all took off you see. I got these commissions and half the time I didn't know what to do with them – so much freedom. Improvisation, all of it.

The play that made me – the one that catapulted me – I knocked it out, half-cut: it was nothing to me at the time.

This was the one that ran again. The one you saw running occasionally. I'd never seen it myself.

At the time he had told me this, Harry, I believed him. But, as an adult now, I no longer bought into the idea of *idiot savant*.

When I opened the landlady's attachment the following day, sitting at my work carrel, I didn't know what I was looking for. It advertised a play running soon as part of the theatre festival and I wondered if she had something to do with it. But when I looked it up, I saw that the workshopping had been done by Harry – in London – it had come from a workshop, from two companies, and his name was there and certainly there.

I zoomed and shrank his full name several times. I bloated it out like something under a microscope. I made it small and distant, like an accident. I got up and I shut the laptop and I left.

It was a Friday evening, closing in navy and nervy with low sun. I walked to a restaurant off Nassau Street to meet my husband.

I put it, Harry, straight out of my head.

In the back room of the restaurant a long table had been formed of interlocking inserts and a large group, piled plates and empty carafes, were being loud. This was strange because they looked like civil servants.

What do you want? my husband asked.

Let's be quick, I said, and anyway I'm not very hungry. Just bruschetta and water for me.

That's all?

That's all. It's quick.

You don't want more? You sure you don't want more?

When our food came he pushed his plate towards me and said, Kitten, eat.

Do you have your notebook? I asked suddenly.

He looked at me in surprise and told me that he hadn't brought it. I'd bought him an imposing notebook and searched for ages, hunted high-and-low, to find one with pages that weren't lined. Thick creamy pages without lines, which I presented to him alongside two fountain pens. They weren't ornate or occasion fountain pens, but the kind of pens we were given at school to use when learning cursive. We used to take the red ones and dot wounds on our palms and hold them up and say, Padre Pio.

I'd given my husband the notebook and the pens as a gift. I'd said, Here is a place for you to write down your very best ideas for speechmaking. Your very best ideas for policy.

I've been using it, don't worry, he assured me now with a grin.

Do we have time for coffee? I asked. When the waiter had left I put my hands across the table and took his hands and said, I love you, I love you so much. His hands were warm and sandy and his fingernails were short, and blunt, and white.

Out of embarrassment I'd shopped for the notebook. It was a symbol of poetry and progression. It required the intimate press of paper and nib. I said: Write in it. I said: I believe in you. I'd come to feel bad for him, almost sorrowful, after the argument. I'd come to think that it was possible I knew nothing anyway. I'd been so sure, you see, of other things, and these – well. *He's divorced.*

So maybe I didn't understand anything.

After eating we cut through the campus of Trinity. There was a large congregation of students in Front Square, by the dying light, with steaming breath, but it was difficult to say why they were there. I had remarked to a colleague, I don't think sometimes they realise, these kids, their privilege; she had said, They are not remotely unaware of it. Have you met them?

I decided that we should hail a cab. The bus seemed too mundane or humble for the task. We were going to an open meeting about proposed cuts to bus routes which would double or stand for a local Party event; which would feature a current standing politician my husband knew. We were going to see him and not really thinking of buses at all.

The meeting was held in a kind of church hall near Dollymount, a one-storey building with a steep roof like a boathouse, in which tongued boards and plastic chairs opened onto a lectern and a sadly damp proscenium of scouting banners and club banners. The space was quite full with humming talk and the crackle of rain jackets. In the doorway my husband received a call from the mother of his youngest child and said, You know I can't do that tonight. We took our seats and a squat sycophant introduced the Teachta Dála, an affable man with a youthful face and a Rathgar accent. He spoke at length about proposed changes, suspensions, and cancellations of Dublin Bus routes, justified by both budget cuts and the extension of the tramline; an extension which, he opined, didn't impact the Bay very much and in fact was not as per the latest poll used to a significant degree by the elderly, the elderly being an important point, since proposed changes, suspensions, and cancellations of routes concatenated in a crisis situation, potentially, with regards to elderly members of the community and access to Beaumont Hospital. Not to mention, he said, the Mater Misericordiae.

My husband sometimes sent me messages in Latin when he was drunk. I would have to Google translate them. One of these was *ignosco tibi*. I could not be sure if that one was a joke.

Oh the elderly, he whispered now. Your enemies.

If they're going to die then they better do it, I said, and decrease the surplus population!

Are there no prisons? he hissed. Are there no poorhouses?

The TD took questions from the floor. It had begun

to rain outside. We knew this because we could hear it, rushing richly against the tiles of the roof, sounding so wet and abundant and poetic that it made the small lodge, its framed and ancient photos of dinner-dances, like the cosy kernel of a nut. It took me back to every rainstorm in my life, an incremental deposit of ambient memories. Most questions pertained to what the Party proposed to do about this and how it related to the imminent vacancy of a Dublin Bay seat, by a member exposed for relatively minor incarnations of corruption, in the coming by-election. Because the assembled crowd were Party faithful nobody dwelt on the corruption bit. I found myself dimly surprised at my acclimatisation to hypocrisy, by which I meant my own hypocrisy, my presence in the assembly a source of amusement and levity to me rather than anything serious or committed. A role I could play, selfishly. I'd sat a day earlier in a lecture hall in Trinity, listening to the trials of Castlereagh, with a similar expression of polite interest.

This is my life a lot, I thought. It is the life, finally, of a civilised person.

After all, I had said to my husband when he renewed his Party membership, I had to accept you as a fascist when I married you. He had turned sharply on me, with anger.

You can't say that, don't say that.

It's what people call you guys.

It's childish. You shouldn't say it.

You don't really think I'm a fascist, he asked, do you?

I don't. I think you are a good man, I replied.

I thought: *every woman adores a fascist, the brute boot in the face*, but I didn't chant it this time – it was tasteless though true in a way that did not reflect the particular situation, albeit remaining *adjacent* to it somehow – and I thought of whipping Harry and the hysterical desire I felt at the time to keep going until I drew blood and put off the inevitable punishment which was, I felt somehow sure, sheer actual death: I expected to be murdered eventually for my transgressions: I expected this in a giddily non-committal way: it was decadent and idiotic and hysterical. It was harsh laughter mounting towards a fit and met with a slap in the face or a boot in the face or blunt force. It was race memory.

And that morning I woke – he was gone – the brute boot in the face – well perhaps that was that.

I felt frightened in the church hall suddenly. There was a ringing in my head. I couldn't tell why I was frightened, but it was as if something terrible had become real.

The crowd was applauding constrainedly and things were wrapping up.

My husband approached the podium and joined a chattering queue of relaxed middle-class people. An old man with a rolled-up newspaper in his hand was expounding on something at length and the TD was nodding and laughing intermittently. Their heads were bent together in intimacy. After some time the TD moved on to my husband, and I watched them from my seat: they performed a polite physical irruption of mutual recognition, shook hands, and actually slapped one another on the back, which is a gesture you read about politicians doing – *a slap on the back* – but which I did not realise existed literally. I thought: people really have no idea about themselves. I saw that the men were not equal because my husband was bowing somewhat, saying, Oh you know yourself, do you ever go back? And I knew they must be speaking about Clongowes, or Trinity. My husband with other people was self-deprecating, but animated intensely by any response. I knew that he must have looked like this, from a distance, on the morning he asked for my number at Connolly.

After a moment he gestured outwards and I sensed that he was saying, *My wife*: I sprung up with an acquiescent smile and walked to the podium. I had dressed entirely in black and straightened out my hair so that it lay over my back. I knew that I looked different to other people but this look was something I cultivated to look sophisticated, and rich; it was a cartoonish approximation, really, of sophisticated and rich.

Lovely to meet you, Lana, said the politician with a smile. Behind us a queue of elderly people was growing irate. The politician's face was more human and weathered up close. He looked like the kind of man who had photographs of his young son on his desk, and a passive-aggressive wife.

Well then, I looked at my husband, regretting the tone at once, since it seemed motherly. But when my husband began to explain his aim the politician nodded while looking over his shoulder at everyone else and at last said: You should drop into the clinic. He suggested, that is, that my husband could join some kind of line, could make first contact with his secretary: he did not, that is, make an appointment directly. A secretary could fudge and bluff, I thought. The whole point of this demeaning shit was the personal relationships my husband was now digging up, the connections they represented. This was Ireland after all.

My husband was nodding now, chastened. But I felt enraged.

He's not going to *drop into your clinic*, I said with disgust.

Before I had finished the sentence the politician began to laugh kindly and I knew he had intended to laugh kindly at me no matter what I said.

I'll see you, said my husband.

Give the clinic a call, the other man said.

We moved off, into the porch of pattering rain and wet carpet.

For some reason I thought of the foot-and-mouth outbreak, which had happened when I was at school. Struck gong of the earliest noughties triggered by nothing more than the shape of a door in a municipal place. During the outbreak, in every public building including the school, rubber grids doused in disinfectant were laid before the door. And at once I had an image of newsreel, bonfires of cow-corpses piled and ablaze, in the front of my head, and this seemed akin with the darkness and unspecific nervousness of my mood.

As we stepped out into the whipping weather, rain and wind, the blurred streetlights glowing beautifully on the coast, I began to click the fingers of both my hands. I wanted to say something disdainful about the TD but I kept this in check: it was not, I saw, my place. It was possible that my husband didn't realise he had been humiliated.

I, sweeping out of Trinity the night before, had been by contrast bleakly and candidly aware.

My husband asked, Are you all right?

I like the wind in my hair, I sighed, as the straightened streaks were whisked about my face. It is a pleasant sensation.

Harry had said: The rest of mainland Europe is mostly windless. It is an Irish thing. It is a thing about islands.

Years ago. I thought of it now, I often thought of it. I had all these habits of thought but I felt as though I wanted, for the very first time, out.

The table in my husband's apartment was as wide as a pool table and brutally laden with errata. There were textbooks of course, and dog-eared tests, but also bottles and clean crockery and unopened post, folded clothes, three varieties of weapon-heavy, decapitated, lampstands, some mason jars with festive straws I could not explain the presence of (Anna, I think, he said), and flaking envelopes of old-fashioned photographs, developed in chemists with beer-dark negatives retained, showing mostly Anna at points in childhood or my husband, squinting, before monuments in Spain. There was a battery of printer parts. There was a stoic orchid in a purple pot that his mother had given me. Behind the table shone the chimney-breast of Anaglypta shuttlecocks.

There were few photos, here, of the youngest daughter, the baby girl – these were all online. I looked at them a lot and sometimes I felt guilty and sometimes I felt nothing at all. Because I was not actually allowed to mind her, because this was yet to be negotiated, I rarely commented; I did not especially want to get involved.

I cleared the table: I cleared everything. I made a political decision not to find places for anything. Instead I packed it into boxes or stacks and secured them all, compressed, underneath the table. I found and washed and dried a tablecloth of Kilkenny lace.

My husband had returned from Spain to train as a teacher and take up dominion here. When he first brought his ex, the baby's mother, home, she baulked and insisted they take a taxi, right away, to her own apartment. He spent, I suspect, rather a lot of time there in the subsequent years. She made a whole world for him in her image and, then, he left.

His own place had remained the same, chilly and drab, rain-lit, a place for darts-playing bachelors and hotplates, even though it had a kitchen-nook and a breakfast bar. My arrival had not improved it much, but I felt slightly more determined on that day. To have dignity. I vacuumed the hideous carpet, which was pathologically florid, like a missal painting.

Please clean the bathroom, I said. When he didn't I wondered – really wondered, in a state of earnest open-handed awe – if this was supposed to be provocation, or if I was projecting. He pottered about all morning, taking on soft jobs like washing bowls and stacking these supplely, chatting or playing the radio. At one point he called me over to laugh at an article in *The Times*. This was the paper he bought because he was, as I always said teasingly and in affection, a total West Brit.

In the bathroom I looked at welts of soap-scum, at smudges on the savage little magnifying mirror. I decided to let it all slide right out of my head. From the coalescence of crap in the hall I isolated and extracted a bone-pale vase.

We'll need flowers, I said.

I'll get them, my husband replied. He was leaning over the newspaper.

Thank you, but don't get the bunches with, like, the bright yellow yokes? And the grass? They look so cheap and discordant.

Discordant, he repeated.

There's no art to them whatsoever. No excuse for that.

Well, what colours do you want?

I realise that you cannot see, I said, what a sadistic question that is to ask. Just not yellow. Just not discordant. I laughed.

This job meant that he could leave the house, which was what he wanted to do. He made use of such marginal slides of time to phone the ex, the mother of his youngest child, and discuss their shared affairs. He did not like me to hear these conversations.

While he was gone I sat down with the paper and a glass of wine. I had a roast in the oven – instructions from my mother – and an Eton mess pre-prepared, sunken in a punchbowl in the fridge. The smell of the beef in the cold old room reminded me insidiously of Sunday dinners at my grandparents', of stony days, of racehorses on television, memories I was as ever helpless before: I drew my cardigan around me and curled my legs into the chair. Between stretched toes my tights webbed opaquely. When the light dimmed I lit candles everywhere. My husband returned with a sheaf of raw roses, like something from another century, still thorny and wrapped in butchers' paper. I decanted them into the vase.

I'd felt for the most part somewhat emotionally tense for much of the week. I was thinking of course of the landlady's email now. I was bringing it close to me and pushing it away, waiting for a firmer *gestalt* to emerge from atomic mass; I was thinking *he is divorced now*, I was saying things like *Motherfucker* in my head, tracing words like *Motherfucker* with my hands. I felt lurching urges to google things I knew would cause me pain.

When the door was knocked a sinking sensation swept over me and left tidemark impressions: bands of anxiety at the ribs. I realised that I would rather stay alone here, with the candles and the roses, in a warm indeterminate limbo, for a warm indeterminate length of time.

You get it, I said. They know you.

And while he did I busied myself by needlessly opening and closing the oven door. Dry heat flared in my face and warmed my hair with the odour of meat juice. When my husband led the couple in, I was standing at the breakfast bar with a stiff smile, aware that this made my face fragment and look less imperious, or sulking, or alarmed. He was a tall and clean-shaven barrister but she was small, and West-of-Ireland dark, with Spanish eyes. She wore a shift-dress with a houndstooth heart-shaped print and carried a toddler, a small boy screwing an eye socket with a fist.

Hello! Hello! I cried. Her bare legs were fake-tanned immaculately. I had never known such women personally.

Jesus, said the barrister warmly, looking at my husband, who had known him for years but was frozen with nervous delight, this looks different now, doesn't it?

The flat? my husband said. You remember it from before?

This lad, the barrister said to me. We thought he would get hepatitis from it when he first moved in. Wasn't it — who was here before?

The groundskeeper.

A groundskeeper, a caretaker or something, from the park.

It reminds me, I said – not for the first time – of something from Anthony Cronin, from *Dead as Doornails*, you know, like, somewhere Brendan Behan or Patrick Kavanagh lived in the sixties. Came around with hangovers after holding forth in the pub. Or, like, the stage set for *Look Back in Anger*.

It has that vibe, the barrister agreed. His wife was looking at him in irritation.

Niall, she said.

At once he swept the child from her and sang at it, How's the boy, how is the boy? The toddler anchored himself by gripping his father's lapel and twisted around to scrutinise the room. Freed, the wife passed me a bottle of wine as an offering and kissed me on the cheeks.

You've made it look well, she said, the place. She turned on my husband and began to cluck. You, you! she cried fondly. We never know, do we, what you're going to do next? My husband seemed confused but laughed along as they embraced. She asked after his youngest daughter pointedly and I thought, a-ha, but also: how disappointing, I had expected more complexity.

You know I saw her the other day, she continued, speaking of the ex. You know she is doing a night course at NCI.

Yes, but she isn't going to the classes, only exams.

Well she knows it all already I suppose.

Oh yes, like, she doesn't need to go.

I told her, the wife said, I don't know how you do it, I'm very impressed!

It's an upskill she needed, my husband qualified. She's in the international department now.

Can I hold the baby? I asked. I wanted to hold him but I also wanted to be seen to want to hold him. He sat on my hip and regarded me tolerantly.

We napped earlier, his mother said.

You are such a handsome young man, I told the child. He had cornflake-coloured curls.

So tell me, so tell me, the wife began: you work in, a college, is that it?

When the meat was done I summoned my husband and asked him to carve it, which he did well, while describing at length the situation with the vacant bay seat he somehow, to my dismay, still appeared to imagine he stood a chance with. He stuck to ideological and imaginative points only, or so I thought, growing excited, so that I felt tempted to ask him to concentrate and at once almost saw myself from above asking him to desist and concentrate; spliced idly but weirdly by a flake of filmy memory, myself walking by the greengrocers on a pretty red-brick street near the British Library, connecting Euston Road to Bloomsbury, and green apples shining gladly in plastic bowls, thinking about buying an apple but knowing it would be coated in smut.

It was a memory of profound if serene aloneness, one of many moments in London when it occurred to me that nobody knew where I was or what I was doing, that my petty thoughts burned off and entered a huge vacantly vibratory ether, like lost balloons, and that this was a horrendous prospect, horrendous and godless; now, watching my husband, a terror of loneliness or a panicked sense of loneliness, here among these people, named itself – wanted

228

to name itself – by streaking by me, unprovoked: an image of apples, and bricks, and sky.

The baby sat on its mother's lap. She let her own food go cold while she fed him patiently from a plastic bowl I'd heated in the microwave. As she fed him, in milliseconds of distraction, he grabbed at the tablecloth and her plate in a brilliantly irrational way. I thought that the whole place, my room, my bed, was going to smell of dinner later. I remembered the cottage and how it was permeated with a smoky odour from the fire. I remembered the day I was balling my coat under my chair at the film institute and somewhere I smelled it, smoke, from somebody's clothes perhaps, and years had passed but the memory pulsed through me with a strangled cry of longing in my throat.

I spent the dinner addressing the baby, for the most part. I found this easier than addressing the couple. The barrister was affable. He teased me lightly in a tender, familiar way. Partly, I presumed, to facilitate this, she was sharp. I tried out a tactic to warm her up by asking questions about a wedding she'd been to recently, inquiring about guests and dresses and location and other things I did not really care about, but realised too late that my bland disinterest was obvious and also that, sounding fatigued, she herself was tired of discussing weddings. At one point she shrugged with what looked like despair, a despair contained by tight birdlike shoulders, at the question of whether or not Cabra Castle still had that corridor of antique tapestries I'd seen there, years ago, at some huge red-cheeked country wedding I attended with my college boyfriend.

My own wedding had given me, recently, an unprecedentedly normal point of access into conversations with the kind of woman I felt dimly nervous of or despised.

Yes I work in a university now, I said. I tried to account for what I did every day. I said, it's mostly reading, even though I had not opened a book, really, for weeks.

You were at UCD, the barrister smiled. He pointed at me, just remembering it.

Yes, I did my undergraduate there, I did English. And I can tell you that we were drunk more-or-less-consistently for three years, and we stuck it to the man. I laughed. We wanted to prove something. My students today are so sedate, it's like they don't even hate anything.

Struck bell of a day with Harry: *Sometimes I think I belong to the most cowardly generation under the sun.*

I was there, said the barrister, and my brother did medicine there, through Vincent's.

Is it true, I asked, that Saint Vincent's is controlled by Opus Dei?

I don't know, but I doubt it, he replied, without laughing this time, which made me think Saint Vincent's was almost certainly controlled by Opus Dei.

Bruton has come out against abortion, my husband whistled.

Oh my. What a cunt, I said. The wife laughed with accusatory surprise but nobody else said anything. I'd had more wine by now.

This lad, the barrister said at last, was at Trinity with half the cabinet.

Back then, my husband observed, Creighton was for abortion and Varadker was against. Now they have reversed positions.

She called it wrong, I said. Wrong side of history. But oh, how cynical. Of both of them really.

Politics, the barrister said.

But why do you think, my husband pressed, they reversed it?

It makes no political sense, for her.

It does, the barrister said at once, forcefully: you don't understand, pro-life, on the ground, is popular.

I don't think it is, I answered simply.

If you go to the grassroots level.

I've been to the grassroots level.

The wife looked at me with interest then. To lighten things, I asked, So you: can you talk about cases right now, cases you are working on?

With a mouthful of food, the barrister smiled and closed his eyes.

Privacy code?

Paperwork, he said. Boring paperwork.

My husband had been called for jury duty twice in his life. I'd never once been called for it. Why twice? I'd asked, when he mentioned it; why the hell *twice*? It's random, he replied. It can't be random, I insisted. It's not random they call a bloody Blueshirt twice but never summon the loose-cannon expatriate. When I asked him what jury duty was like he only said, you'd never believe how much drink they give you in the hotel overnight.

I regret not doing law, I said, sometimes. I had my head in the clouds when I was eighteen.

Where did you go to school? the wife asked me then.

You flatter me, I cried, assuming I went somewhere worth telling you! I made a point of not asking her back.

The child became fractious in the later afternoon and, with apologies, they left. As we cleared up my husband chuckled at me and said, Cunt, my God; but *cunt*.

Baby, they were terrible, I replied. Well, he wasn't so bad.

What? He looked widely at me.

Terrible! I moaned. I raised my hands in mock-defence, or like Eurydice. A horror show. I did not break his gaze for a moment: I allowed my eyes to harden against him.

When we had put away the clean dishes and balled the tablecloth in the washing machine, when the cloth was turning like soapy snow, I said to my husband, Let's go to the Castle for one, and he looked at me with happy surprise.

On a school night?

Are you going to protest?

I'll just jump in the shower, he said.

I poured another glass of wine and waited for him in the armchair. On the arm of the chair, the book I'd been reading earlier lay open like a bird. The spine was tight and kept it springy: not a dead bird, but a live one, still in flight. The clean kitchen – my kitchen – became overlaid with that other kitchen, the centre of Harry's cottage, and the night it came apart at last as I dried up crockery and crackled into action suddenly, a kind of heave or expiation, muscular and peristaltic perhaps.

But no – not suddenly. There was forewarning, certainly.

Harry and I came apart properly, I thought, in the final week – in the third week of the cottage – due in part to the turning of my mood. A turn to familiar, flatter darkness, to a steadier melancholy.

The mimetic mill. Death at the edge of the river.

Carsick curve in the road.

Conspicuous Big House watching, cyclops-eyed, from the other side, winking out-then-under from behind sedate haystacks paced beeches slipway old boathouse.

There was an old woman who lived in the public house we passed: Harry had told me about her, but he may have been thinking of a different public house.

I for my part was unable to tell if my urge to inertia was sickness or cure.

Oh, be *gentle* with him: gentle with his hands, gentle with his first sweet dry and hesitant kiss. Gentle apprehension of his approach, and gentle awareness of his proximity, there, beneath the pennants and a maritime scene of spindly wind-tilted skiffs, in the landlady's drawing room.

I remembered it then, the grief. The grief didn't know how to escape me. Raw wailing failed or came out crimped and cultured like the sound an accordion makes. Silent tears went sour on my face. I leaned my body on the countertop of the cottage, bent wholly at the waist, and wept, and when I opened my eyes I saw my open feet. Chipped polished toes. The voice that asked

why are you crying?

why are you crying?

was the voice that once said *there's the moon* and *who is singing here?* The voice of someone else's mother, or a fat practical neighbour carrying a fat practical bag. *Well now it can't be as bad as that.* It can't be as bad as all that. It was a barren day that God forgot about. Nothing got started and nothing got done. The clouds were doused, sagging over the fields like soiled wool. All the trees to the east had been sawn but for the laburnum.

Someone had put an old table out there and it was warping nicely in the rain, stripping and silvering like a birch, sheltering a slick of leaves. Learning how to camouflage itself.

With Harry, in the cottage, and gradually, I grew feral again.

I was like a person with too much to do, even though there was nothing to do.

Really it had not been like this before.

Before: dry pills sticking like gum, a walk down and up the Strand, where the Eleanor Cross is hell. The Eleanor Cross is pure hell. Buses multiply scatter like beads towards Westminster and all the while the Eleanor Cross is hell, a beacon, church bells inverted so that sound is sucked into a well.

Before, on the floor, when I felt the tube slither beneath me — floors and pipes and plague-pits beneath me — as a princess feels a pea. All night on the floor, lying there, paralysed. A drunk in the street passing singing, No woman, no cry.

Different this time.

I met it once on some stairs like a devil. Now I had encountered it in a man.

This was refreshing.

In that last week, one still day: out the cottage door, past the wintergreen tree, through the mist of pampas grass as high as the roof, out the door I went with rubber gloves on still and barefoot in the part-damp woodland morning rough and sour like a dishcloth or a dog. Making an erect angry beeline for the gatepost. He didn't chase me, did not follow me, and this quite pissed me off because I'd heard the tales of woe involving his wife who threw things – knives and ornaments, a plug of peat – and orchestrated suicide attempts when I was well-behaved, when I was accommodating. Nobody dared go off on one in my house growing up because of my father's temper – until my breakout, that is; until the severing. Now I had a chord sprung tight and violent in my temples again, and why not, I thought, why not let it fly? One half of my head pictured revenge and the other was terribly sorry for it, extending fingers to be twisted and a heart to be destroyed.

I will tell her.

I will tell your wife.

I will ruin it for you.

I will let her hit me in the face; I will see it sliding like a comet.

I will see it breaking into rain against my cheek.

When I'd calmed down and apologised Harry said, I circle my own void, so I know what you mean.

It's fear, I said. It feels like fear.

Fear, when it came, shot through me suddenly as a lean geyser between my ribs, or a stick stirred thickly through me, and really I was overpowered every time, no matter what I tried.

In London in snow sprinting down the stairwell near the Tabard and bustling onto Borough High Street, a figure in a black jacket, practically clapping my hands in an effort to exorcise it, swiftly scissoring arms and scissoring legs, to wholesome places like the council library with its wall full of comic books and televisions showing Sky News subtitled intuitively – subtitled painfully – words in blocks of black remade and deleted – slowly and associatively

– like the commentary of a concussed person. In London I thought of the witchy monologue, Not I, saying a – *ha ha ha! – merciful God!* On fluoxetine the world would be dulled underwater for a while and this wasn't so bad, though it wasn't so *good*, it was all a bland insipid slough, it was like a swimming pool gauzy with disinfectant.

I circle my own void, Harry had said. I know what you mean.

Or perhaps he did not say, *I know what you mean*: perhaps I only tacked that on afterwards, wishfully.

Which is to say I wished he'd responded with empathy instead of self-interest, self-declaration, again.

Which is perhaps the nub of it: let me start again.

My husband appeared, dressed and wet-headed from the shower, as radically real and surprising and welcome as he had been on the very first day of our acquaintance, at Connolly Station.

Ready to go? he asked.

Somewhat dazed, an empty wine glass in my hand, I nodded at him without saying a word.

Are you OK?

I'm good, I'm good, I said.

If the flat was naturalism, the sweet suburban streets were a pleasant reprieve, with old rain sliding from canopies and cement knuckled up by the roots of sycamores.

At the Castle there were two stone lions, roaring, relics from its former identity I suppose as an actual castle – or supposed identity – and you reached them by winding underneath a wire arbour trained to trees. The first time that we came here my husband had said, When Anna was a baby she used to put her hand into their mouths and pretend they had bitten her, and every time I would have to pretend to give them a smack.

I loved this story like I loved the story of driving in

France, because I heard so few of these, little scenes from his world long before I was ever in it. And I wondered, reflected rationally, if this was love, because I believed that it was love – care and nostalgia, even, on behalf of the other. Anna would never be a small child and so trusting again.

I knew as I took off my coat in a snug that I was going to get very drunk. I was going to do so deliberately. I felt wound up and I wanted to oil every knot in my body, to come apart disgracefully, to career giggling home, or crying, or retching, or whatever, and to sleep the sleep of the intoxicated, waking with a paranoid wrench at five o'clock in the morning. I was old enough to know the score and still decide to enter into this, something which my body wouldn't get over for days.

Oh and yes, the latency of rain: the day in Harry's cottage, climbing the stairs after he had said *Stop*: wishing to drink, and to be perhaps annihilated. To at least have this abbreviated. Tension – stretching – latency. This.

It is marriage, I thought. What have you done?

I once thought I could walk away, leave, anything, and that this was the soundest defence against being left.

Harry and I came apart, I thought, in the third week, due to a turning or swivelling of my mood, and I still can't say if this was pathological or symptomatic of something grinding, slowly but surely, between Harry and I, or between me and reality, or between optimism and cruelty, or between my inner child and the unfortunate character cast as unwilling father, demigod, satyr and sympathiser, saviour, base betrayer, ordinary man of middle age with predilections.

I really do mean I felt uncertain even then, sitting in

a snug and waiting for my husband to return. Oh but everything was in this you see. I had to do justice to it. Its combustibility.

I really hate saying *I was ill* because I don't believe it is illness in fact. If something is staling and going awry in an atmosphere, in a space or house, and nobody names it and so one begins Cassandra-like to jerk against it in a nervous dance, this is essentially rational actually; this is the ghost articulation of facts. There is a tic-like synchronicity to it.

In London, before, I had presented at the college counsellor and said: I have a terrible sense of dread, of terrible wrongness to everything, and suspect this derives from a fundamental badness or awfulness inherent in me. And this woman, with glasses on beaded string, asked, But what is wrong? Nothing concrete, I said, or many things. The woman replied: We are not in the business of giving out free and scarce therapy appointments to people who feel merely *unhappy*. At the time I experienced, at this, a rush of shame and despair; now, with the wit of a grown woman, I only think, stupid bitch. She directed me to the GP and a prescription. This was right before the night on the floor and the trains, the plague-pits, rattling beneath me. The night of No woman, no cry.

How I wish now that I could re-inhabit myself at twenty-three and tell the counsellor, you're a foolish, clueless bitch. But what would that do? She reminded me of the chaplain at school. I was dispatched to the chaplain when my father left, and she said, You will have problems relating to men for the rest of your life. Nobody had ever mentioned either men or the rest of my life to me before; I had no sense of time unfolding ahead of me in patterns and templates, a concertina or an ornamental fan, the mill-of-God.

In the cottage in that third week Harry told me, I circle my own void, because I don't love any of the work I've done. I consider it all in some way flawed.

I replied, with thought, what you said just there, it made me think of a poem: 'An Irish Airman Foresees His Death'.

The Yeats?

Yes. Uncertainly, I recited it, and when I was done, Harry asked, will you say it again? And then, I'm not sure I follow you.

Lonely impulse for purity, I explained. Beyond good and evil or good and bad: lonely impulse to write. Can you think of it like that? Could you think, I pressed, of love like that?

When I talk about art I get earnest and confident and feel foolishly free to move into the territory of love, discursively. People back away in embarrassment. I don't know if I blame them. They think I'm insane. People are so boring.

Pure, cold love? Harry asked.

Untrammelled, I said. I liked that word so much.

A bit Joan of Arc, isn't it?

I laughed.

You look like Joan of Arc, he said.

I sort of did, after the haircut.

That was a nice moment, but maybe the last.

After my tantrum and my threat he said, I circle my own void you see, with work, and began to explain the years of uncertainty and the recurring uncertainty and the backlog of emails from the director, and explained to me,

You cannot get pulled into work, you should take care not to follow the darkest thoughts into the abyss, do you understand? There are ways of avoiding this. He was paternal and kindly with me. I nodded, rhapsodic. He went back to his office and stayed there for days.

Harry emerged to eat and sleep, of course, but only this. For two nights he slept next to me, or lay awake tensely next to me, in his clothes. His withdrawal was like a growing, sickly odour. I had cracked up and misbehaved and stalked into the garden, between pampas grass, in rubber gloves, mid-way through washing up, a task I'd been doing when at once the imp of bloodlust was in me and I said, I've been to your wife's place, escalating – old tight wound-up spring of badness – I had cracked up and lashed out (why? I don't know: bear with me: I am mapping every impulse I can map) and now, post-tantrum, when he lay beside me stiffly in his clothes I couldn't say a thing or rock the boat, you understand, I clung to an illusion until it broke.

When, I asked Harry, do you plan to go back to London?

I thought in a few weeks. We'll see.

Only I, I said. I may not really want to go back.

What do you mean?

I had not expected him to face into it so openly. I felt sure on some level he knew what I meant.

I might, I said haltingly, visit my mother, or something. He looked at me with some compassion. This look made me nervous because it was as if he was seeing something in me, some vision of me, I couldn't see; something to be pitied, you understand.

What, I asked, will you do with me in London?

Where, I asked, will you put me?

Put you? He was stalling for time.

I said, You know what I mean.

I had a great love, then, of giving things up – of packing things in – of writing things off. I quit jobs. I was especially wont to quit jobs. Temping made the non-commitment easy and relatively acceptable in terms of my résumé. I loved that I was able to quit, that nobody could prevent me from leaving places, stations and situations: I loved the feeling of agency and power this compulsion for cutting ties sustained in me. It was the opposite of childhood you see. It was the opposite of pained rain-light, endless afternoons, concrete schoolyards and seagulls skating idly overhead against a sky like yellow snow; it was the opposite of ashtrays and altars and bas-relief, of sour fields and unfinished housing estates, of boredom – always ambient plangent boredom – and of the policing policies instigated by adults, especially women: you-were-seen-here and you-were-seen-there. It was irruption. I went to London, I left London. I came here and I could because I wanted to. I could become the lover of a rich man nearing fifty and quit my job as a temporary receptionist to five psychiatrists; give up my room in the council flat with a gourd of damp; cut off my hair with nail scissors; throw my phone into the sea. All this freedom you see breaking now against the wall of his effortless influence over me. I had found something I didn't want to give up, I had found something I wanted ferociously *for me*, and here it was slipping away, passing by, the terrible pendulum of the inevitable.

All these women, I said bitterly. I was in the kitchen. I was stacking plates. Harry was standing at the counter with a laptop computer and not looking at me.

Always in a kitchen for these showdowns aren't I? Such

a female thing, really. Struck bell of my grandmother, stacking plates by lamplight perhaps, seeing suddenly the peeping tom standing against her kitchen window, watching her, his breath a close blood-chilling mist against the glass: a horror show.

All these women, I repeated to Harry then, in your chaste harem. The landlady, your wife, the women you have brought here – all your retired women; you keep them around, you will do this to me, you will keep me around but take it away. Your prick, or whatever. You would have a hold over me.

Calm down, Harry said. At this I let the plate slip, plate with a chaffinch on it, and stepped back and burst into tears at the sandy crack.

And actually I felt remorse even then, in the snug, to remember it. I had lost.

Why relive this? I thought. I thought this in the Castle – in the snug.

It is boredom, I thought – it is tension.

Anguish, at those people in my dining room, my husband's dining room, being so disappointing, the petty limits of their interest in everything; of the *grassroots level*, as I sang for my husband now; of that agile absence of curiosity you see in the Irish middle-class, arid and frigid but slipping around it all somehow – tension, tension, I said, Jesus, they'd make you tense just looking at them.

My husband was laughing again. It had to be *cunt*, he said.

I laughed too although I was wound up, sharp beyond sharp as if something were rising within me, disappointment or terror or rage. You should know, I said, that you have married out of that now, I will never be so constipated. I ran away, I found myself saying: I ran away from things, when I was younger. I couldn't wait to get out of this country once.

The landlady, her husband, Harry: these I pictured in her drawing room, all of them elegant as a conspiracy, my shoeless shiftless girl-self with her cheap clothes on the steps of the big house – cornices, undulating equestrian mouldings, rhapsodic putti and muses swooping into a milky twist in a copula, such lovely things, the landlady had told me, within – on the outside of everything. Oh, smallest violin.

My husband now bought cider for himself and wine for me. I liked that he did not patronise me by buying a small glass.

I love you, I said, as he sat down.

Oh me too.

No I really mean it though. God, it is dangerous!

What I meant was: I love you even though not only will you never break into politics nor make anything of yourself professionally, but also you will store any possible shame or self-realisation attaining therein in your subconscious, letting it manifest as slights and acts of emotional violence against me, forever and ever, or at least for a couple of years, and I am old enough to know the score and see all this. I love you even though I can't even begin to deduce the elegant arbitrations of your private morality.

I meant: I love you although I am jealous of your privilege and you are jealous of my industry. Even though I have stravaged and suffered to reach this peak when you sit on top of it like an idiot, you sit on it like an *idiot*; even though you've lost two families I am going to make a third with you, a bolshie *sprezzatura* gesture, because there is something in you I can't get over and I'm done, really – I am worn out.

I meant: I have watched you so closely, I have watched Harry so closely, and I think I know you both in my own beguiled style. I think you will grow with me, and in me, and never let me down.

I meant: but I've *made my bed*, you see. The sheer limit of it filled me with a cosy glee I remembered from childhood – from being, oh, *very, very* young indeed.

You don't want to spend too much time with them again, he supplied. He was talking about his friends.

Well I doubt they thought much of me.

They were impressed by you. Or not. I like, he winked, I like to think people are surprised by you. The things you come out with sometimes. I don't know what to do with you.

You're just protected, I crowed: you're just innocent. Even though he was avowedly not. There were shadows in him darker than anything I had known or acted out. And yet he never so much as swore most of the time, his adenoidal accent rising to affront at speed but never breaking into serious obscenities.

I love you, is what I meant, even though I don't think I respect you very much.

The bar was stocked with Sunday families finishing heavy meals, pushing soiled plates aside and starting to talk loudly and fretfully about how and when to deliver elderly relatives home. Mammy is tired, one woman said, constantly – several times, I mean – Mammy is *worn out*. To our right sat an incongruous foursome of American tourists, late in the year, attempting with genuine puzzlement to ascertain what kind of salmon was available.

Is it, like, wild? they were asking. The waiter, who seemed to be Korean, nodded blankly and said, Yes, it comes from the sea.

Isn't salmon from a lake? a woman asked.

Yes, the waiter laughed indulgently. He laughed as if they had made a permissible mistake. Yes, and the sea, both water.

What did you think of her? my husband asked.

I said, You don't want to hear my opinion, before adding, she looks like she goes to Ladies' Day.

Yes. I imagine she does.

Why weren't they at the wedding?

I don't know. Didn't invite?

Would have been your job. I laughed into my wine, and coughed. More, I said, standing up pointlessly.

Sit down, my husband said as always: my round.

Later he said, Next time we'll have friends of yours over. People from work maybe.

Intellectuals.

Maybe.

Artists.

Maybe. You met Maeve and Donagh that time.

Yes, he was all right. We could ask your dad over.

Are you curious?

What? No. Well, yes, I mean, I'd like to meet him.

Maybe I'll arrange something. I felt tired then.

How did you get on with him, what was it, two weeks ago?

Oh, the usual.

What does that mean, though? I don't know what the usual is.

It's difficult to explain. I countered, What do you talk to *her* about, when you call her, always – I was shredding a beermat now – when you are out of my earshot?

The baby, he said shortly.

Yeah. You could talk about that in front of me.

250

What are you suggesting?

Nothing, nothing. I don't even care. I don't want to be a hypocrite.

I don't even know what you mean.

We fell silent. After a while, my husband nodded at the Americans. They come over expecting something completely different when they see the word *Castle*, he laughed. I felt my mouth smiling serenely and relaxing into this expression with alarming elasticity, slackening, as if cut loose from my face.

I remember next emerging from the arbour, all things tilting, to clap my open palm against the soft expressive crenulations of the lions' manes, sighing loudly to release a toxic impulse; my husband tugging me by the hand, my saying, Usually this is me pulling you, isn't it? Usually this is me, dealing with your shit. I tore around to face the hotel again and saw the doors drawn across it, the lights half-extinguished within: my God, I shouted, is it closing time already?

It's nearly one.

Fuck's sake, I said.

How do you like this? I asked as we stumbled. How do you like me? My husband, I felt, was genuinely taken aback at my state and the change it brought over me. It's all right, I said, you'll have it against me. To hold I mean. I got the impression that I was being scolded. I was led home and sat in the kitchen. He'd disappeared. I shook my head. I saw the sink, shouting whitely; washing machine. But where? I whispered. And then I stuck my head in the door and there he was, passed out in the bed, clothes melting into substance on the floor. OK, I said. OK. I lay down.

My heart was ranging dryly through my chest and up my throat and into my head. The room dipped cruelly backwards and I spoke, saying, No, no, no, this is not tolerable. Can't lie down if it's going to tilt like that. I found this clarity comforting. I found shoes and, head clearing ever-so-slightly, let myself out and walked down the street again, towards the sea, banding my arms around me.

At the bottom of the street I stopped and looked back up. It was dry and mild, with wind flushing freshly through the sycamores now, with streetlight siphoned into orbs on the bonnets of cars, gathered into pools of galvanised gas – with festive blasts of streetlight, sometimes, in the canopies. I swaggered and sang a little but, at once, felt my sadness tip over me once again: I sat down on a doorstep, I believe, by a gnarled little boot-scraper. I couldn't cry. I mean that I felt alone and petulant but also deliciously ridiculous, because now I had somewhere to go – now I had something to lose. I was over my tantrum at last and I climbed to my feet.

This is here, I am here, this is here, I am here: it swung in my head like a seesaw, it was urgent that I know: it is here, I am here, I am staying here, I live here – I am here, alive – I am staying here, I have made a promise, and I can't be turned out, I have rights.

Houses slept. Houses were shut obediently under the slumber of their occupants, confident people who knew where they were and what they could demand and who protected it – protected themselves – in ways I needed to learn how to do.

I must have made my way home, animally, and when I woke up there were leaves and debris in the bed.

Part Six

Harry left. And I awoke to find him gone. I let the cat in and walked my thoughtful circuits by lamplight.

Some cold defensive carapace returned.

All lights extinguished and a purity of black.

Harry had gone. Well then, I thought, baiting the universe really, if that is that I will have to kill myself. Absurd as it sounds, at that very moment it seemed banally obvious. I would need to cycle to the coast when it got light and walk into the tide. Numb but singing shanties I would wait for currents or steel-traps to catch my legs.

Waves would wallop over me, like washerwomen, thoughtlessly, and do the rest: to me, just then, it was obvious. I was not even frightened by the thought. It was almost consoling. I had come to the end of some great precipice. I had followed its bawdy logic to the very end.

Can you not offer me anything better? I asked, baiting the universe again. Is this the very best I can expect?

I stood barefoot, my soles as black as coal, in a peacoat, stiff, and my fragrant derangement found its object in the thought of suicide: quick, jolly, singing, in the tide.

Idly I scraped a cold sole against a bare calf. Idly I pushed fingers across my scalp and tugged, dully and all at once, at the roots of my hair, to calm myself. The pain felt earthy and authentic.

He would come back, but in the meantime, I would have to kill myself.

Nobody knew I had come here, to Ireland, with him. I had been eating my fill and lazing about and lying open as a bottle of champagne, kept cool with silver spoons: I had been taking it, being fucked, so satisfactorily and unabashedly he could no longer look me in the eye – he jumped to the side, in the morning, when I came ringing down the ladder, even before the day of the void and the tantrum and madness. Even before that.

My mind, now, was spare as the mind of an animal, an amphibian. Death was a brag that held no horror for me. In retrospect it is evident that I had, by this point, gone insane. But it must be said that as I stood there, coal-soled, dead-eyed, black-hearted, I did not feel defeated: I felt uncommonly alive. Now that Harry was gone the tension was gone and the system of manners between us eradicated. Things had been revealed.

Also I suppose at this point it was my story now.

Lights appeared in the landlady's house. I knew that her lights were a signal to me. I lifted the latch and stepped out the front door, where I saw, by the splash of the sensor-light, a shrew that had been torn open and laid out on a step by the cat. The cold grit of the step shocked my feet and I returned inside for shoes.

The cottage was set off the boreen, and shaded by layers of trees, but you could still see the first floor of the land-lady's house: a Grade 2 listed farmhouse clad in red brick with two columns and a portico, drive sweeping before it grandly and the dawn glowing behind. Wind rinsing in the many trees – the trees, the pines and limes and green-oaks, hawthorn, silver birch, against the sky – the whole hollow alive with industry. I still wore the peacoat with wellington boots. She was struggling with a shag draft-blocker as she pulled open her door, towing it to and fro so that the knocker, a love-knot, swung. She wore a long dressing gown like a mother superior.

I heard him, she announced at once. Off – early. I heard the motorbike, I woke up. It must have been sudden.

Yes.

London?

I was grateful she did not smile. That her face was show-ing her age as she adapted to the porchlight by degrees. All around us breath rushed through the trees, making them thrash softly as distant glass, but still she did not invite me in.

It was not cold: it was mild and lively.

Look, if he rings, he will be ringing you, because there is no phone in the cottage.

Don't you have a mobile?

No, I said. The sim was still somewhere: I'd never installed the sim. I did not want to go into it. In fact, I asked, would you mind if I phoned him from here? Not now – later today.

On his mobile?

But then she realised that she would be privy to it. All right then, she said.

I returned to the cottage. The day began.

Shortly after the sun had risen, early in fact, the vege-table man arrived with a three-note blow of the horn. I wondered if he wondered who I was as I emerged. In the box were squash, tomatoes, aubergine, apples, blueberries, bananas and a green gourd I could not identify. At first it felt like a kind of blessing, but then I grew depressed thinking that all of it but the bananas would soften and rot. I felt his absence piercingly and began to cry, and my crying is difficult – my crying is embarrassing. Like all little girls I used to cry at my mother's dresser, in the mirror, as a child, while plaiting and unplaiting my hair. But as an adult I cannot even bear to look at myself when I cry.

When the weeping ceased, I climbed upstairs and lay on the bed. A book he had not finished lay open on its jaw next to one of several pairs of spectacles. He had tidied away the whip in the inlaid box. The cat purred in my spot and stared at me. The night before this man had pushed my head to the side and ground against me fruitlessly, and then lay still with a stunned or absent aspect; I serviced his broad beautiful penis and shook semen onto my chest in warm dashes. With an older man there is less of it.

In the afternoon, I drew a bath. The light had limpened and the horizon grew feathered and grey. The tin tub filled from a hose and I sat in it derelict, rubbing oil into my hair. My feet were scabbed and worn-looking, but my breasts were heart-breaking; my cunt has always been a coquette. Through the window a robin flitted kitschly on a branch overhanging the stream.

At three I trudged back to the landlady's door. Now the air was lower and cold, mist was building on the fields, and burning wood gave an incense to the air.

Aha, she said on seeing me, pretending to just remember it, he called.

Why didn't you get me? I cried.

Well I knocked, but I got no response.

I was bathing, I thought. Good. He would imagine I went out. I would not mention it; I would let him think that I went out. The landlady looked sorry for me now.

Come in and call him then, she said, and I'll make some tea.

I crossed her herringbone floor briskly. It was the kind of floor that made one want to brisk and flit. This room was the most beautiful room, the one they had restored entirely, down to the fireplace and the wrought iron chandelier of candle stubs. She intended it to have an impact on everyone and it did; the first time I came over I whirled about in delight. By the phone, where it hung from heavy saffron-coloured tiles, were a great many lever-arch files and brochures.

We are trying to source a stag's head, she explained: taxidermy.

She moved some of these now and tipped the switch on the kettle. She braced her hands on the Belfast sink. You take your time, she advised, because I can get back to it later. I prayed that he would not, in front of this woman, fail to pick up on me. Two vegetable crates were on display and at the lived-in, looming dresser, smoky flutes stood half-unpacked from wax paper.

Oh, oh, I pulled an expression of ecstasy, pushing the receiver away. Party? I mouthed.

Just a little thing, she said.

Hello? The man, on the other end of the phone, flooded back to me through his voice, sounding English and tinny and clipped.

I maintained a mellifluous note to my own voice as we spoke. At such times in life I think back to the comportment class at school: adopt a *smooth melodious tone*.

You know that you can stay as long as you like, he said.

But I want to see you, I replied.

Of course, and I you. But it's become difficult.

Are you with your wife?

Well, he gave a dry frustrated laugh, of course; I am home.

I wouldn't bother being jealous, if I were her, I said. My eyes travelled to the landlady, judiciously unpacking champagne flutes and holding each one to the light. They looked like the wedding flutes my parents would toast from at Christmas only, in the pebbledash semi-d of steamed windows and dinner-smell, and not the kind of champagne flute you buy to seem chichi. I stood always in awe of her taste.

If I were her, I continued, I would simply give you a good thrashing.

Precisely because the landlady did not swivel archly around I know for sure that she had heard.

Now, now, the man spoke softly. There is no need for that.

Shortly afterwards we finished up. I had intended to laugh and make light of it, but cried.

Well now, remarked the landlady, addressing a flute.

I reflected on my economic circumstance; on my hopes and dreams, on the unease in my stomach and heart. It was mildly thrilling to be this imperilled, but the truth is any situation runs the risk of getting old. The landlady placed at last a mug of something leafy before me. A witch's brew.

What should I do? I asked.

Leave, of course.

I told her that I had no money.

And what about a job? What do you do in London, apart from study?

I'm a temp.

There you go, she said. She was cruel. Go back and do that. You know. The landlady had seized a baton of roses and was snipping them into the sink. That surprises me. I hear you speak, I would think you came from money. After a moment she asked, Did you go to Trinity?

For my Master's, before.

Very impressive, she said.

I have my doctorate.

You should finish it, she said.

Yes. I drew breath for strength.

I couldn't think of anything other than him. I felt *quite mad*, *quite mad*, and the words ground through my mind: *quite mad*, quite insane, I could smell him under my fingernails, dirty and dark. He was the seam of grit defining every distal edge collected when I scraped my hands across his back and chest, gored through, or riding on his lap. I had never loved a man with my body before, which I supposed meant I had never loved a man before. I wanted more and more and more. Even the odour of my own sweat, spiking underarm, made me think of him, but I couldn't tell this woman it was serious or that I was mad for him: people never believe you, it is as if you are disclosing belief in the paranormal and want to convert them. They look away.

If you're having people over, I said as I looked out at the leaden day, I could help.

The landlady straightened and glanced askance at me. I couldn't pay you, she said.

At four o'clock I returned to the cottage alone. None

of it was funny any more. I stood in the odour of wood-smoke and raised my arms to reach for something – raised them about level with my shoulders, where they froze. There was no pain or suddenness, but a short-circuiting, whereby I found myself picked out sharply against the light suspended in a half-animate pose or silhouette. Each joint arrested where it is. The swell within was worse than tears. My expression in the slit of mirror I could see was so private I was quite unable to interpret it. I felt like my own likeness, my own spirit, or my own death caught in a photograph. In this moment, I experienced a deep and profound terror that it would never end, that I would never breathe again.

I cannot do it, I thought.

I cannot do.

When motion was restored I began by closing my own fingers around my throat, feeling thumbprints bearing in, wondering if dead-of-heart hands could finish a dead-of-heart life. How sore it would be and long it was likely to take. I imagined my own detonation, waiting, latent, like something at the end of a long fuse. I could choose a beach I was familiar with, with a bad old tide. I pulled out a straw-bottomed chair at the table and thought about it. I allowed my eyes to roll over my lover's collected posses-sions – a map of Canada, bikes, a pick-axe, a strange rock shaped like a loaf of bread, some paintings, pots and pans with gold-bottomed hues like flinching pools of parallax, a space-heater we towed behind us into rooms, a nineteen-twenties wood-burning stove – with new coldness. If I could disappear from your life. Not only your life, but mine.

It can be soothing to think about it. What life asks of

you is so often too much. Not only occurrences, or lack thereof, but sprockets in your head: the question of what is normal and what is not, of what is pathological. Of whether it's true that nobody loves you, if God is listening, if there is a God. If it will always be like this and you will never move again. If you will ever know yourself. I don't mean existential questions, or not only these, but the very *nature of truth* as this impinges immediately on you. On me.

Take, for instance, myself, sitting in a straw-bottomed chair. In Ireland of all places. How I had gotten there. Truth is too large a frame of reference. Say perception instead. I perceived, if dimly, myself, sitting in a straw-bottomed chair. Lonelier than I had ever been in my life. I knew certain facts about the world as I was placed in it at that instant.

I knew I was forgotten here; he was, among other things, the only person besides the landlady to know I was in Ireland; even if I wanted to it wouldn't be easy to call on friends or family.

I knew that nobody could see me, I was alone and inert to the point of being a proverb in myself – it is quite possible I *did not exist* beyond my own tenuous and habitual sense of self. Any vanity I experienced in the bathtub that morning could not comfort me. Perhaps I was, in fact, ugly, or just dispensable; hobbled somehow, or marked. Born under an unlucky star. Supposed to winter quietly out and finish life on a silent note but not resigned to this – not resigned to be invisible and as materially irrelevant as an unheard, falling, tree.

Should I open my wrists at this table, beneath the gape of the fireplace, *someone* would find me, even if it were days. They would say, Stupid girl, she had so much ahead of her. But nobody can say that for sure. You might have nothing ahead of you but torment for all they know.

At six o'clock, evening began to fall.

I remained where I was in the straw-bottomed chair.

By the bulb of a burgundy lamp I saw my silhouette in a pane returning to its nightlife as a mirror; saw one half of my face lit sharp and the other in darkness. Saw my hair kinky from the wet air and the damp from ground-water, from the land-stream, from the mist. Radiators hissed in wasteful contemplation on the walls. Still it was cold, *as cold as stone, as cold as stone*, truly that cold. I watched my silhouette and wondered if it was a beautiful silhouette. I saw the serious face of my paternal grandmother. I saw the turmoil of my curls and the blunt bit at the end of my nose. I saw my thick bottom lip, my trick; it melts out when I cry so you see only a terrible hole.

How could I see the night out without violence?

All I wanted was for the man to come back, for the man to be here, strong and warm, my arms across his chest and my head resting on his arm. In his absence my hips and ribs and lips diminished; this was the beginning of full disappearance, of numbness. Perhaps I would leave only a faint inscription on the air, like the final smile of the Cheshire Cat.

After a week, there is no such thing as a beautiful corpse after all. But is that how you want him to remember you?

No, actually: a *controversial inquest* would be enough.

See now there's your sense of humour back.

Eventually, I arose from the straw-bottomed chair stiff and chilled to climb upstairs.

I lay in his bed for a while, peeling off my fingernail-tips, leaving jagged surfaces behind. Condensation built on the window and then broke up mincingly; the moon was fuller still, I thought, but smothered under cloud.

When I'd warmed up the first thing that I did was go through his belongings. I threw open the deep wardrobe, a warped mahogany monstrosity, waiting for the butcher's hooks; there were only coats and boots. With the bone-handled knife on the sill I scratched *Bluebeard* into the wood, but shallowly, and at the back, where he might not find it for years.

In a stout bag like a bellows there was paperwork of no significance, some ticket stubs, and then a slight vial of whiskey, which left me surprised. It also left me warm and took the edges off my mood. I looked through papers – this was sacrilege, a karmic reflex I expect to be richly revenged on for eventually – in search, in truth, of evidence that I had somehow impacted on this man: I couldn't tell, since he wrote dates illegibly. By this time I was hungry.

I ate tuna from the can and oranges. I felt oppressed by an intense respectfulness and couldn't trash the place, nor even bring myself to tip a single thing. Why wasn't he worried about this? Did I seem so sincerely sane?

I sent an email. I have not gone, I wrote: I am staying here, to wait for you. I switched the computer off and I felt I must do something with my hands, letting them fly about like butterflies, in the upper room. It was night. I made tea and I lit candles. I poured out the tea and made coffee instead.

Harry would read the email at once, but not answer immediately. The stalling would have nothing to do with strategy and everything to do with honest shock; also, he didn't like to be gruff with me, or anybody – all the fighting was mine, all the raging was mine, and Harry was merely intransigent, quiet, cowed-looking, but never defeated.

The night deepened. I decided that I would go out again. The very idea of sleep was absurd.

A car was coming down the boreen, and this was unusual enough to make me stop at the door of the cottage to watch it pass; a man and a woman, talking animatedly, taking the pits and gashes of the irregular lane, swallowed up towards the landlady's house as up some narrow dark canal. It was late, about nine, and the spikes of the brick factory in the distance – over stubble fields, flat as be-damned – shone eerily.

These ones are late, came a voice. When I turned I saw the landlady's husband walking up the boreen with a torch, pointing the cold stalk of torchlight ahead, in a gesture at the car that had just slid by me, and passed.

Oh, I answered, in confusion.

Stephen took me in shyly now and asked, Were you not at the house?

Oh, I said; no. Is there something going on?

There's a few people here. Come over, if you like.

I was just going to go for a walk.

Do you have a torch? You'd need a torch for the lanes; it gets very dark further up, very easy to stumble into a ditch. If you don't have a torch, we have several at the house.

I'd like to go to the house and see people, I said.

I think she must have forgotten to ask you, he replied.

When we arrived at the house she was still on the steps, having admitted the two latecomers, and wearing a black velvet dress which, with her piled hair and creamy complexion, made her look like a neat little half-pint of stout.

We thought you might be gone! She wailed for effect when she saw me, raising her arms in a Eurydice attitude of dismay: we thought you might be going – we were going to call and ask if you wanted a lift to the airport. We thought that maybe you'd booked a flight.

No, I'm not going yet.

Would you like to come in, and take something to eat? her husband asked.

Oh it's OK, I said.

Help yourself, help yourself, she cried behind me.

In the house there was a series of tableaux.

In the parlour, underneath the dark cascading cabinets and the huge dresser, its polished plates of glass and shining stalactite decanters, in the cold, cold parlour, food. There were platters of meat frilled with lettuce, tabbouleh and salad, cold potatoes, screwed-up tubes of bread, and everything had been demolished or ransacked at speed, if civilly: someone had dashed flash skirts of foil over sever-al dishes, decently. The table was like a Dutch *vanitas*. I found I was not hungry because I was too anxious, so I moved to the second tableau, the kitchen, down the stairs.

There, a girl in black with an apron tied around her waist stood playing the radio. She had set out the food and was dealing with dishes now, and a great many plastic containers, slaw and salad tubs; she was picking peas and chips of red onion from the teeth of the sink. She sang. She was younger than me, and red-faced. She turned and said, Anything you need?

I'd like, if I could, to make some coffee.

Aw no problem! The girl was bright. Her hair was fine and blonde and she was plump; her nails were shocking talons of electric-blue. I'm about to serve coffee upstairs.

Something, like, instant will do, I said.

Pfft. The girl looked at me. There's gorgeous coffee. Why would you bother with that shit? I'll make you some and you can have it here.

Are you – related? I asked.

I help out sometimes, I live out by the crossroads. She does my nails for me. The girl held out the blue talons, which were terrific, and hideous.

Are you telling me, I asked, that the landlady does – *shellac*?

She's a trained beautician. She'll do my makeup for my debs and all. It's next week, Sacred Heart.

The landlady does makeup? I felt exhilarated; my nerves gave unto mirthless and unnecessary chuckling. I thought, I said, she was an aristocrat.

Oh she's well-off anyway.

The kitchen was sunken, and lit by an inverted

punchbowl of smoky light. There was even an oilcloth on the table and a slab of butter so forgotten it had turned soft and sour-looking underneath another dish of glass. A crowd of potted herbs filled the small window over the sink, like spectators. Despite the window it felt internal or womblike. The girl filled up a cafetiére and hummed to the radio, which was playing incongruous dance music. Or not incongruous.

When I was a teenager my father and his new wife brought us to the house they were renting, somewhere desolate, somewhere in the fens – there was very little furniture, boxes everywhere, no heat, a new-build with blunt and simple-minded fixtures, I was screwed up inside by the unfamiliarity and overcrowding, since this new woman, whom he would marry, had daughters that were older, louder, franker, than me. I remembered now the empty window of the room I was given, looking onto the abbey churchyard, the darkness so complete there was no outline of a single tree, no relief, only a sucking solid boss of space – no abbey gable in this memory, though I know it was there. Something about it made me need to look away and lie face-down on the undressed bed, my school-bag full of homework, poems, clean underwear, while my new stepsisters played loud pop music next door. They played it all night as I lay awake in turmoil and I could not connect, I could not go to them and ask for anything – when was this? I was about fourteen. It surfaced in a solid knot of strain. My fingers clenched at all the horror once again.

Are you OK? The girl asked, as she began to push the plunger through the cafetiére quickly, pumping really, causing bubbles to erupt.

I'm OK.

Are you a visitor?

Sort of.

The others are all in the dining room.

I'll help you take that in, I said.

In that house in the fens it was always cruelly bright – the light of bulbs that were never dressed, just like the walls were never painted, and the boxes not unpacked; several lives spilling together as if nothing meant a thing, and everybody arguing – or pitch-black, grave-dark, since the house was in the centre of a half-finished housing estate. That was the boom, so such brash freezing houses had sprung up all over the country. I would drift around the crust of the estate, past yellow diggers tipping into recesses, engines cut out on Friday evening, and plastic-sheeting flicker everywhere. I would wear fingerless gloves and earphones and listen to the Smashing Pumpkins. I decided that Ireland, with its wet fields and the surge of the plantation on a distant hill like pyroclastic flow, was the ugliest shithole in the world, and that as soon as I was able, I would leave.

If ever I complained someone always said, Stop it, your mother is having a hard time.

My father left when I was twelve. I foresaw it some weeks before. It was the winter after the twin towers. It is like a play: two girls in a piano room at school, old sodality scrolls and morality manuals. Practising for the Christmas concert. Singing 'Poor Wandering One'.

Rain sheeting and pleating beneath the streetlights in uphill wind. So cosy it is. The girls are still ungainly and on the lean unlovely cusp of puberty. I was practising for a concert. I was not a bad singer at all, though I played piano terribly, and gave up trying altogether when I discovered boys. On this rainy night we packed our things and left, and the smell of soap in the orange corridors was comforting. And I was taking a half-lit shortcut through the community college – during the day they might chase us away or spit on us, for being convent girls – and I realised a man was coming towards me in the rain-slicked pavement and that it was my father, whom I had never seen abroad, alone, outside of his car, in my life. My father was walking in the rain.

What are you doing? I asked.

Only walking, he said. Go on home there like a good girl. And weeks later he left, and I had foreseen it. In my heart I knew it when I saw him coming towards me, so strangely in the grainy rain, like his own ghost. Although I did go home, like a good girl, and ate reheated food in front of the television.

Here I was, back in Ireland, with no good reason any more.

The hired girl and I now carried trays from the sunken kitchen of the farmhouse, through a hallway lit sedulously by sconces, to the dining room, to meet the third tableau. We pushed the doors to with our respective hipbones.

I left the cottage on the day after the landlady's party because Harry sent me another email and, indirectly, instructed me to. It said: I have booked you flights. He had thought out every bit of it, the time it would take to the get to the airport, and to pack. The flights were booked for the following afternoon.

You, he wrote, may want to say your goodbyes to the landlady.

I cannot tell you what I thought when I read that email.

I wrote, and erased, several times, I am going to kill you, I'm not even joking, I'll find you and bind you and strangle you, I'll fuck your life up absolutely every-which-bloody-way, but each time I erased it, and finally I took the bone-handled knife and opened an essentially harmless aperture in my arm. This, I thought, is getting a bit crazy now. It did not stop bleeding for some time and my arm, my knuckles, my dress, the white enamel of the bath, became stained with blood.

Bloody motherfucker son-of-a-bitch bloody motherfucker, I yelled. Fraud, bastard, coward. The cat stopped in the doorway and sat down in sympathy.

When I had bound up my arm I found my shoes. I moved with lizard lust and speed. I took the bicycle from its place, tossed behind a modest mound of firewood that had been sealed off with tarpaulin, weighted down with breezeblocks, took the bicycle and scooped, scooped, scooped a foot for speed before I had so much as steadied on the saddle. I could hear only my breath and my pulse, but I thought, suddenly, of the fact of an anechoic chamber, of something a fellow student, a musician, had said to me: she'd been, this musician, into an anechoic chamber in the Netherlands, and said, It is the most distressing thing.

Is it like a seashell? I asked. This was in London.

What?

Do you hear your blood, rushing like the sea?

You hear a high-pitched, electric sort of sound, she explained. It is your nervous system.

As I sat and pedalled down the boreen, steering wide of chasms and dried-stiff tyre-tracks like lizard backs, I imagined a fleshless system of transmitters, in the shape of a human, buzzing dryly, the demented ring of instinct, it was such a rich image! I thought of ghosts composed of nervous systems, interrupting satellites and hard drives, flashing like the blank bomb-light of climbing fluorescence in public bathrooms. It came to me now, the boreen and the bowering of trees, the road before me and the turn I took, cycling towards the village. I needed to hurt and burn energy. There were mirrors resting in the bosoms of hedges; there were midges glowing over everything. The land was flat. The sky had little input. I was but a fizzing neural incident. I sang loudly to myself.

In the village I became afraid. The fear was somehow ancient and familiar. I felt a tremendous sense of guilt.

When the bus to Drogheda pulled up, the driver shook his head at me.

Extra for the bike, he said. Twenty euro.

It doesn't matter, I replied. I only wanted to get out of there, to make it as far as the bus station, to travel from there to my mother's house.

The driver – people being such busybodies – tried to dissuade me, as if I were only calling his bluff. I had to lie and say that somebody would come and get the bike, shortly, that it would not be stolen, that it was perfectly all right with me. This meant everybody was looking at me by the time I found a seat, and curled up, catching my knees in front of me, digging my heels into my buttock cheeks. I'd dropped the key through the letterbox of the cottage. I'd let the cat out and, as it turned towards slaughter in unthought provinces, it looked right at me. None of this was the animal's fault.

As the countryside unfolded around and the evening approached, I thought, Bluebeard, your bloody key. You'll rue the day.

I thought these things: my profit is, I can curse thee.

Is this you back for good? my mother asked.

I had shivered three tubes of sugar out on the Formica table top. My mother wore her work lanyard. I have always felt *lanyard* to be a beautiful word, like the name of a Romantic poet who died of tuberculosis.

Yes, I said stoutly.

And what about the PhD?

I have twelve months of stipend left; I will write up over here.

Will they mind? The Institute?

They won't notice. I tried to be bold. The Institute. They never notice anything.

Won't you need the library?

I thought of the Institute: the hot wiry furniture of the library, the microfiche, the strange smell of hospital dinners inexplicably eternally circulating; I'd found a dry little nest there, flicking through papers and thinking of images; *image* is to *picture* as word is to sentence, as sound is to musical phrase. I can still remember dreams I had at two and three years of age.

It was a man, I found myself saying. It was a man. My

voice seemed to collapse into itself: I can't go back. I couldn't face going back after that.

Lovey, she told me, there will be so many men.

That October I was tired all the time, and my favourite release was sleep. When I was in bed, I really did sleep, deeply and easily, and I dreamt simple poignant dreams. I hung from unseen ropes over a seabed where the sunlight through the milky currents winced, towed gently or else held inert and cool as bog butter, in some space webbed and steady as a womb. My dreams were not distressing. All day I looked forward to them. I hardly ate; I went to bed at dinnertime. Peddling air, flying only as a balloon or a broken bird is thrown around by wind, I came across the man I'd lost – I came across him everywhere, in all kinds of places, fairs and firework displays, a cabin in the roots of an aspen grove, a party full of people. Sometimes in these dreams I stretched my hands out, and sometimes Harry would take them, but at other times he blanked me just as he would blank my emails and refuse to take my calls or send any message at all.

Without dinner I got thinner and soon my appetite withered away. Some people praised me for this, some people criticised me to my face. My daytime life became of less and less concern to me, just as it had in London, shrinking to a low relief like wallpaper or some grinding refrain you ignore to remain sane. One day I woke up and the room said, This is your hubris, you have earned this. You are bad and dishonourable.

I went to London one weekend, met some girls for coffee at the university, and after this drank wine alone in my budget hotel at Paddington until the sun came up, the tube cranked into action, and I packed my satchel, checked out in keen dark winter dawn, walked hammered with my teeth stained down deserted broadways where newspapers bloomed like jellyfish and drifted on delinquent winds, stepped in-and-out of self-awareness, stepped into the blur again.

When the cafés opened I ate breakfast and sobered up. I had nowhere to go, so I went to where my books were, in a hot press in Stratford. This was the greasy sublet of a friend.

I am sorry, I said, as I knelt before the hot press and put my hands on the covers of books, that I can't take these yet.

My housemates might steal them, warned my friend.

I'll take a few then. I'll take the Friedberg, and the Ettinger, and the Joseph Campbell.

There came the sound of a housemate clapping through the front door; it resounded through the house. In the sink there was Pyrex and porridge bowls, the permanent lurk of old curry, decaying dishrags and three spin-lines in the garden, like Golgotha. It was hard to believe these terraces were ever loved before the international expendable administrative class found itself living in morbid portions of them.

Let's go to the Seven Bells, said my friend.

In the pub, I said, You see, I can't give up. I feel it so strongly, that he will come back. And by the way *everyone*, I laughed at him harshly, looks at me like that, when I say it. That is not an original look.

He sounds like a piece of shit, my friend observed.

I had asked in a bar, another bar, right before leaving London to join Harry, what would you do, what would you surrender, for love?

I asked, What are you willing to give up for love?

All asked at once what I meant, as I knew they would. A group of girls from the university.

I am Mephistopheles. Say, I explained. And I can promise you the undying love, the eternal devotion, of the man you choose. What would you be willing to give up?

How much would you surrender for love?

All said at once that they didn't know. Some seemed to want to change the subject.

I, I told them freely, have prayed, on at least one occasion – I have asked, or offered up, maybe to the devil, who knows – and I have said that, in exchange for love, I will give up my talent. I will never write anything again.

This is true, and as I recalled it I realised that I would promise it over again.

Would you give up your looks? I turned to a beautiful girl.

Looks will fade anyway, another said.

A girl asked if you can surrender daylight, or family, or the ability to have sex: which would, she added, defeat the purpose anyway.

It is not an unusual question – I sipped from my glass of wine. People have done it before. Women only I think. Ariadne gave up something. I looked to the girl who studied Classics. What did Ariadne give up?

Her string.

It was more, I think, than her string.

The girl who has referred to looks also said, For love, Medea killed her children.

Yes, that is what I mean, I said. Let's say I can promise you love, the eternal devotion of the man you choose, but you can never have children, ever: could you accept that?

No, answered one girl quickly. A second said, I don't want children anyway.

Well then, the Classics girl laughed.

Your bargain would be you would have to *have* children!

No way! The girl made a campy gesture, batting her palms: no way would I agree.

You would surrender your talent?

And my career. I would be nothing but a lover, for love.

But what if it went wrong? What would you have to fall back on, without a job?

You don't understand. I was patient with them: This is Mephistopheles. It is a pact. It can never go wrong.

We drank and looked at the tabletop, scarred with age and stains and character.

A candle guttered wetly in a mason jar.

A gang of men shouted a toast at the bar.

Some of us were plump, some of us slender, some of us beautiful, some of us plain. All of us were intelligent.

The Little Mermaid, I remembered, surrendered her voice. I raised my fingers to the hollow of my throat.

That would be easy, I said. I would find that a relief.

For love I would certainly give up my voice.

I don't believe you, announced the girl who had mentioned Medea, gently. I don't think you could really go through with something like that, if it came down to it. The others were laughing and rolling their eyes or changing the subject and there was discomfort, I knew, in the air, among us, but I couldn't stop at that point – I was past worrying what people thought.

I would, I insisted.

A lot of you would, if it came down to it.

All of you would, if you had any sense.

Part Seven

On a calm afternoon, I came home from work. I took out a pale-pink woollen dress. It was not the kind of thing I usually wore. I left my hair wet, in a slick down my spine, drying and curling like fur at the back of my neck.

My husband had bought for me a writing desk, a bureau, lined with baize and framed by beams of smooth rosewood that had been scratched all over and, in places, seemed to have been branded or have words and sentences dug into them. On examination and no matter how closely you looked, these never claimed coherence, they were just like television snow. Years ago, if you crept down into the cold front room and turned the television on, there would be nothing but static, just snow, demonically indifferent and mesmerising.

It had come from a fire sale at the central bank after the building was dispatched by the national assets agency. The furniture on sale ranged from bockety swivel-chairs to extraordinary throne-like seats with piped ecclesiastical devices and masonic devices. My husband wanted desperately to buy something. The bureau fell somewhere within budget and after he had paid for it and arranged delivery we crossed to a queer little café and drank fingers of limoncello. Everything was glamorous as a dream. My husband was the most thorough and least repentant snob I'd met since the landlady.

At the bureau I sat and traced some promising nonsense in the wood. It was too early to leave yet.

Were you there when your daughters were born? I had asked my husband. He was there for the second one, the baby, now a year old. The first was born in seclusion and secrecy. Her mother had gone to hide out in a convent. Can you imagine? It wasn't all that long ago. That was the world. I hated him for being there for the second birth. I hated them both for the intimacy they had shared. What a scoundrel to leave her in the end. Practically right away. To sit beside me in the bucket-seat as I sat harmlessly, young and lovely, at Connolly Station.

In argument, I shouted, I wish you had never crossed that platform to me; in the night, sometimes, I still sobbed tiredly, imagined saying to Harry, I wish you'd never crossed the room. What are the odds that you should end up living here, where I was born, part of the year? I used to think this meant something.

I sat now at the writing desk. There lay an opened un-lined A5 notebook and a fountain pen. There were curled inserts for letters and documents. On the top a porcelain swan, neck curled, wings parted to reveal a hollow on its back. In this were chinks of copper change and curls of hair, of dust, of scrapes, of waste. If you see real swans pressing their wings out, half-opened, on the canal, you can see that there are real white exquisite chambers in their wings, along their backs, and how much they resemble the architecture of clouds.

I had found the swan in a charity shop.

Earlier than I had expected him, my husband banged in.

Drinking already? he asked.

Just a bit. Our wine glasses were tiny, like wine glasses in a play, lined with a strip of golden paint around the rim. Do you want some?

Sure. My husband loosened up his tie. What time is this?

Doors seven-thirty. Not to worry. Lots of time.

I have to have a shower.

I know. We have plenty of time.

The buses were slow. The traffic was held up. Coming the whole way across town like that is such a joke.

There is loads of time, I said.

Suddenly, he smiled. There was something to the smile that was high-pitched. Loads of time then? he asked. He came behind and closed hands over my shoulders. Maybe we should? he said. A thumb rose and began to compress forcefully the hollow of my head. I arched my back and sighed. Hands slid to cup my breasts beneath the woollen dress.

Even now I can't say what came over me, but perhaps I was still twenty-three, pulsing upper legs dumbly and thickly, trudgingly, against the pedals of a bike.

I stood up and caught him by his lovely hair. Lightly, but assuredly. Kneel, I commanded and, when he obeyed with surprise, I slid off my underwear. I opened my legs and stood vulgarly above him, stroking now, so that his face pushed into my pith and he understood my instruction.

Up, I breathed, and then said, soft. I braced my hands against the back of the settee. I tried and tried to push his face out of my mind. I bore down on him carefully at first, and then less carefully, until I was swinging with strangely wooden movements, sawing swiftly, and imagining that I myself, my mouth, was buried in the pith, until I came with ragged breaths and a gesture that was a caution to him not to break the rhythm, or stop, or retract it. My frame relaxed against the beam of the settee. Beneath the plush there were the hard bones of its frame. In this state, flaking or dissolving at the edges in seltzer, I didn't care what he or anybody did; he fucked me happily, on the cushions, coming quickly and with gratitude, with whoops. He hadn't seen this side of me since we had been married; the woman who had no ties to him or cares for him and was, therefore, heedlessly greedy, literal in all things sexual. I lay against his chest and felt darkness. Decided that I didn't care if I went out smelling of sex.

He was as happy, getting dressed, as a pet. We spoke kindly and fondly and hysterically to one another. I left my face naked and ground my wedding band against the webs between my fingers, the little blind chambers of flesh dried out by cold and detergent. My husband asked, Should I wear a tie? No, no, I answered, no. It's not the Gate. There will be people under seventy. We walked into a hard-pink sundown. Over the sea, over Poolbeg, the sky was poetry, obviously, it is so rarely anything else; the sky is superlative, is always surplus in a story. I have laboured so much over skies. Its prettiness irritated me, as did half-a-glass of syrupy Merlot, although I wondered aloud if the sky matched the shade of my dress.

Taxis sailed gaily, as they always did, along the coast, metallic and propelled. It never took more than a minute to flag taxis in Fairview. Radios rumbled into news. The keys on my laptop, I remarked casually, had crumbs tucked under certain letters, between keys, and I had almost signed myself off as *Allah* that afternoon.

You're in a good mood, said my husband, censoriously.

And why not? barked the driver.

Exactly. I poked my husband. Exactly. I knew by the side of my eye that he was looking at me.

We are six months married today, I said.

Oh yes?

If this were probation, it would be up. I laughed goofily. I continued to watch him, coyly, from the side, like a bird, like a swan, but he struck up conversation with the taxi driver. What do you think of that? he asked, referring to a news segment on the possible pedestrianisation of College Green.

Bullshit, said the driver, pure spin. Never going to happen. How – there are hotels and that, yeah? All the way up to Christchurch. How are tourists going to get up there without cabs, huh? Tell me how that's going to happen. How are people going to get up the hotels, right, if the place is pedestrianised? Tell me that now. Can you tell me that?

I lay back in the taxi, sticky from the wine, my eyes closing. Searching and finding every interstice of silence in the evening. Taking silence from where it has been tucked between things and forgotten, from the vacant flashing junctions of Ballybough, from lit windows with drying clothes hanging from curtain poles, from the stasis between radio stations, the flakes and haste and snow.

When the celebrated self-constructed activist and beauty Maud Gonne arrived in the life of W. B. Yeats, the poet who fell in love with her, it was he later said as if a gong had been struck and the reverberations of this continued dimly but persistently throughout the rest of his life.

The gong that went off in the life of Yeats, then a young man, its melting mimetic metal variant on *OM*, became a symbol, obviously, in poetry – gong-torn oceans, gong-tormented seas, Maud Gong, all of that. A gong will film the air with severe sound. And then one day I was reading an interview with the musician Nick Cave and he spoke about the death of his teenage son and bereavement and how memories, or great events, or things like that, were not anchored in time as far as affect is concerned (these weren't his words) but more like *ringing bells* (his words) reverberating through a life, not only now or in the future but also through the past – a fluid movement extending forwards and backwards, tidally, recurrently, altering everything. I would say *imbuing everything* but I reviewed a substandard academic book recently and the writer could not stop saying imbued, every damn thing was imbued with this and imbued with that, and I cannot write *imbued* without wincing now. You understand.

The bells and the gong, these things being so similar, struck me, *chimed with me* as it were, I comprehended well, and you have two artists working with language but in ways which slide and ache towards a form before or beyond language – music, in the case of Nick Cave, and images, in the case of Yeats. Yeats was all about images and damned to verse, and a lot of the time he literally misspelled things, and some critics in retrospect described him as *dyslexic*.

The gong and the bell struck me as such passionately accurate reflections of my own life and experiences and especially in the way they broke down time frames through the levelling distension of solid sound. Especially the way they came from without, but filled and even interpolated the body, saturated, with sensation, and seduced. Of course this isn't a flawless category of metaphor because gongs and bells eventually go silent. And, I suppose, people eventually die. So there you go.

I wanted to write about this, about Maud as a gong, frozen or flattened into a statue or daguerreotype, albeit writing her own pretty ridiculous autobiography, but really I knew what drew me to it was the operations of mnemonic and emotional gongs, often tormenting, in my own life, and the making and re-breaking of my heart with every swing of the tongue. It was the palimpsests I meant.

On a mirrored dresser in the hallway of the landlady's house, on the ancient ordered tiles, there had stood the wrought iron frame of a dinner-bell with gong removed; the naked frame of a gong with a socket of soft air, the hiss of radiators, the occasional whistle of a draught, suspended in it instead of a gong. There were fire-tongs and a dish of pot pourri adjacent.

Married, and panicking, I dreamt of flocked wallpaper fading into plaster, I dreamt as though my gaze was tracking slowly all along the paper. Houses inside me and houses outside, and houses all around. A great house is a statement that was made, carefully and firmly, a long time ago: now it iterates and exfoliates and regrows wings that only ever existed in dreams.

Awake and alert that morning, when I was alone, I had composed a list of things I was sick of, bored with, all the more forcefully because they had been marshalled as symbols previously. Tea-sets patterned with willow or family devices; umbrella-holders of bamboo; woodcuts of Saint Cecilia; ancestor portraits from the eighteenth century showing sloe-eyed snub-nosed women caressing children; masonic obelisks; stone-bottomed lily ponds ruffled by robust wind; follies; bell-jars of artisan cheese; blunt white unchipped jugs; cornices creamy as meringues; horses; box-cars; headscarves; heritage check; cut-glass decanters; busts; taxidermy. In a separate aesthetic, wood-chip, anaglypta, holy water vessels shaped like Our Lady of Lourdes, fire screens showing pastoral hunting scenes, oilcloth, sewing machines, boot-scrapers, tinned-meat pie. The border with Northern Ireland. Every squat and de-faced bunker on the barracks beach. The map of the world that hung in the back of my wardrobe when I was a tiny child, like Narnia. The Celtic Tiger. Ghost estates. The smell of resin, sound of saws. That omnipresent odour of organic garbage lingering in the lifts and stairwells of every apartment block built hastily during the Boom. The Big House with its violent tympanum of armour and courtly weapons, spreading flowers, Latin mottos, baying dogs, over the great hall and my back to the fire, the slimly-licking flames and slim shoulders, the shoulderblades, my body strategically starved, a glass of wine, my wrists shaking.

You don't know what I can do. Nobody knows. I've been so good, so damn obedient, I've been so acquiescent, so pleasant!

The gongs accumulated and chased one another, conglomerated, filled the still familiar scene of early winter Irish countryside, the trees in shades of gold and red and bluish-green, a world at last I fully understood, and not only understood but *rejected*: I said, begone now broken heart. Fuck this. I'm hungry. I am tired. I am bored. I want to fuck and to be fucked. I want to walk into the tiled and splendid hall of Brown Thomas and buy a stick of lipstick or a scarf scored with the knots one sees on cherry wood.

That morning I had lain across the bed in my husband's apartment: all interest passed over and lifted like a spirit finding no abode.

The first corridor in the world compressed itself into diamonds outside, and I tried to travel back to old emotional states, pulling out old images with a flourish.

Where I began.

Cycling into a village flung on some fan, from the pivot-point, the butterfly-pin, of Meath, somewhere I struggle now to pick out on a map; where I began, warm with exercise.

Some townland wriggling on a pin.

It is not heroic. Although it may look heroic. Some people have trouble thrust upon them, but I went looking for it. I was beginning to understand.

It changed me – of course it did – I could not turn back or go back or bear to look back – I went forward, furiously.

When I married I felt I was up to it, clever and competent, but I'd skidded and worried in these weird weeks after the landlady. I felt a fresh callousness towards Harry and towards my husband. I realised that no one had ever been watching me, really: all those side-eyes, surface measurements, were skin-deep, and I couldn't – I thought now, warming to it, feeling thrilled – I could not remain still long enough for anyone to gain the measure of me.

And now we were riding in the taxi, my husband and I. Beneath a pink painterly sky. I was numb with anticipation. My body was stiff and specific as a doll. We were going to the theatre. At Smock Alley, snap of car-doors, sound of promise on paper air.

Life does not have a narrative. This is only a way of choosing to see and usually for sinister purposes. To explain oneself and give substance to the greater dangerous lie of consensus and common sense. I have done with narratives and now I only walk into memories like cold-spots or sensations sometimes and accidentally, with no need for a link between these only something like a déja vu or last night's dream. No more of the spontaneous labour narrative demands, like a catechism: what is this memory of, what is its nature, where did you meet it first, and when did you see it last? What lesson is to be drawn from it? What story opens, buckles, drops, surrenders, or refreshes here? What story finishes? As if you owe life narratives. Like everything must be tagged with some mnemonic quality to be crated and stacked.

Really if you think about it whole memories and energies can be dispersed to the wind: imagine yourself standing at the edge of the lane and facing the stubble-field and letting not only your own history go but many other histories too, the history of the Big House you see sunken under parkland or the tractor-trails, the shape of blades, the cattle hooves, the sombre troughs of boots. Established meaning stamped against the sky in winter trees – typewriter keys – as sentences lengthening inelegantly into Meath.

Let go. Let it blow away, retaining only useful information, the route back to the house perhaps. Days lost like chaff: days blasted, cut down, leaving gleanings, towing crows, leaving all *possibilities* or better still second-growth. Trees can reclaim an abandoned building within thirty years you know.

And you, he cried when he saw me in the lobby, you owe me a bicycle.

All my things, I said.

Your things? He spoke loudly, he beckoned people towards him. He looked at me the whole time with a look I couldn't tolerate, of such wonder and affection it was too much like staring into the sun.

Oh yes, he remembered at last, your clothes, your things. He looked hard at me, as if trying to decide something. Your hair is so much longer now, he said.

What do you do? he asked.

I teach a bit. In different places. English and Art History, I write—

You draw?

This was something pointed and impatient, something my parents would say. As in, you tell them you have done something, and they say, sharply, yes, but have you done the *other* thing.

A little. Not much.

I have the picture you made.

The satyr?

Is that what it is?

It's you! It's supposed to be you!

But I saw that he was laughing then, joking with me. It felt surreal. The bar was brimming with people and some were circling us tensely, waiting to speak to him, one or two I thought with eyebrows raised but they could not know who I was, I thought, could they? His eyes were locked into mine. He had grown a beard and it was tremendously ageing, although not inaccurately.

You're an old man now, I realised.

Of course I'm an old man.

A dirty one?

Not any more.

I am married. I remembered it abruptly, with triumph, like an errand I had almost forgotten: I am married! I shot out my married hand. I looked about. He is, I said, taking a phone call probably. I might, I said, introduce you some time.

Congratulations. You are a genuine *dotorossa* now?

That was ages ago. But yes, I am.

Ages ago?

I am over it.

At that he laughed, and suddenly we were conspirators laughing, and some well-dressed woman I didn't know wafted angelically into my ken to close a hand around my arm.

They are calling us in! Her eyes were wide. Hardly anyone has had a chance to chat. I have hardly touched my wine.

I must find my husband.

I began to click the fingers of my hands.

Breaking at that point was like making a fresh tear,

instead of wallowing in some existing wound; it felt delicious then, it felt correct, although I'd also wilted underneath this woman's solicitation and felt a scrubby serf again, as I so often did.

My husband was standing just outside, speaking into his phone.

It's starting now, I said. He flipped and snapped the phone at once and smiled jocularly at me and whispered, to my initial surprise, Sure thing, kitten; but then I remembered that I had sawn over his face and let him fuck me on the couch and I took his hand – I did not feel guilty – I felt self-conscious.

During the play my heart raced until I grew restless. It was not acted especially well. A Brechtian bag of sand – some prop or weight – hung dumbly as a gland and in the glare of the stage lights.

I couldn't see where Harry had sat and this unknowing made me feel as though there were a sniper somewhere, his gaze taking in, perhaps, some cruel or unflattering angle, such that I bent my head low and let my hair curtain the planes of my face and picked uncouthly at the lipstick dried into my lips. I sucked my front teeth. My husband's hand crept and wound around mine playfully, until at last I sighed and let the electricity spread into my fingers, and turned to kiss him, tasting soured wine and the thick shining surplus of his lips; his finger stroked, then dug into, my clavicle.

When he withdrew his breath strafed my face for a moment, heavily, and he laughed lowly, so that several people looked at us, across the dark extinguished space.

But when my child was born I stopped writing and began painting. I had no ideas or abstracts, only colours, colours in helixes and streams, in double-serpents and seaweed. Colours flushing and retracting in tidal currents like musicians bent over wind instruments; colours obeying the currents of orchestras.

If you look through the surface of a lake, light coalesces in seams, reflects on the floor of the lake like twisting gold.

I painted stretched and treated bedsheets to begin with and, when I became more confident, I painted the entire chimney-breast with poster paint. I painted colours running together, sometimes spattered or blasted for effect, like cable-cords, or like the veins in the neck of a severed head. These knit into each other organically.

My colours were heather-purple and squid-ink, with greens, and sore-corrupted yellows stencilled through by bristles applied stiff and tight – I held the bristles together myself, with painted fingers, toothbrush-tight, to achieve grinding combs throughout the paint – and from a distance it was fish-scales underneath a nightmare sky; up close ordinance-survey impressionism, a map; at times, especially in the mornings and by the whitest oatmeal light, a sonogram of emotions, a galaxy of cheap mood-stones, and coral, most of all a coral reef, although, as I reflected afterwards, there was no real red there, no oranges, no *coral red*, the shade which happens to most flatter my complexion.

I painted onto the chimney-breast of the basement flat because it presented itself as differentiated, smooth and declarative, coated, like all the walls of the apartment, in ancient Anaglypta. When my mother visited she double-took and said, My God, did you do that?, and gave me a firm sideways smile.

Well I am awake in the night, I explained, with the baby, and I can't write: I can't bring myself to write, it makes me sick.

During my pregnancy I threw up every time I tried to write – or if not every time, enough times to develop something of a neurosis. I'd come in fact to loath writing quite atavistically. It had held such a grip on my identity for years. It made me live inside my head, where everything was terrible. After my child was born I began to surprise myself with feats of flagrancy and shiftlessness that I would never have allowed myself before.

Milk-soured laundry built around me and, instead of washing it, I threw a whole lot of it out; I went around topless a lot, in the apartment, with the heating and the fire-bars whacked up, obscenely, until summer came; my bosoms as I reasoned had always been small, cox-pippin sized in fact, and so it didn't matter that they swung more heavily or frankly now; my clavicles were still exposed and neat as gracenotes without strain. In fact my ego billowed in me and I had to be careful not to make this too obvious in case they thought I'd gone insane.

After all, I explained, I am alone so much, and my sleep is disturbed.

The baby slept in a cot beside the bed. I knew that when it got older I would put it in the bed with me, not for any ideological reason, but out of laziness; it was too much, *too much*, to contemplate night-feeds between two separate rooms. I slept when the baby slept. I always drooled. It was six months before my husband reappeared, as I told people – six months of age the baby was before that man materialised! – and, afterwards, they all assured me this was totally untrue. By then I was convalescing.

One day my stepdaughter was there – I am sure – a column or a medieval monarch in the sleek niche of a church, in a tympanum, smiling *l'inconnue*-style on a scene of hell: her hair the duck-blonde, down-blonde, egg-blonde of her father in her childhood: she dipped over the baby and her hair slid loose again.

I wanted to say I was sorry for all the things ahead of her that she could not know about. But then, what did I know? Perhaps it will be easy and sweeter for her, growing up.

Another thing I did when all alone, with the baby, was lie in near-sleep plotting like a clock, digging at the coarse skin of my feet. I peeled the callouses from heels, and progressed to my poor insteps, scraping the scales and sandy bands of battered skin, revealing pink. In time I sawed stiff plaques of yellow from my heels with little blades. I went too far and, after I was done, my feet were almost purple, and my toes were milky-blue; colours not unlike the cold colours of the chimney-breast or of an amputated limb, a curly-toenailed corpse.

I did this dementedly. It brought me back to the time I contracted impetigo at school, on my lips and chin: the hot tingling crust which built all day and, when detached, came off in strips of oily grit like mineral felt. Relief of raw skin underneath. The tingling crust re-established. I was given iodine by the pharmacist's wife. The impetigo persisted for so long that a teacher wrote a note to my parents chastising them for sending me to school. Tearing the tired rinds off my feet left me relaxed. The baby looked at me with hunger. It had a wonderful wet slit of lips. I think in retrospect that this was only a couple of weeks, I think: when I remember it, it trembles like a coiled snake in my ribs, a coiled snake in my stomach, a spring in my clitoris. A rush and a push. And then I was in hospital for a bit.

These are wondrous memories, thrilling and terrible and precious. They are also forbidden. I visit them alone only, sometimes, at night, at the table, under a safe fluorescent light. Even this light threatens, however, just a bit, when a certain memory peels from it. This is the memory of a fluorescent light that once was tacked over the dining-table of my grandmother's house. In the nineties a spider crawled in when the light was just installed and, when the light was first switched on, the spider fried. Its exoskeleton remained, outlined, within the body of the light. I was struck with terror whenever I looked at it as a child. Nonetheless, of course, I stole looks at it. Surreptitiously. Because the fried spider was all I knew at that time about death.

With the child I visited beaches of childhood and adolescence, almost entirely intact. The long brawn of Laytown becoming the Boyne Estuary; rocks and rats and navigation stacks, and birds. Birds of looping human cries.

The great irritation of other people, kites and dogs and kids and ridiculous bootcamps pedalling legs in the air. The buggy left slack tracks in the sand. March came in like a lion and limped out in daffodils: Always, I said, this phrase had made me think of men in bed.

The baby was buttoned into an airproof suit, and a trail of shine ran from its nose – I caught this with screwed tissues, chattering always to the child, saying Look, look, look!

Returning in the car to a café in Drogheda, flinching at any black-headed man but never running into him, where I met my mother for coffee, and we descended to department stores for linen and baby-things, for bowls and urns and pestles we took any liking to. I tried not to go to Drogheda too often. I never visited the head of Saint Oliver Plunkett.

On other days, the buggy hissed swiftly over wet sand at Dollymount. On the pier beneath the yellow lighthouse we saw the bone-white prow of a freight ship slide from the bay, so close and so immense the baby screamed; I felt afraid too, crouching down and crowding it out with the shape of my body, turning the buggy into a safe cabriolet, warm with body-heat and fragrant of gripe water. Women gave me grimaces of sympathy. Men didn't look at me anymore.

Sometimes I took coffee and scones like a wealthy leisured mother, obliging waitresses to drag plastic high-chairs to the table as I serenely unpacked a paperback, a small toy. The child would howl at last, the spell broken.

On still more, different, days the buggy kept up a warm growl against the gravel of Glasnevin cemetery, where my husband and I courted one another gauchely, where he pushed his fingers into me and held them beneath both our noses, bending close.

One day when straying from the old graves – pork-butchers and locksmiths, city elders, masons, unmarried daughters of agents, big farms, mills, eel-weirs, boring country places where they spent their life probably darning and picking flowered samplers, sex a weltering beneath stale skirts and pungent colonial kitchen-gardens, skeletal screed of trees on a horizon of prairies – one day, straying from these old graves, which were wryly comforting because the dead, long-mouldered and reduced to bits of twig, did not care at all about anything, seemed to urge through the weight of clay on top of them, *Stop giving a fuck*; one day, wandering from these graves, I found a suicide I'd known at college several years before, I found his grave, shot up newly like a springtime shoot.

It was Easter and the air severe, and I was wearing gloves. It had to be him because he had an unusual name and the dates lined up and it had to be suicide because that was what *tragically* meant, in the obituary I found quickly online, with my phone. I stroked the headstone for a moment in a daze.

I held back the barrage of interest, the swaggering womanly demand for gossip that had become more of my lot since having a baby – women disclosed much easier, as if relaxing into chairs, sighing with pleasure to take the weight off their feet, because, you see, you too had something now to lose – and tried not to be ghoulish, common, coarse. I had not seen this grave before.

Not even when courting my husband and spending every afternoon here, practically, because this was one of the only places in the city where no one could see us.

308

Always we preferred to be alone together only. Those were the happiest times. Everything had been imminent then, even immanent. I progressed to the beribboned still-births plot but realised that I could not look at it now – I couldn't bear it – so I turned and returned to the suicide, patting the headstone absently.

A boy who sat before me in a lecture hall. That was all.

Above ground, in the sunlight: breezes, occasional crackle of flower-foil, birdsong, baby's cry, wind chimes.

Acknowledgements

This book was written with financial support from the Arts Council of Ireland, for which I am immensely grateful.

Warm thanks are due to Brendan Barrington, who worked editorially on the text at an early stage. Thank you to my agent, Matthew Turner, for shaping it and finding it a home, and to my editor Lettice Franklin, for her brilliant work and for making it into a better book.

Thank you, finally, to Donna and Darren Corcoran, Aoife Frances and Colin Mifsud, the McNultys, Sydney Weinberg, Joanna and Michael Hofer-Robinson, Roisin Brennan and Nick McCormack, Josephine Campbell and her family, Pauric Havlin, Nathan O'Donnell, Julie Bates, Christodoulos Makris, Richard Kirkland, Colin Graham and the Department of English at Maynooth University, the Gen X '16/17 crew, Meath County Council, the Tyrone Guthrie Centre, Greywood Arts Centre Cork, Desperate Literature Madrid, and the Irish Research Council.